Lora Leigh's novels are:

"TITILLATING."
—*Publishers Weekly*

"SIZZLING HOT."
—*Fresh Fiction*

"INTENSE AND BLAZING HOT."
—*RRTErotic*

"WONDERFULLY DELICIOUS . . . TRULY DECADENT."
—*Romance Junkies*

D0052832

ALSO BY LORA LEIGH

Rugged Texas Cowboy

THE BRUTE FORCE SERIES
Collision Point
Dagger's Edge

THE MEN OF SUMMER
Hot Shot
Dirty Little Lies
Wicked Lies

THE CALLAHANS
Midnight Sins
Deadly Sins
Secret Sins
Ultimate Sins

THE ELITE OPS
Live Wire
Renegade
Black Jack
Heat Seeker
Maverick
Wild Card

THE NAVY SEALs
Killer Secrets
Hidden Agendas
Dangerous Games

THE BOUND HEARTS
Intense Pleasure
Secret Pleasure
Dangerous Pleasure
Guilty Pleasure
Only Pleasure
Wicked Pleasure
Forbidden Pleasure

ANTHOLOGIES
Real Men Last All Night
Real Men Do It Better
Honk If You Love Real Men
Legally Hot
Men of Danger
Hot Alphas

LORA LEIGH
AND
VERONICA CHADWICK

one tough cowboy

St. Martin's Paperbacks

ONE TOUGH COWBOY

Copyright © 2019 by Lora Leigh and Veronica Chadwick.

All rights reserved.

For information address St. Martin's Press, 175 Fifth Avenue, New York, NY 10010.

ISBN: 978-1-250-30948-8

Our books may be purchased in bulk for promotional, educational, or business use. Please contact your local bookseller or the Macmillan Corporate and Premium Sales Department at 1-800-221-7945, ext. 5442, or by e-mail at MacmillanSpecialMarkets@macmillan.com.

Printed in the United States of America

St. Martin's Paperbacks edition / February 2019

St. Martin's Paperbacks are published by St. Martin's Press, 175 Fifth Avenue, New York, NY 10010.

10 9 8 7 6 5 4 3 2 1

For Piper Ann. Gammy loves you.
—Lora

For April and Miss Pam. Thank you for your constant encouragement and your unfailing friendship. I love you both so much.
—Veronica

acknowledgments

Thanks to my co-writer, Veronica, for her patience and friendship.

—Lora

prologue

Finding the middle-aged woman dead, alone in her home, was a shock that mild summer night. It damned sure wasn't something anyone could have expected.

Sheriff Hunter Steele stood on Dorthea Coulter's porch and watched the EMTs solemnly wheel her covered body to the waiting ambulance.

It was a damned shame and despite appearances, he just couldn't go with an accidental death, or God forbid, suicide. That simply wasn't Dottie. Yet someone had gone to a lot of trouble to make it appear it was.

"Looks like an accident, Sheriff." The coroner spoke finally, stepping out of the doorframe where, oddly, he'd been standing silent for a while. "The pills were right there on her bedside table."

Hunter didn't reply, he just listened as the man shifted his weight from one foot to the other before continuing, "Pain medication's a tricky thing sometimes. People forget they took 'em. Wake up still hurtin', take more, which only confuses 'em further, and then they take even more."

Hunter nodded, narrowed his eyes on the coroner, catching the hint of unease in the other man's eyes. Bill, the coroner was a squirrely, fat, little man who cleared his throat a lot when he was nervous.

He was nervous now.

"Yeah, older folks don't always pay attention like they should," Hunter stated. It wasn't an agreement.

"It's sad," the coroner agreed a little too loudly before clearing his throat again and gripping his case with both hands. "I still have to do the autopsy and all, of course. I'll be sure to let you know if I find anything else."

"Thank you, Bill." Hunter shifted his position from where he leaned against the porch post, watching as the EMT closed the ambulance doors and climbed into the cab.

"Mayor Henderson said he'd call her kin. I guess he knows her brother's family." Bill sighed. "They're from these parts, he said."

"The Ryders." Hunter gave Bill a side glance. "They used to live next door there." Hunter motioned to the two-story white house next to Dottie's. "Moved about oh, sixteen years ago, I guess."

For a second, vivid blue-green eyes and a gamine grin sparkled through his memory. The flirtatious flutter of dark lashes and a woman-child destined to break hearts had regret tugging at his chest.

Dottie's niece, Samantha Jolene Ryder had been a wild child. She'd cried when she and her family had moved, he remembered. Staring back at him as he watched the car drive away, tears whispering down her cheeks.

There was more to the Ryder family leaving than they told folks, though. When Dottie was questioned about why they left, she'd just smile wistfully and shake her head.

"Oh, they're on to bigger and better things. This wild country life ain't for everybody, ya know." He always noted the empty way she said those words. Defying the pleasant expression she'd presented.

"Well, I'll be goin' then, Sheriff," Bill interrupted his musings. The coroner breathed out slowly, an affected sigh. "I'll send you my report tomorrow."

"You do that, Bill." Hunter glanced at him as he started down the first step; he looked up and watched the ambulance pull out of the long driveway onto the street.

"Sure is a shame," Bill said, then paused, looking back at Hunter with suspicious brown eyes. "Dottie was a friend of your uncle's too, wasn't she?"

Hunter nodded, his gaze moving to the little man once again. "Yeah, she was."

"Too bad about that too," the coroner said, lowering his balding head as he shook it slowly. "Hunting accident like that. Older folks. Go figure."

"Yeah, go figure." Hunter didn't bother to hide his sarcasm.

If any man he'd served with in the army had heard him say that, with just that tone of voice, they would have been watching their backs. Instead, the fat little bastard gave him a parody of a sympathetic smile before he waddled quickly down the walk to his work van.

He bounced a little to gain momentum before hoisting himself into the driver's seat.

Bill Markham wasn't much of a coroner. He'd been given the position by the mayor just after the old coroner resigned three years before. Hunter remembered the disgust that had filled his uncle's voice when he'd talked about the other man.

According to Zachariah Steele, Bill Markham was sloppy at best at the job. He should have lost his medical license years before and no doubt would have if he hadn't retired instead. Five years later, Henderson appointed him as coroner. At the time, it simply hadn't made sense.

Maybe it did now, though. Hunter watched the van turn onto the street, catching up with the ambulance at the stop sign ahead.

Three deaths in an eight-month span of time. First, the mayor's wife, Lillian Henderson. She'd drowned in the little fishing pond not too far from her house. Accidental drowning, the coroner had ruled. Before the then-sheriff, Zachariah Steele, could protest, the body had been cremated, eliminating any chance of proving murder.

Zachariah had still worried over it, though. Certain the woman that had held his heart as a young man had been murdered, he'd been determined to find her killer. Before Hunter could get home to help him, his uncle had allegedly killed himself accidently while out hunting. Tripped and fell. The gun went off, shooting Zachariah in the chest and killing him instantly. Zachariah had been on vacation at the time, and it had been more than a week before he'd been missed. Well, according to the deputy sheriff at the time anyway.

Of course, all evidence of foul play, if there had been any, was gone by time the body had been found. At least that's what the coroner's report said.

Strange thing, that. A man who never went hunting, to be killed while hunting. Hunting alone, as well. Zachariah owned a hunting rifle, even took it out when Hunter was home and wanted company when he went hunting. But he never fired it nor had he ever gone hunting by himself.

"If I cain't eat it, then I ain't killin' it," his uncle had told him once, years before.

Zachariah wasn't fond of venison, and he was especially against eating "vermin" as he called it, like squirrel.

Now, Dottie Coulter, who just happened to be Lillian's and Zachariah's closest friend, was dead as well.

Accidental overdose, his ass.

His teeth clenched as the two deputies that had arrived on the coroner's heels stepped from the house.

"Coroner has the pills," Ray Decker, the once deputy sheriff, drawled with just a hint of disdain in his tone. "These old people need to learn how to take their meds, I guess. Her family should have put her in a home some time ago."

The other, younger deputy, Shane Warren, didn't reply. Shane didn't often say much. He watched. The boy was a hell of a watcher. He paid attention to everything, hyperaware of his surroundings. Hunter liked that about him. It made Shane exceptionally good at his job, which made him a valuable asset to the sheriff's department.

"And someone needs a few of those classes the state offers on showing proper respect for the dead," Hunter drawled. "Shall I sign you up for a few, Deputy? I certainly don't mind."

Decker's lips thinned. "Apologies, Sheriff." His smile was all teeth and carefully veiled dislike. "I'll be watchin' my manners in the future."

"Uh-huh. You do that." Hunter highly doubted that would ever happen. "While you're at it, I want your report on my desk before you head home tonight."

"Like hell." Decker's eyes widened. "I wasn't even on duty."

"Then you shouldn't have arrived in uniform, Decker." Hunter gave him a less than friendly smile, a cold one. "You should have headed on home instead of racing out here to get your nose all up in this. Now, since you put yourself on duty, you can write up that report for me. In detail, if you don't mind."

"I can turn it in tomorrow morning . . ." Decker grumbled through his teeth.

"Sure, and you can turn in your badge with it," Hunter finished for him. "Do the report tonight or you won't have a job come morning."

Anger flushed the other man's face, giving it a mottled appearance as he tore his hat off, pushed back his thinning blond hair, and glared at Hunter from beady, brown eyes.

"You cain't fire me without the mayor sayin' you can," Decker reminded him before slamming the hat back on his head.

"You don't turn in that report, I can." Hunter didn't bother rising to the other man's anger. Decker really didn't want to see the day Hunter let his temper get riled over him. "Mayor can't help you, Decker, if you don't follow the rules. You showed up, in uniform, and you went through the crime scene. As senior deputy on the scene, you get to write the report. Before shift change. That's in"—Hunter looked at his watch—"about three hours, not in the morning. I'll be looking for it on my desk. Tonight."

Decker's eyes gleamed with pure hatred before he stomped from the porch, one hand clenched on the butt of the weapon holstered at his side.

One of these days, Hunter thought, the bastard was going to get stupid enough to think he had the balls to use that weapon.

Hunter watched the deputy jerk open the door of his cruiser, slide behind the wheel, and slam it behind him.

He took a toothpick from his pocket and placed it between his teeth before glancing to the other deputy. "You got something to say, Shane?"

"He'll not face you, Hunter," Shane said quietly. "He's the type to shoot a man in the back. I'd be careful."

"Not for a while yet," Hunter drawled. "I wasn't elected to this office; I was appointed, remember? Kill me off now and that governor might get a little pissed. And another accident would look awfully suspicious."

"Especially considering the fact the governor, your aunt Madeline, might send the National Guard in to sort it out. Sure would put a damper on killing you just yet." Shane snorted.

There was always that. Aunt Madeline wasn't someone to challenge, especially where her family was concerned. And she often said how fond she was of her nephew, Hunter.

"Whoever killed Zachariah wasn't aware of that," he

murmured. "They forgot Zachariah had family. Powerful family. Never underestimate the power or the rage of a woman whose family is threatened or harmed, Shane. Especially when that family's her baby brother. Remember that."

"Aunt Madeline even scares me," Shane assured him, his voice quiet. "And speaking of her, she called this afternoon. Says to let you know she expects an update soon."

Hunter didn't doubt that one a bit.

"Yeah. Too bad I don't have much of an update." Bitterness filled him over that one. He'd been here eight months, and still, there wasn't a shred of evidence to point to the killer.

"Think Sami Jo will come back for the funeral?" Shane asked as he stepped closer. "Dottie was awful fond of her."

Sami Jo. He smiled at the nickname Sam had hated with a passion. She hadn't been fond of being called Sam either, but he liked pushing her buttons.

"Boy, you better not let her hear you calling her that." Hunter gave him a sideways glance. "She could get you in trouble."

"And how could she do that?" Shane's grin was a little too smug to suit Hunter.

"Because." Hunter stared at him from beneath the brim of his hat. "She'll pick a fight with you, and I'll have to step in."

"Hell, I don't wanna fight her." The suggestive tone in Shane's voice had Hunter lifting a brow, but he stayed silent. "How come she don't pick a fight with you? You called her Sam all the time."

Hunter chuckled. "That's 'cause I'm special." He met Shane's gaze and dropped the smile. "And I can be a shade possessive."

If Sam came back, there was no way in hell he was letting another man have a chance with her. He'd already put claim on her years ago.

Shane groaned. "Oh man, that's not right, Hunter. You can't pull rank that way."

"Watch me, kid." Hunter stepped back to the open front door.

Damn, this was going to break Samantha's heart anyway. No doubt she'd be gone before the funeral ended, with her husband and kids in tow.

"Hell, she's probably married anyway," Shane said as if the kid read his mind. His voice softer as he expressed Hunter's thoughts. "I doubt she'll stay long."

"Yeah, no doubt." He stared into the house, remembering Dottie's pride in it and the memories she had cultivated there. "Lock up for me, Shane. I'm going to head back and make sure I get that report tonight. I'm sure her family will be here come morning."

"Good luck on that report, Sheriff," Shane muttered just loud enough for Hunter to hear.

If he were lucky, Hunter thought, Decker would neglect to turn the damned thing in so he could get rid of his sorry ass. That was the problem right there, he simply wasn't that damned lucky.

chapter one

Samantha wouldn't be back if Aunt Dottie hadn't died. Deerhaven, California, held too many bittersweet memories. Samantha didn't have a lot of family, and in some ways the close-knit community had filled that loss. Leaving it had been heartbreaking. At the same time, there was no room to grow here when she'd been younger.

Leaving was good in the sense that she went to college and found her niche in life. Being here, however, reminded her of what she'd left behind and what she had lost.

Now, she was back in the home she'd never wanted to leave so long ago and facing the loss of an aunt she'd loved nearly as much as she loved her parents.

Only hours after her aunt's burial, she was trying to deal with the memories of her past and the aunt she'd so missed. Reminders of a happier time, when family meant everything, filled the house.

As much as she wanted to avoid them, Samantha couldn't ignore the people who had come to pay their respects. The gathering had begun slowly, but now the house was filled with friends of her aunt's, and Samantha had to face them.

In the kitchen of Dottie's home, she found a moment of peace, such that it was. She never expected this many people would attend her aunt's funeral, much less come by the house to offer condolences. Aunt Dottie hadn't been very social. The woman was an enigma, really. As bold, smart, and outgoing as she was quiet and private. She had few friends, but they were those rare, ride-or-die kind of friends. And they had all died as well.

Or so Samantha had believed. She'd obviously been wrong.

The hushed conversations were muted and indiscernible, a muffled background hum that Samantha could easily tune out. That was good enough, for now. It was just a moment's reprieve, but it helped.

She put her hands on the counter, closed her eyes, and took a deep breath.

Aunt Dottie's home was too small for so many people and Samantha wasn't fond of crowds. Still, it was kind of them to come. Well, some of them had genuine motives. Most of them just wanted to gather fodder for their gossip circles. Small towns were like that, and Deerhaven was notorious for it.

Cute and quaint, her hometown was just as innocent in appearance as they come. People lifted a hand in greeting or nodded with a smile at passersby. Even so, little backwoods country towns were also known for corruption. Deerhaven was no different. It was all just a lovely cover while underneath the surface was a fetid, decaying mass of excrement.

That was the ugly truth no one wanted exposed. Maybe because they were afraid they'd get some of that stink on them, or maybe they were afraid someone would figure out that part of it was of their own making. Keep it all shoved down and hidden.

"Don't trouble trouble, and trouble won't trouble you." Wasn't that William Henderson's favorite line? Mayor Henderson was the ringmaster after all. He didn't cotton to people poking and probing around, her aunt once said. Still, even with all that nastiness, Deerhaven was home to many goodhearted people, people like Aunt Dottie.

Gentle, fragile Aunt Dottie.

Samantha stood five foot nine inches tall, curvy with a "sturdy" bone structure. Her aunt Dottie, an elegant and diminutive but plump woman was a giant in Samantha's eyes. Not just her family, her mentor, her friend, Dottie was her hero.

And now, something, no, some*one* had taken her hero away from her.

Accidental overdose, the coroner's report had read. That was bullshit. Dottie refused to take prescription pain pills, no matter the amount of pain she was suffering. She was terrified of them due to the addictions she'd seen so many others succumb to.

Someone had killed her aunt, and Samantha swore she'd figure out who.

She'd taken leave from the Detroit police department indefinitely. Captain Bradshaw officially gave her two weeks, but Samantha wasn't leaving Deerhaven until she ripped the cover off the whole disgusting mess this county had become and revealed every bottom-feeder involved in her aunt's death. If she lost her job, she'd just have to lose it.

With another deep breath, she reached up into the cabinet for the extra plates she'd come into the kitchen for in the first place. She needed to get back out there. She didn't give a damn about what the gossips had to say about her or her family, but she wouldn't ignore it either. She'd learned that in every fabricated story, there was a fragile thread of truth. So, she'd smile sweetly, accept the hugs, the condolences, and listen closely to the whispers exchanged once her back was turned.

It was her aunt Dottie who taught her to be "wise as a serpent and harmless as a dove." There were many valuable lessons she'd learned from Aunt Dottie. That particular one was her favorite.

Aunt Dottie was an intelligent woman of faith; however, she didn't pander to religion. She was wise and imparted that wisdom to all her nieces and nephews. Some of that wisdom came from the teachings of Jesus, some from brilliant wise men and prophets such as Gandhi, Buddha, Martin Luther King, Jr., and some were from the sharp sting of Aunt Dottie's wooden spoon.

In the dining room, Samantha set the plates at the end of the highly polished mahogany table filled with covered dishes, casseroles, pies, cookies, and cakes. Of course, there was that one lone bucket of Kentucky Fried Chicken. She couldn't help but smile at that. Lord but ranchers knew how to cook. Cowboys ate a lot. With so many people there, at least all the food would be eaten.

If not, she'd take what was left down to the mission. If that mission were still there.

Sadness was a whisper that settled over her softly. When her father's job offer in Michigan had taken her away from Deerhaven, she left a part of herself behind. Now it felt like that part of her was gone forever. Faded away like a wisp of smoke as time in the little town trudged on.

Everything changes.

Samantha turned to face the assembly of people and expressed her appreciation as these strangers hugged her or laid a sympathetic hand on her arm as they whispered their condolences. Accepting hugs and touches from these people was becoming more and more difficult, yet she smiled, nodded, and thanked them politely while she attempted to focus on individual discussions going on around her.

". . . happens in threes, they say." Samantha didn't look in the direction of the women.

"That's true. So tragic, though. And all three of 'em was awful cozy, if you know what I mean."

"Oh, honey, I know. There was talk of—"

The doorbell interrupted the ladies' discussion. Samantha kept her smile in place as she made her way through the small crowd. Her jaw was beginning to ache from the forcing a smile, from clenching her teeth in frustration.

"I'll get it." A woman waved to her as she stepped to the door and opened it.

"Thank you," she said as she leaned down to accept a hug from yet another little old lady who said she knew her when she was a baby. Then *his* voice captured her attention.

She didn't look up right away. Standing there stiffly, she smiled down at the lady. "Oh, Sheriff Steele is here. You remember him. Don't you, dear? Maybe not so much. He's a little older than you, I think," the grandmotherly woman said gently with an impish gleam in her eye.

Oh, Samantha remembered him.

Hunter Steele, the righter of her accidental-on-purpose wrongs, the conqueror of irksome, wannabe bullies that she couldn't resist provoking. He'd been her champion.

She nodded to the lady. "Yes, ma'am. I remember him."

He'd never seen her as anything other than a pesky little kid because that was exactly what she had been. She had constantly pushed the boundaries and was forever getting into trouble.

When she was seven, Hunter had swooped in and saved her from being beaten by the Collins boys for daring to defend her friend Jesse after they knocked him around and stole his Gameboy. Donnie and Robbie were three and four years older than her and twice as big, but she was mad and had lost all rationality.

Hunter was popular around town. His family ran the well-known Steele Spur Ranch. Samantha had known him all her life, but when he made it clear he would bury the boys if he ever found out they'd picked on her or anybody else, in her mind she'd gained a champion. It only made her bolder and more mischievous. That's when he nicknamed her Pixie Pest.

Four years later her parents uprooted and moved away from her quiet, country hometown to the cold, often cruel city of Detroit. She'd been torn away from the only life she'd known, the rugged, beautiful open spaces, from friends she'd had since birth and grown up with, people she cared about and who cared about her.

Several families came by to wish them well and say goodbye. Hunter had been there with his uncle. He'd smiled down at her as he tugged her ponytail and told her to behave and stay out of trouble.

The next time she saw him was in town while she was visiting Aunt Dottie with her daddy, several years later. They were going into the restaurant as he was coming out with a very pretty lady on his arm. He greeted her dad with a grin, finally turning his gaze to her, and his expression went blank.

She'd never forget that look on his face. He probably didn't recognize her. But at the time Samantha was seventeen. All teenage angst and romantic dreams. He had been twenty-five then and apparently attached. His companion was stoic but didn't let go of his arm.

Samantha no longer saw him as her own personal bodyguard who kept bailing her out of her shenanigans. He took her breath away, made her heart race. Heat bloomed in her cheeks even now as memories flashed through her mind. She had been awkward but shameless in her attempt to attract him.

He had looked at her like he didn't know her and then completely ignored her. Lord, she hoped he didn't remember.

"Sheriff!" the sweet old lady called to him. Samantha cringed inwardly but managed a weak smile as she looked up and watched him saunter toward them, Stetson in hand.

Always the gentleman.

He hadn't changed much. He seemed bigger, his shoulders broader. His signature thick, black hair was cut in a shorter style. As he got closer, Samantha noticed his face had changed quite a bit. Any boyish softness he'd once had was all gone and had been replaced with hard planes and angles, except for his full, well-defined lips. There were fine laugh lines fanning out from the corners of his steel gray eyes. Those eyes were more intense, hard. The easy laughter that lit them when he was younger seemed to be gone.

"Ms. Bell." He nodded in greeting to the diminutive lady.

"Good of you to come by, Sheriff. Little Samantha is handlin' all this by herself." She winked and patted his arm. "She could use a little help, I'm thinkin'."

Samantha wanted to walk away. She also wanted to throw her arms around Hunter and hold on for dear life. Not just because he still made her heart pound, but because he was a part of her life she thought she'd lost. She wanted to hold on to a stable, warm part of her past where she was happy and safe. Seeing him again brought those memories and emotions all rushing back.

"Hey, Sam." The smooth, deep bass of his voice was quiet and soothing.

"Hey, Hunter." His name left her lips with more composure than she felt.

"I'm sorry I couldn't make it to the funeral, but I wanted to come by to extend my condolences, and to see how you're doin'." He stepped closer and rubbed her bare upper arm. "You holdin' up okay?" His hand, a bit rough and callused from real work, was warm, reassuring.

She crossed her arms over her chest. "I'm okay, Hunter, thank you." She cleared her throat. "Everyone brought food. The dining room table is overflowing. Help yourself."

He followed her through the living room to the dining room. She turned and almost jumped back. He was standing inches away, looking down at her. His brows furrowed, his gaze sharply assessing her. He smelled incredible, and he stood so close she could feel the heat from his body.

She opened her mouth to say something but forgot what she wanted to say. She must look completely ignorant gaping up at him like that.

"Are you sure you're all right?" Sympathy and concern shadowed his expression, softening the harsher lines of his face.

"It's been a long day. I'm fine, really." She was a basket case, and not just because of her aunt's death.

Hunter gave her a gentle smile and pulled out a chair. "No doubt. Sit and talk to me for a while. I haven't seen you in what? Ten years?"

Samantha welcomed the chance to get off her feet and get away from the crowd for a bit. "Yeah, about ten years, I think."

He pulled out the chair beside her, turned it toward her, and sat, staring at her solemnly. "I'm real sorry about Dottie."

"Me too." She looked into his eyes, assessing whether she could or should continue. "I really didn't get enough time with her. I'll always regret that."

Hunter shook his head. "Sam, you know Dottie thought the world of you. She knew you loved her and she loved you."

Had she? Samantha couldn't help but question the observation. School, her career, and far too many emotions had seemed to always get in the way of returning to Deerhaven.

"Yes, I know, but I look around at these people and think of how some of them probably knew her even better than I did, her own niece." Samantha frowned and gestured toward a blue-haired woman sitting on the couch sobbing, clutching another woman's hand. "Mrs. Holt is devastated."

She obviously had not talked to her aunt on the phone enough either, because Dottie had never mentioned the other woman.

A small smile touched Hunter's far-too-sensual lips as he lowered his head and leaned closer. "Sam, Irene Holt never even met Dottie. She attends any and all funerals and wails and carries on like that at every one of 'em." Amusement touching his gaze.

Samantha looked at him incredulously until he raised his hand and said, "Hand to God. Every one of 'em."

"Wow." No wonder her aunt Dottie had never mentioned the other woman.

"Yep." Hunter's smile broadened. "As for the rest of them, they're just being neighborly or nosy. Most of 'em still remember your family and you. You were pretty hard to forget . . . Pixie Pest." His brows lifted playfully. Teasingly.

Samantha narrowed her eyes. "Ugh. That nickname. I don't know which is worse, that or Sami Jo."

She protested it. Just as she always had. That flare of warmth she felt whenever it passed his lips was still there, though.

"You earned it."

"Psh, whatever." She'd actually worked at it at the time.

Hunter chuckled and she nearly sighed. Lord, she'd missed his laugh, his smile, even the way he'd tease her. She'd missed him.

"Aw, you know I was always fond of you, Pixie. You were a great kid, even if you were a pest that was constantly following me around and giving my girlfriends hell."

She had been such a tomboy with wild, young girl fantasies of being swept off her feet by the cutest boy in Deerhaven, or the whole wide world, for that matter. He'd called her his Pixie Pest whenever he'd seen her and tugged at her long, tangled hair.

"I'm not a kid anymore." She held his gaze and couldn't imagine how she'd gotten so bold.

Hunter's gaze traveled over her body, a single black brow arching slowly in acknowledgment. "I've noticed. I'm trying really hard to remember what a pain in the ass you used to be."

Samantha lifted a brow. "I can still be a pain in the ass."

"I bet you can." The look in his eyes was making her feel way too hot, way too needy.

She didn't want to go there. Not now. After Tom Novak, the very last thing she needed was another relationship. Besides all that, she was here to get answers, not to get laid.

Clearing her throat again, she changed the subject to the one on which she had to keep her focus. "Hunter, what really happened to Aunt Dottie?"

His smile faded and his gaze sharpened. "What do you mean?"

"Aunt Dottie had a sharp mind. She didn't overdose accidently, no way in hell would she overdose on purpose. What happened?"

Hunter never broke eye contact. "We're in a cornfield, Sam."

It took her a minute to realize he meant there were too many ears around.

"Fine. I'll ask you this question again later. But, just so you know, I'm not leaving Deerhaven until I get the answer."

Hunter nodded. "Understood."

Samantha stood. "I'm being rude sitting here. I better go mingle. Please, get yourself something to eat and fix a plate to take home."

His lopsided smile gave her pause as he stood and took a plate from the stack. "There's iced tea in the kitchen. Make yourself at home," she added warily.

With a deep breath, she turned away and walked into the living room. There stood William Henderson, shaking hands with everyone, his practiced smile in place. He wore expensive suits and kept his hair slicked back and combed over to hide his bald spot. He thought himself attractive and carried himself like he was the king of everything.

Samantha straightened her spine and pasted on a smile of her own as she forced herself forward. Henderson looked up and tilted his head, a sympathetic expression on his face.

"It is good to see you again, Samantha. I do wish it were under better circumstances."

She took his hand. "Yes, thank you, Mayor."

"I'm truly sorry for your loss. Dottie was a fine woman and a beloved citizen. It's a shame."

Samantha looked up at him. Mayor Henderson was intimidating physically. He'd had a little more than his share of fried chicken with gravy and biscuits. Add to that his broad shoulders and height, at least six three, the man tended to block out the light. He didn't intimidate her, though. She'd taken down men his size before, both figuratively and literally.

"Mayor." Hunter held out his hand as he stepped beside her, surprising her. She hadn't known he had followed her.

"Hello there, Hunter. I thought I might run into you here." The mayor smiled jovially.

"Of course." Hunter was an inch or two shorter than Henderson but had a lot more muscle and good sense. He wasn't the least bit intimidated. The hard look in his eyes belied the tight smile that curved his lips.

"Listen, Hunter, how about using your infamous charm to get little Samantha here to transfer back home? It'd be good to have her home again, and I hear she's got a good reputation with the Detroit PD," the mayor announced abruptly.

A myriad of emotions flashed through Samantha all at once, and she steeled herself against letting them show on her face. Besides the misogynistic comment, he'd obviously been inquiring about her with the department. That didn't sit well at all.

Hunter chuckled easily. "I don't know about charm." He glanced at Samantha and what she saw in his eyes didn't match the amiable smile that curved his lips. "But I'll do what I can."

Samantha's grin was more like a grimace. "While I appreciate the compliment"—she had to concentrate to unclench her jaw so as not to growl at the men through her teeth—"I have to say, regardless of the volume of charm being displayed at the moment, I'm happy with the Detroit PD and have no plans to leave."

Henderson's grin was condescending as he shook Hunter's hand again, slapping him on the shoulder with his other hand. "You do what you can, Sherriff. We could use another deputy."

"Excuse me." Samantha managed an affected chuckle. "I should go . . . mingle." And with that, she escaped without losing her temper.

Time plodded along as Samantha sat in the dim living room with its bold magnolia prints and crocheted doilies. She listened to and laughed at stories of Dottie's escapades. She answered questions about her parents and didn't pull away when visitors held her hand and patted it sympathetically as she explained that her father had died three years ago of a heart attack.

Their concern for her seemed genuine and the kind words and gentle touches were a surprising comfort to her. She found herself remembering that rare country hospitality she'd missed for fifteen years.

It was late when the last person, none other than

Mrs. Holt herself, hugged her, patted her cheek, and left. Samantha closed the door and leaned against it, shutting her eyes with a sigh. It warmed her heart that at least some of these people not only spent time cooking for her, but also gave up their entire Saturday in her aunt's memory. The feeling was bittersweet in that she did have happy memories, but she'd been cheated out of so much.

"Everyone finally leave?" Hunter's voice, so unexpected, had her reaching for the weapon she hadn't worn, then attempting to cover the move by propping her hand on her hip self-consciously.

"I thought you'd left," she exclaimed, her heart racing as she laid her hand over her heart a second later.

"Sorry I startled you." Hunter smiled, watching her with observant gray eyes.

"It's okay." She pushed away from the door. "Everyone has left, except you."

Something in his eyes made her heart leap. She swallowed and gestured toward the dining room. "You should take some of that food home."

Hunter shook his head. "Already put up. There wasn't much left, but it's in the freezer, labelled, dated, and everything. Dishes are all washed and put up too."

He'd done dishes?

"Well. Thank you." She was a little more than surprised.

"No problem. You're tired. Hated for you to have to deal with the mess." He stepped closer, his expression stern. "There's a plate for you in the fridge. Make sure you eat it."

She smiled up at him, nodding. "Okay, I will." She

paused. "Is now a good time to talk? No more ears." She gestured.

His eyes narrowed. "I'm working on it, Sam. Let me deal with it. Will you be selling the house?" he asked quietly.

She sighed and furrowed her brows. It would sell rather easily. A great starter home. Small, well-maintained, two-bedroom home on a lovely three-acre plot of land. It had briefly crossed her mind. The memories were too bright, the pain too raw to seriously think about it at the moment. "I don't know yet. I had thought about it, but now . . . I don't know. Stop evading the question."

"I'm not evading. I told you, I'm investigating. This is just not something you need to poke around in."

Oh really? Narrowing her eyes on him, she stared back, assuring him that wasn't going to happen. "Yeah? Well, too bad. I'm poking." The decision had already been made. She wasn't leaving, she couldn't leave, until she knew what had happened to her aunt.

He watched her intently, as if he was sizing her up.

"Look, Hunter. I know you don't know me anymore. I'm not that kid you liked to tease. I'm an officer with the Detroit PD now and—"

"I should have expected as much," Hunter interrupted. He wasn't smiling, however. That's okay. She wasn't either. She was dead serious.

"And . . . I'm here to find out what happened to my aunt," she continued. "I know there's a connection to your uncle and Lillian Henderson. You have to see that."

"How long are you on leave?" His gentle words contradicted his hard expression and the sharp intent in his gaze.

She braced herself and looked him in the eye. He may try to run her off, he may even call Captain Bradshaw. Either way, he'd better be ready for a fight. "Officially, I have two weeks. I'm not leaving until I set this straight."

She held her ground under his intense glare, refusing to break eye contact.

"Fine."

Well, that was unexpected. "So, Sheriff, are you gonna work with me or am I gonna have to fight you every step of the way?"

The corner of his mouth curved into a slow smile. "No, Pixie, I'm not gonna fight you. *You* can work with *me*, however. My town. My rules."

"Psh, the hell with that. It's my town too." It always had been, whether she lived there or not, it was home.

"God, you're still such a pest." His mischievous grin irked her, and she narrowed her eyes. "I'm the one with the authority here, Sam."

"Yeah, but that doesn't make me any less qualified or skilled to help with this investigation. Someone killed my aunt, Hunter!" she hissed.

"Someone killed my uncle, Samantha." His voice was deep and held an edge of growing anger. The muscle in his jaw pulsed as he clenched his jaw.

Samantha uncrossed her arms but didn't reach out to him. She had been so self-centered, so wrapped up in her mission that she hadn't considered his pain.

"I know. You're right. I'm sorry."

His body remained as rigid. "So, yes. I get it, but you will do things my way. This town is my responsibility, and while I'm as eager to uncover all this shit as you are, this is gonna take finesse and time."

It wasn't just her arguing with him that caused the frustration she saw in his expression. "Okay."

His shoulders relaxed a bit. "Don't worry, I won't leave you out of the loop. Hell, you and I are the loop."

She nodded, wondering if he would really keep her informed, or was he just placating her? The Hunter she knew was extremely protective and wasn't above keeping things from her if he thought there was even a remote chance she could get hurt. Maybe that wasn't so bad when she was a starry-eyed teenager. Now, she was quite capable of taking care of herself. She didn't have tight abs, her muscles weren't defined and prominent. Having a body that was curvy and feminine gave her an edge. People didn't expect her to be physically strong, quick, or dexterous. She was all three and tactful enough to know how to use those qualities most productively.

"Hunter, I trust your word." She knew his word was important to him. He knew she was using that fact too, judging by the way he narrowed his eyes. "Please, don't make me regret it."

He rolled his eyes and changed the subject. "Do you like living in Detroit?"

She had to think about it for a moment. Honestly she had, but being home reminded her of all the things she missed by living in a highly populated, metropolitan city. "Detroit is a great city. So much history, culture, and art. There's always something to do. It's Motown! The Motor City!" She grinned.

"Yes, it is. But you didn't answer my question." Hunter lifted a brow.

With a sigh, Samantha looked around the room at the things that reminded her of her youth and a part of herself that she'd left behind when they'd moved away. The truth was, she felt whole here. "Yes. I like living in Detroit. I love being a cop." She met his gaze. "But Deerhaven is a part of me that I didn't even realize I missed."

He smiled at her then. That crooked, sexy smile that always made her feel like she was the only girl in the world he smiled at that way. He made her feel special. She smiled back, wondering just how many women felt special because Hunter Steele graced them with his wicked smile. "I better head out; I've stayed too long already. The hens will be talkin' about how long my truck sat in your driveway."

Samantha laughed, following him to the door. "Since when have I cared what anyone thought or said about me?"

"Point taken." He stopped, turned to face her, and to her surprise he pulled her into his arms. "It's good to see you again, Pixie."

A moment passed, maybe two, before she wrapped her arms around him and hugged him back. His warmth enveloped her, and she breathed in the scent of him. The embrace had already passed casual. She pulled away, but he didn't completely release her. "Good to see you too." Her voice was way too breathy sounding. Lord.

He pressed his lips to her forehead then met her gaze. She watched in fascination as they darkened and turned stormy. She opened her mouth to say something, and he lowered his head and kissed her. A small kiss, lingering only seconds, but the impact was powerful. When he let her go, she felt suddenly cold.

"Come by the station Monday morning." There was an edge to his voice, rough and dark. She couldn't let herself analyze it.

Even as the thought bloomed in her mind, she knew she would. She'd be thinking about that simple kiss all night. Dammit.

"Okay." She nodded, folding her arms over her chest.

He turned and opened the door. "If you need anything, call me." He walked out onto the porch. "Lock up."

"I will." She fought her desire to ask him to stay.

"Good night, Sam."

"Good night, Hunter." He pulled the door shut, and she chained and bolted it. Samantha walked into the spotless kitchen, her body humming with arousal. She ran her fingers through her hair in frustration. Sleep was definitely going to be hard to achieve tonight.

chapter two

Hunter shook his head, sitting in his truck, watching Sam's silhouette through the windows as she moved through the house. Just keeping an eye on her, he told himself. The circumstances behind her aunt's death weren't sitting well with him, and that worried him. It made him worry for her.

Sam would protest that she could take care of herself, and no doubt, she could in most circumstances. But he couldn't seem to help the impulse, couldn't help following the movement of her shadow from one window to the other, and wish he were in there with her.

A grin tipped his lips at the thought. In the little time he'd spent with her since she'd been back in town, she'd fascinated him. She was quick. She was smart. And she was damned dangerous to a man's heart if he wasn't careful.

It didn't help that he'd missed her with a surprising

strength when she'd left town all those years ago. He'd keep expecting to see her just behind him, waiting to sabotage his date to slip into some kind of mischief. And slipping into mischief was something she'd been real good at.

As the windows went dark, he waited until the back bedroom light came on to start the Jeep and pull away. But it didn't stop thoughts of his Pixie Pest.

He had been willing to bet she'd have a family by now. He certainly never imagined she'd be a cop. He'd imagined Sam married, maybe with a kid or two of her own. Undoubtedly no threat to his bachelorhood, or sanity, whatsoever.

Yeah, right. She had no husband or kids to protect her from him. Or him from her. Over the years what he'd seen in those pretty, wide, blue-green eyes of hers had gone from wild, innocent wonder, to yearning curiosity. Independent, badass cop or not, there was still that same sweet, mischievous innocence in her eyes along with a fiery determination that only made her all the more intriguing.

Hell yeah, he was going to be distracted. That was an understatement.

Maybe she had changed. They both had. Life had a way of doing that to everyone. But Sam was still the same in a lot of ways. He'd be willing to bet that she'd caused a ruckus or two with that balls-to-the-wall approach to anything and everything she went after. There was no doubt she was a damned good cop. It was in the way she watched everyone, gauged their actions, kept her eye on everything without seeming to. She was suspicious, and no way would she sit back and leave this investigation to him.

He almost hadn't shown up at all. He hadn't gone to the viewing and deftly avoided the funeral. It wasn't all that hard to do. He needed to stay on top of this investigation, and no one was making it easy for him. Add to that, the fucked-up mess of paperwork he'd inherited with the position. It was more than fair to say he was swamped. The truth was, in spite of all that, he knew he'd have to see her. Not really sure why the idea of seeing her again put him off so badly. But it had been easy for him to follow his instinct.

Where Sam was concerned, his instinct had told him to keep a good, safe distance from anything outside the parameters of friendship.

She had been a funny kid, always getting into jams and running to him to get her out of them. She'd pretty much used him as her own personal guard dog. He hadn't minded so much. The girl thought she was invincible and could take on the whole world. It seemed she still believed she was.

But when she came to town with her daddy to visit Dottie, everything had changed. She had just turned seventeen, but she sure as hell hadn't looked seventeen. He'd been nearly twenty-six and engaged to Kelly. His reaction to seeing her scared the bejeezus out of him. So, he'd stayed away.

Even if he hadn't been about to get married, he would have stayed away.

Maybe.

As tough as Sam liked to think she was now, she was

still a tender, innocent little thing, and he wasn't interested in being the one to destroy that. It was too rare. What he'd wanted to do was protect her and keep her that way forever. Damn stupid notion, that was.

His gut had been right. It never let him down. He should have heeded its warning about Kelly. Distractions like Sam were more than he needed right now anyway.

No way in hell was she going to be easy to deal with, though. If there's one thing he knew all too well about Samantha Jolene, it was that she never let go of what she was after.

She wanted in on this investigation, and she wouldn't let him get in her way. But his intense attraction and need to protect and shelter her made the situation dangerous. The whole combination of woman-child was messing with him on too many levels.

Ah shit.

Yeah, his fucked-up situation just got worse.

Somehow, he was going to have to ignore his libido and keep his focus on his investigation. It was too important. The last conversation he had with his uncle Zachariah, the tough, ex-marine turned sheriff who had helped raise him, played through his mind.

"I gotta tell ya, something's up, son," Zachariah confided in Hunter quietly as they sat on the porch of the Steele family home. *"The mayor's dirty dealin'. I can smell it."*

He spit a stream of tobacco juice off the side of the porch before leaning back in his chair. Zachariah was in his late fifties, robust and healthy, and as agile-minded as he was in the marines.

"How so?" Hunter watched him curiously. He knew Mayor Henderson all his life. The man was a sleaze-ball, but he never thought was a criminal sleazeball.

Zachariah shook his gray head slowly. "Not sure, but I'm tellin' you, Hunter, I know a good deal about the man. He's flashing money he shouldn't have and meeting with some real slick characters of late. He's edgy, and Lillian's death was too suspicious to suit me. She was a fine swimmer. Granted, that don't mean a whole hell of a lot. But that was a fishin' pond. She didn't care for fishin' in the least. What the hell was she doing out at the pond?"

Zachariah's voice had been somber. Lillian Henderson had been Zachariah's girl before she married the other man. When Zachariah had joined the marines and gone off to war, she had married the only son of the caretaker rather than waiting for him to return.

Zachariah had never gotten over it, as far as Hunter knew. And Lillian had deeply regretted it. They'd become good friends, and Hunter had often wondered if they had been having an affair.

The possibility that his uncle's relationship with Mrs. Henderson had something to do with his suspicions concerning the mayor had crossed his mind.

Now, Hunter wasn't so sure.

Zachariah's sudden "hunting" accident was just bullshit.

Hunter understood that most of the men in the area lived for hunting. Zachariah, being the outdoors-loving mountain man he was, gave the impression that he'd be a hunter.

Somebody didn't do their research and screwed up

royally on that hit. He had no doubt it was indeed a hit. Whether it was a crime of passion or something much more sinister, that was what he needed to find out.

Hunter pulled into the parking lot of the sheriff's office and parked in his space. He sat in the gathering darkness, staring at the aging stone building that housed the jail as well as his office. That he didn't trust his men or the mayor meant he was on his own in this investigation. He didn't have the luxury of being less than discreet.

The few friends he had grown up with were mostly gone now. Not that he was an outsider, except in the sheriff's department. There, he felt more and more alone and scrutinized amid the few deputies who were much too friendly with Henderson.

Shane Warren was smart, quiet, and he watched things. He had been Hunter's only addition to the force. Shane wouldn't be there if it hadn't been for Hunter's brother-in-law, Mark. Shane and his younger twin brothers, Levi and Ethan, were Mark's nephews and he got them jobs helping Hunter keep the ranch running smoothly for a while before Uncle Zachariah was killed. But, Shane had his mind set on law enforcement, and, Shane's mom, Mark's sister, Gracie Anne, wasn't able talk him out of going to the academy.

"Hire the boy," Mark suggested quietly after Hunter took office. "He's dependable and needs the experience."

At the time, Hunter was well aware of the general atmosphere of insubordination that he was facing. He could try to fire them, but he knew Rodgers and Decker, the two deputies causing him the most concern, would whine to the mayor, and he'd end up being forced to reinstate them. Plus, it would be harder to keep track of them if they were there under his watch. It was best if he could just stay low-key and appear to be oblivious.

On the surface, everything looked about normal. There was the usual influx of drugs into the county. Not as much of an issue as the meth cookers up in the hills. That was a constant strain and irritation on him. There weren't many strangers moving into town, and fewer people just driving through. Unless you counted the short, mysterious disappearances Henderson made on occasion.

Those times when he went missing were odd, though. Where the hell he went, Hunter had yet to figure out. He wouldn't be gone long, but no one could track him down when he went poof. Usually only lasted a day at the most. No one else seemed to pay them any mind. Hunter, however, figured it was part of all the mess that didn't add up.

He got out of his truck and hit the lock button as his thoughts drifted back to Sam. Dammit. Despite her in-decision about the house, she was a city girl. He could see it all over her. Once the real reason Dottie died was exposed and the case was closed, Hunter was pretty certain she'd go back to Detroit. Best thing for him to do was let her help him.

He drew in a deep breath, thinking about how pretty she looked standing there, enduring. Her eyes filled with sorrow, her arms wrapped around herself for comfort. She was as strong as she was beautiful. Holding her for that brief moment had felt so good. She fit in his arms so well, it was hard to let her go.

Hell, maybe he had been too long without a woman.

The last thing he wanted from Sam was a one-night stand. He'd had plenty of those after Kelly. If he'd wanted more, there were plenty of "Kellys" in the county to choose from. Sam was no Kelly.

A relationship just wasn't in the cards. It would be so fine, though, damned fine to curl up with Sam, feeling her warm softness against him.

"Dammit," he grumbled low, as he unlocked the door and stepped into the dimly lit office. Decker was sitting at his desk, typing away at his report. He didn't bother hiding his anger as he lifted his gaze to glare at Hunter.

"How's it comin', Decker? You about done?" he asked with false joviality.

Decker mumbled something under his breath.

"What was that?" Hunter asked from his office.

"I said, I'll have it to you shortly!" Decker shouted back.

Hunter grinned, entered his office, and sat at his desk to begin sorting through the paperwork that had been deposited there haphazardly.

He busied himself reading reports, and then filing them as he waited for Decker to finish, all while trying to keep his thoughts off one Miss Samantha Ryder.

It wasn't a long wait, but he got all his filing done by the time Decker dropped his report on Hunter's desk.

"Happy?" Decker's voice was a bit too high with residual outrage.

"Well, now. That remains to be seen," Hunter said, as he picked up the report and read it out loud. Slowly. He pointed out grammatical and spelling errors, then circled them with a red pen.

Decker balled his fists at his sides but remained silent.

His face turned as red as the ink on his report. No matter how hard Hunter tried, he couldn't piss the deputy off enough to make him quit. And evidently, he hadn't pissed anyone off enough to try to kill him yet either.

With an exaggerated sigh, Hunter dropped the pen back in the holder and handed the report back to Decker.

"Fix those mistakes," he ordered. "I better see it on my desk, corrected, when I get here in the morning."

"Fine." Decker managed to get the word past his clenched teeth as he snatched the report from Hunter's hand.

"All right then, you have a good night." Hunter motioned for him to leave his office.

Hunter shook his head and resisted the urge to sneer. He finished straightening his desk, grabbed his keys, and followed Decker out of the building.

His cell rang as he locked the door.

"Yeah."

"Hey, Sheriff. You still at the office?" Shane asked, his voice quiet.

"I was just locking up. What's up?" Hunter asked a bit absently, aware of Decker deliberately gunning the motor of his car as he reversed from his parking slot. That kind of adolescent aggression only made him look ridiculous, but no doubt, Decker fancied himself a bad-ass in his brand-new muscle car.

"Can you wait for me out by where you usually park? I wanted to discuss something with you privately. I'm almost there." Shane sounded far more serious than normal.

Hunter's brows lifted in surprise. "Yep. I'll be there."

The thought occurred to him that Shane could be

trying to get him out alone to make it easy for someone to target him, but he didn't think so. It didn't fit really. It just wasn't in the kid's character. Besides, his brother-in-law trusted him. His aunt trusted him. That spoke well of the younger deputy. The current state of affairs had Hunter second-guessing everyone. Unfortunately, he couldn't afford to be trusting, he had no other choice but to be suspicious of everything and everyone right now.

It was a beautiful night, the kind of night when a man could enjoy a cigarette, he thought with fleeting regret. Aunt Madeline had bullied him into giving them up years ago, and he was glad she did. Still, nights like this he sure as hell wanted one. He took a toothpick out of his pocket and put it between his teeth instead, as he leaned against his Jeep and waited.

Shane pulled into the parking lot moments later. He got out of his Mustang and scanned the area as he walked over to where Hunter waited for him.

"Sheriff?" Shane nodded, his expression creased with indecision.

Hunter narrowed his eyes on the deputy. He liked him, couldn't help it. But he'd learned to be on guard. The boy was family by marriage, but like Hunter, he'd been raised in Deerhaven and could well have stronger loyalties to the wrong people.

"What did you need?" he asked.

Shane glanced toward the sheriff's office then back to the shadows where they stood and stepped closer, leaning against the truck as Hunter did, with his back to it, watching the parking area.

"Okay, here's the thing," he said quietly, having finally made up his mind. "Rodgers got a call earlier today, and whoever he was talking to evidently got pissed enough to start yelling. I was standing there . . ." Shane grimaced as Hunter's eyes narrowed slightly. "I feel like a tattletale. I mean, it's probably nothing, but the man was cursing him loud enough to wake the dead. Or I think it was cursing. Sure sounded like it. Anyway, I couldn't help but overhear."

It was obvious Shane wasn't comfortable tattling as he called it, but he had good instincts it seemed, and those instincts were warning him that something wasn't right where that phone call was concerned.

"You're good, Shane. Go on." Hunter frowned, tension invading his body as he felt another piece of the puzzle falling into place.

"It was just damned strange. I could have sworn the words weren't English. I couldn't place the language, though." He shook his head, grimacing at whatever he heard. "Hell, it's just been bothering me."

Now, wasn't that interesting.

Hunter shrugged, feigning indifference. "Who knows who Rodgers has pissed off this week?"

Rodgers was known to piss off everyone except his good buddy the mayor. But whatever Shane had heard, whoever he'd heard, it wasn't normal or it wouldn't be bothering him bad enough to bring it to Hunter's attention.

Shane scoffed. "Hell, if that ain't the truth. I figured it was nothing, but you know, with everything that's been happening lately . . ." Shane sobered. "And Rodgers, well, he looked a little freaked out too. Got my Spidey senses tinglin'."

Hunter chuckled. The kid was such a nerd.

Shane grinned. "Anyway, I figured it wouldn't hurt to tell ya."

Like Hunter, Shane sensed Decker and Rodgers couldn't be trusted, or he would have kept his suspicions to himself.

"Yeah. You're right. Didn't hurt anything at all." Hunter nodded. "Thanks for lookin' out. You know how Joe Rodgers is, though. He's an abrasive fella, keeps everyone pissed."

It was the best he could do to waylay those suspicions. Shane was young and idealistic; Hunter didn't want him going off on his own to investigate something that would get him killed. Mark might never forgive him if Hunter let something happen to his nephew. Gracie Anne sure as hell wouldn't forgive him, and her husband, Clyde, would just kill him. Simple as that.

Hunter suspected Clyde was one of the few people who could actually do it too.

"Yeah, guess so." Shane sounded as uncertain as Hunter felt.

Shane shifted from one foot to the other as though standing still was too much for his body to handle for too long.

He was like a pup, always ready to dive into the next adventure. "I better get goin'. I'm gonna drive out to the lake. There's a few friends meeting up there tonight."

"Be careful. Give me a call if anything starts looking rough. You're not really a superhero, you know," Hunter reminded him, grinning.

Shane grimaced. "You're as bad as that danged brother-in-law of yours. I'm not stupid either, Sheriff."

There was a shade of offense in the kid's tone. Hunter

sighed. *Damned kids think they're indestructible. That's how they end up being dragged out of the lake . . . or worse.*

"I'm aware of that, Shane." He nodded. "Just a warning I'd give to any of my men. No offense intended."

Shane paused, his gaze intent as it met Hunter's before he seemed to accept the explanation.

"Yeah. Okay then. I'll be careful." Shane smiled sheepishly. "Sorry, Sheriff."

"No apology needed. Night, Shane." Hunter watched as Shane turned and headed across the parking lot to his car.

He searched the area carefully, his eyes narrowing as he assured himself no one had overheard the conversation. It might be nothing, as he had tried to convince Shane, but it wasn't the first clue like this one he had come across.

Now, he just had to figure out what the hell it meant.

chapter three

Samantha kept herself busy most of the day. She had spent the morning neatly folding Aunt Dottie's clothes, organizing and carefully boxing them up. Who knew her aunt had so many clothes?

She realized she didn't know as much about her aunt as she believed. They'd talked on the phone every month or so. Samantha had kept promising to come visit, but she never did. That guilt would be a thorn in her side for the rest of her life.

When she was younger, she and Aunt Dottie been closer, but after the move, Dottie seemed more distant whenever Samantha talked to her. Thinking back, she wondered if that had been deliberate. Had Dottie purposefully cut herself off from her brother and his family?

The ladies from the mission came by after church and picked up the boxes. It was clear they wanted to stay and chat a while. Samantha was quick to apologize, telling them she would invite them in but she had so much to do to get Aunt Dottie's affairs straight. It wasn't a lie.

Aunt Dottie's business paperwork was spread all over the dining room table. She promised to call them if she had more things they might be able to use.

It took Samantha more than a couple of hours to go through all of Aunt Dottie's bank statements. Nothing looked suspicious, but she put them all back in the accordion files they'd been kept in. She had five of them, one for every year over the past five years. Thank God Aunt Dottie was so organized. She'd found the deed to her house and a key to a bank safety deposit box.

Now this could prove interesting, she thought, pursing her lips as she examined the little silver key. Or, it could be nothing at all. Only one way to find out. She slid it onto her key ring, grabbed her purse, and locked the door on her way out.

Not much had changed. She noticed there were a few new fast food places closer to town now. Town being a stretch of road that had built up a bit. They had a new co-op feed store, some business offices, and a dollar store, still no Walmart. That was not a bad thing in her opinion. The bank was on the square, though, and the only thing that had changed was the little shops.

Some were new, some had changed out with something else, and some were empty. Samantha loved the nostalgic feel of the square, like she'd stepped into an old western movie set. The architecture of the shops gave it that air, the little mom-and-pop pharmacy looked the same as it always had. She wondered if the Abernathys still ran it. The antiques shop was new but fit right in, even the bank gave Deerhaven personality.

There were probably hundreds of these town squares all over the country, but this was Deerhaven's, and it would always be Samantha's home.

She made it into the bank just in time, with only thirty minutes to spare. After showing the banker her documents proving she was the executor and sole beneficiary, then wading through some red tape, Samantha was led into the vault and the safety deposit box was unlocked with both her key and the bank's. The banker set the box on the table with a forced smile and left her to open it in privacy.

Samantha wasn't sure what she expected to find, but she didn't expect the small flash drive. Aunt Dottie didn't even have a cell phone, much less a computer. There was no note, nothing else inside the box. She slipped it into the zippered pocket inside her purse and left the vault.

Her heart was pounding, her mind whirling with questions. The secure, department-issued laptop was in Detroit. It wouldn't be easy to get access to a computer without people prying. The library had a computer, but that was not at all secure. Hunter had to have one. She'd have to wait and figure out a plausible reason to go see him the next day. Being inconspicuous was no easy task in this nosy little town.

Back at the house, Samantha made a pot of coffee and got back to the business of clearing out Aunt Dottie's things to take her mind off what might be on the flash drive. There wasn't much left to do.

In the bathroom, Samantha put three bottles of medications in a Ziploc bag and set it aside. Aunt Dottie was very practical, she had the typical toiletries, mostly store brands, two tubes of lipstick in very tame shades of pink and coral. Samantha smiled at that—she had a cool color and a warm color. Aunt Dottie was a lovely woman and hadn't needed makeup even if she had wanted to wear it. She always said it made her face feel dirty. However, she never went without her lipstick.

Samantha chuckled at her reflection in her aunt's gilded bathroom mirror, remembering the wild and crazy girl she used to be.

Her face had always been dirty. She'd been such a tomboy. Her hair, now often kept up in some way, had been a wild mop of tangled curls back then. Her freckles were more prominent and plentiful from always playing outside in the sun, forever running all over the county getting into mischief. She had such great memories of fishing in the lake, swimming in the deepest part of the creek, climbing trees . . . falling out of trees.

She finished tossing out the partially used bottles and boxing up the unopened ones for the mission, then carried the box to the living room. She looked around at the few knickknacks that sat collecting dust here and there. It was very likely they were all given to her, and Samantha didn't have the heart to get rid of them. She sighed, thinking about what to do with them now. What about the doilies and the furniture? It felt like she was disassembling the beloved woman's life.

She shook her head in a feeble attempt to clear the cobwebs of sadness and nostalgia, and walked back into the bedroom. Two weeks wasn't going to be enough time to settle everything. Any longer and she'd be jeopardizing her job, possibly her career. She loved being a cop, but she'd been disillusioned with her life in Detroit. Honestly, she wasn't sure what she wanted to do.

Hopefully by the end of the two weeks she'd have some kind of clue what she wanted to do next. Maybe by then she'd miss the noisy city, annoyed by the slow, boring days in the country. She sat and flopped back on the bed, staring up at the ceiling. The peace and quiet in Deerhaven was something she hadn't known she needed. Lying there now, listening to the crickets and the frogs, was oddly soothing. She turned her head and stared at the glowing red numbers on the bedside alarm clock that told her it was six o clock. Really? Six already? She sighed again. It was going to be a long night.

A flash of inspiration had her grinning.

Night Hawk Saloon!

Maybe Sadie was still there. It would be so good to see her again. Sadie couldn't fuss at her this time. When she was ten, she'd been determined to sneak into the bar to watch everyone line dance, maybe annoy the hell out of Hunter by playing a trick on one of his dates. They'd always been so fussy.

She still laughed when she thought about the time she set that little frog on Chelsey Horton's shoulder. She didn't know it would slide down into her cleavage. Hell, it was barely a frog, just outta tadpole stage. She didn't know why Chels was carrying on so much.

Pixie Pest, he called her, trying to hide his smile and look angry so as not to piss off his date. He tugged at her long, tangled ponytail and threatened to tell her daddy, right before Sadie kicked her out and did worse— she called her mom.

Samantha laughed out loud remembering Chelsey's caterwauling. She looked through her suitcase for something to wear. She wondered if any of her friends from back then were still around. Probably not, most everyone she knew moved on. She might be able to scope out the current locals and eavesdrop on some gossip, though.

She stepped into the steamy shower. She couldn't believe Hunter was still there. Since he had joined the military like his daddy wanted him to, she had thought he would be overseas or at least stationed far away from home. She'd heard that he'd been in Special Forces and that he'd been deployed and had seen combat. She'd make a point to ask if all that was true when she saw him tomorrow. Well, unless by some chance he was at the Night Hawk tonight.

She stepped out of the shower into the small, humid bathroom, wrapping a towel around her. She wiped a washcloth across the mirror then carefully applied a little makeup and blow-dried her hair. She tilted her head, giving herself a quick check in the mirror, then went into the bedroom and dressed. She hadn't been a country girl for fifteen years, but she seemed to slip right back into the hick look easily enough with a baby-blue sleeveless, button-up, cotton shirt, blue jeans, and leather sandals. It amazed her how comfortable she felt. She wouldn't dream of going out to a bar dressed like this in Detroit.

It felt good to have her unruly hair loose and hanging free past her shoulders in big thick curls. She frowned at herself in the mirror and tried to picture what she'd look like with her hair cut short. May not be a bad idea, she thought. The severe bun she wore while at work gave her a headache.

She was excited at the prospect of seeing some folks

she knew before. She might even have a little fun. She checked to make sure her clip was full and slipped it into the inside pocket of her little leather cross-body bag. For a moment she debated about taking the flash drive out and stashing it somewhere. No, it was probably safer on her.

The parking lot wasn't too full but it was only seven o'clock. The nightlife wasn't even getting started yet, and it was Sunday. Some country folk had a thing about going to a bar on a Sunday. She handed her five-dollar cover to the man at the door and ignored his toothy grin and roaming eyes. She decided against sitting at the bar and made her way to the small booth in the dark corner in back where she could see everyone who came in.

She sat there a moment, scanning the faces. An older woman in a halter top and jeans sashayed up to the table. Her hair was aggressively teased and piled on top of her head like blond cotton candy, the prettiness of her wide brown eyes was lost in the heavy black mascara caking her lashes. "What'll ya have, hon?" she asked around her gum. It was all Samantha could do to keep from gaping. She hadn't seen Sadie in years, and she looked exactly the same. A couple of wrinkles here and there, but still the same.

"Sadie!"

"Yeah?" Sadie frowned then looked down at Samantha, narrowing her eyes. "Hey, I know you, you're . . . ah . . ."

Samantha couldn't help the grin that spread across her face. Sadie tilted her head to the side as she tapped her pen against her chin, thinking back.

A large hand rested on Sadie's shoulder. "That there is the Pixie Pest herself, Sadie."

"Oh my word!" Sadie's warm brown eyes widened in surprise. Her bright red lips spread into a grin. "Little Samantha? You better get up here and give me a hug!"

Samantha jumped up and embraced the woman. Over Sadie's shoulder, Samantha's gaze locked with Hunter's silvery-gray eyes, sparkling with humor. A slow smile slid across her face. The dark blue shirt he wore opened at the neck and tucked into his well-worn black jeans. His sleeves were rolled up, revealing muscular forearms. In one strong hand he held two frosty bottles of beer.

Sadie held Samantha away from her and shook her head. "Just look at you. All grown up." She glanced back at Hunter then rolled her eyes. "Oh boy! Well, I guess I can't kick your smart-mouthed little ass out this time. So, have a good time, but stay out of trouble, you hear? I bet I can still call your momma," she said, grinning. Sadie patted her cheek. "It's so good to see ya, hon. Y'all want somethin' to eat?"

"Maybe in a bit, Sadie." Samantha didn't take her eyes off Hunter.

"Okie doke. Y'all holler when you're ready."

"Will do," Hunter answered, as he slid into the booth across from Samantha and pushed a bottle across the table for her.

"Thanks," she said, keeping her eyes on him as she took a pull from the bottle. Those old butterflies that made her feel queasy ten years ago were coming back to life in the pit of her stomach.

He was leaning forward, watching her. "I saw you come in. Didn't expect to see you here."

Samantha rolled her lips inward to hide her grin. Something about sitting across from Hunter Steele in the Night Hawk, drinking a beer, seemed funny to her at the moment. "I thought it'd be fun to visit legally."

"Well, I'm here alone this time, Pixie. I don't have a date for you to harass." The way he held her gaze was like a dare, a challenge. It sent tingles rioting through her body.

"I guess I'll just have to harass you then, huh?"

He raised a brow as a slow grin revealed straight white teeth. He must have given up smoking, Samantha thought. Those teeth were too white for a smoker. "Uh-huh, well, you just be careful that you don't bite off more than you can chew." His eyes were full of mischief, making her want to test that warning. "So, listen, Sam. I've been thinkin'."

"Uh-oh." She winked at him, as she took another drink of her beer. "That could be dangerous."

"Ha. Ha." He narrowed his eyes, but his smile stayed in place. "About what Henderson said. It would be an awful lot easier for you to work with me on this, if you were working *for* me."

"You mean as a deputy?" Stunned, she stared at him.

"No. I need a housekeeper," he grunted, then chuckled when she kicked him under the table. "Yeah, as a deputy."

No way. There was just no way. There were a million reasons why that wouldn't work.

"I appreciate that. But I'll have to decline," she finally breathed out heavily, regretfully.

Working with Hunter was far different from working for Hunter in the sheriff's department, she assured herself. Yet, she couldn't help but be tempted as he stared back at her, his expression determined.

"Sam, you know this isn't likely to wrap up all nice and tidy in two weeks' time." He watched her too intently as he took a drink from the bottle.

Unfortunately, she had a feeling he was right, not that she wanted to admit to it. At least, not just yet.

"Yeah, well, we'll see." She looked down and picked at the label on her bottle as she sorted through the tangled web of responsibilities in her brain. "I've sent an email. I'm hoping the captain will maybe give me an extra two weeks."

She seriously doubted it. She hadn't accrued that much vacation or that many sick days. She'd be taking them without pay. Everything felt so open-ended and up in the air at the moment. It was going to take a lot of focus.

"Look. I know you don't have a lot of time to decide, but sleep on it. Let me know what you decide. I can get all the paperwork taken care of pretty quick. Henderson is all for it, so it won't be a problem."

If Henderson was all for it, then they might have a problem, she thought, frowning. She didn't like the mayor. There was something just wrong about him. That oily false charm of his set off warning signals in her like fireworks.

"Yeah, as if that's a positive." She snorted. "What's it pay?"

"Really?" Hunter chuckled and shook his head.

The amount he stated was ridiculous compared to what she was making.

"You're kidding me." That was probably the best they

could do for Deerhaven. She just wanted to give Hunter a hard time. She feigned a scowl, crossed her arms and leaned back against the padded booth. "Dude, I make twelve grand more than that, and I only have five years' experience on the Detroit force."

"*Dude*." The corner of Hunter's mouth lifted. "That's all I got to give you. And benefits."

Samantha narrowed her eyes. "What kind of benefits?"

"Well." With a suggestive glint in Hunter's eyes, he leaned forward. "Besides bein' under me"—his eyebrow lifted—"you'd get medical and dental. Optical too, but to be honest, it's shit."

She smiled at him before finally shaking her head. "I appreciate it, Hunter, but I'm going to pass."

She waved at Sadie to come back over and ordered a bacon cheeseburger with fries and a Coke. Hunter ordered the same.

"So, did you miss me?" Hunter asked with a smirk once Sadie walked away, apparently dropping the idea of her taking a position as deputy.

"Nah, haven't really thought about you," Samantha lied, holding his gaze. Since the last time she saw him, she'd thought about him often. It had been little more than a brief glance before he'd turned away. But the memory of how he had looked at her had stuck with her over the years. That was the first time anyone had looked at her like anything other than a little girl.

"Well, it has been awful quiet around here since you left." He grinned.

"Really?" She didn't hide the sarcasm.

"Yep. Nobody has gotten me into as much trouble or as many fights, that's for sure," he stated.

She laughed, remembering some of the problems she'd caused him. "Aww, sounds so boring."

Lifting her beer and sipping again, she noticed the way his gaze slid to her lips before easing back to her eyes. That flirtatious glint had an edge of arrogant demand as well that was far too sexy to ignore.

"True enough. You really haven't changed all that much either, have you?" he suggested.

"Psh. Have too." She laughed, thinking about the wild child she once was.

"Well." He paused, tilting his head as he looked her over. "You have brushed your hair."

They both laughed. He had a soft, bass rumble of a laugh that made her wonder how it would sound with her ear pressed to his chest.

"And you've filled out." Hunger darkened his gaze. A male sexual hunger that had her breath catching a bit.

"Is that your way of saying I'm fat?" She scowled at him, trying to lighten her own response to him.

He scowled back at her. "You know what I mean. You're no longer a waif."

He looked pointedly at her cleavage, lingered there a moment before clearing his throat.

"Nah, I'm just 'Pixie Pest,' remember?" Her brow arched mockingly.

"Oh yeah." He grinned. "You drove me nuts. You know, Amanda still hasn't recovered from the time you dumped that plastic pail of sand and duck poo on her head at the lake."

That memory was one of her better ones. She hadn't liked Amanda Whatshername at all.

"Good, I never liked her. Oh Lord, you didn't marry her, did you?" The idea was horrific. Amanda was a pretentious, feckless, attention-seeker. Being stuck with her would have been the worst!

"Hell no! I didn't like her all that much either, but she was easy, Sam, and I wasn't choosy back then." He took a long pull from his beer.

Samantha nodded slowly, watching his throat work, feeling her body heat.

"Oh man, thwarted by a devious, ten-year-old pest." She sighed, almost laughing. "I'm certain you were devastated."

"Yeah." He nodded, his smile wistful. "I'd spank you, but you probably did me a favor at the time."

Her eyes widened at the thought of Hunter warming her naked backside with his hand. She quickly drove that image from her mind. "Hey, maybe does this mean you owe me?"

"Hell no. God knows I couldn't afford it, knowing you. I did get married, though." His smile fell as he continued. "I married Kelly. You might remember her. She was with me the day I ran into you and your dad—"

"Yes! I do remember," she interrupted. She'd never forget it and was surprised that he remembered.

He dropped his gaze and nodded. "Yeah, that didn't work out." He took another drink and cleared his throat. "We've been divorced for a while now."

"Oh, I'm sorry." She could tell there was some residual pain but didn't pry.

"Don't be. It is what it is." He shrugged and smiled,

meeting her gaze. A thin ring of dark stormy gray bordered the cool silver of his irises, yet there was warmth in them. That wicked smile that curved his well-defined lips had always made her heart skip a beat. Maybe she'd had a little crush on him from the beginning.

It was becoming all too clear that she still wanted his attention, an altogether different kind of attention than she had wanted as a kid. Having the most popular guy in high school watching your back was awesome. She'd been cool by association. Well, within her circle anyway.

Probably didn't help his reputation much that she was always running to him to get her pre-adolescent, ornery hide out of trouble. Years had passed, they weren't kids anymore, and they knew very little about each other. Strangers really, but somehow there was a familiar, comfortable connection between them. A very strong and hot connection. Oh, she had to shut that down quickly. An affair with Hunter would seriously complicate everything.

"What?" His question broke her train of thought.

"What, what?" she asked a little too quickly.

"Your expression completely changed. What were you thinking?" His brows furrowed.

Scrambling for a reasonable explanation, she took another drink and cleared her throat. "Just thinking."

"About?" Suspicion was clear in his tone.

She sighed heavily and went with a half-truth. "Well, let's see. My aunt just died and was most likely murdered." She held out a hand, gesturing toward him. "I have two weeks to work with you on figuring out who did it *and* make sure they're brought to justice, all without getting us both in trouble or worse."

He grabbed her hand and held it. His thumb brushed over her palm, sending tingles rioting through her. "We'll be fine. I've always kept you out of trouble. Haven't I?"

She looked down at his thumb making suggestive circles in her palm before lifting her gaze back to his. "You know, I can take care of myself now, right?"

He nodded, smiling broadly. "Yeah, I'm sure ya can."

"I just might be the one keeping you out of trouble this time."

"Hey, could happen. Ya never know, crazy stuff happens all the time." Amused doubt filled his expression as well as the teasing flirtatiousness from earlier.

Samantha snickered. "Indeed."

She wondered how in the world the icy bottle of beer stayed cold in his hands when she felt so warm from his touch. In truth she didn't want him to stop at all. She wanted much, much more. It wasn't until he lifted one brow that she finally pulled her hand away. "Back to your playboy status, Hunter?"

"Nah, not really." He grinned. Laugh lines fanned out from the corner of his eyes, softening the hard, edgy expression he often wore. Same with the lines that bracketed his oh-so-sexy mouth. "How 'bout you? You get married?"

Samantha thought of Tom Novak and cringed. "Almost, but not quite. I escaped just in time."

Boy, was that a true statement.

Hunter's eyes narrowed as he leaned forward. "What happened? Was he mean to you? Want me to kick his ass?"

Her eyes widened, and for a second she wondered if

he actually saw something in her expression or he was just joking around.

She quickly decided to go with the latter and laughed. "Nah, I think I handled it fine. What makes you think I wasn't the mean one? Maybe I just got tired of him and kicked him to the curb."

He watched her silently for a moment, his eyes glittering with something she didn't want to define.

"I don't. Maybe you did." He shrugged, finished his beer, and set the bottle aside. "Still kick his ass for ya."

"Aw, thanks, Hunter." She winked at him. "I keep trying to tell you I'm quite capable of doing my own ass-kicking."

His laugh was deep and rich; it rumbled low, and she could have sworn she felt the vibrations from it. "I have no doubt, Pixie. No doubt at all."

Samantha shifted in the booth as her body reacted. She felt too warm and tingly. She watched him, amazed at the way she was feeling. She wondered if he was feeling the chemistry between them or if it was her imagination. Just that teenage lust in full bloom.

Sadie saved her from possibly doing something wicked by bringing their food. She set their plates and glasses in front of them. "Y'all good?"

"Yes. Looks great! Thanks, Sadie." Samantha smiled up at her.

"Yep. All good," Hunter confirmed.

Sadie looked at Hunter then to Samantha, then back to Hunter again.

"Mmm-hmmm." Sadie narrowed her eyes. "Y'all holler if you need anything else."

"Yes, ma'am." Hunter grinned up at her.

Sadie kept giving him her narrow-eyed stare.

"Mmm-hmmm," she murmured again as she walked away.

They ate, chatted a little in between. Hunter got Samantha up to speed on the folks still in town and those that had left.

"So do you actually have an opening in the department or were you going to create one?" she asked.

"Create one."

"That's really sweet of you," she said sarcastically, rolling her eyes.

"Yeah. I know." He grinned before taking another big bite of his burger.

He studied her intently while he chewed. It was damned disconcerting. She took an equally big bite of her own burger and lifted her brows.

Hunter took a drink of his Coke and chuckled. "Does everything have to be a challenge with you, girl?"

She shrugged, the corner of her mouth tilted slightly as she swallowed. "Don't know what you're talking about."

He shook his head and kept eating.

"So how many deputies do you have?" she asked him several minutes later.

"Three." He was watching her too closely, too intently.

"Do you trust them?" Honestly, she was just trying to focus on the subject at hand, instead of Hunter's mouth. She watched the muscle in his jaw pulse as he ate, and she wondered how his stubble would feel gently rasping over her most tender areas. *Ah jeez*, she thought. Lusting after Hunter was only going to muddy the waters. She needed to lead with her brain, not her libido.

His eyes met hers without lifting his head. "One. To an extent." He finished off his burger and wiped his mouth with his napkin.

"To an extent?" Her voice was a little too breathy.

"Does anyone really know someone?" His eyes narrowed slightly.

Good point. She knew very little about who Hunter was now, but she had no choice but to trust him. "I found something today. Do you have a secure server at work?"

His gaze sharpened and his voice was low. "Can't talk freely here. Let's go. I know a place we can talk without being overheard. And woman, if you keep lookin' at me like that, people are gonna notice."

"I wasn't looking at you a way." Her denial wasn't one bit believable. "Where are we going?"

He paused for a moment, thinking. "Do you have a pen?"

"Probably," she drawled. Of course she had a pen.

"Slip it to me under the table?"

Without looking away, she felt around in her purse at her hip, found one, and did as he asked. "Is this really necessary?"

"Girl, you know this town. Let's at least attempt to keep this on the down low." He smiled for effect.

"Right." She picked up his lead. Just casually hanging out with an old friend. "Have the burgers here always been this good?"

He nodded and glanced down briefly. "Best burgers

in the world as far as I'm concerned." He placed a crumpled napkin on the table, sliding it a little closer to the middle, then patted her hand. "It's great to see you again, Sam. Hang out here another half hour and then head out." He scooted out of the booth. "I got the check. You have a good night."

"Aww, thanks. You too, Hunter." She watched him walk away, lips pursing just a bit.

Damn, he still looked just too good. She was in trouble here and she knew it.

chapter four

Jacob Donovan's cabin was empty while he was away, and being that Hunter was the only person Jacob trusted, he had the key. He was reasonably confident Sam would be able to find it; his directions were very detailed.

Just in case, he'd added his cell number to the note.

Times had changed a lot, even in Deerhaven. Civilization had begun to creep up the mountains. Broken-down shacks had been torn down. A few of the old sprawling homesteads had been divided up into smaller lots or quaint little subdivisions.

George and Drusilla Golding were one older couple that sold their family farm and moved down the mountains for the convenience of being closer to town. Like most folks in Deerhaven, they waved as he passed, and he honked in return.

He turned onto the narrow two-lane road that curved and twisted its way up the mountain. There were still places farther up that were off-road and secluded, and therefore, private. Jacob's cabin was one such place.

It was a bitch and three quarters to get to. Good thing Sam had an SUV. It should be able to handle the long, pitted road with its large rocks, deep eroded ruts, and broken brush. As long as she found the spot to turn off, she'd be fine.

However, he didn't feel all that comfortable going too much farther up Jacob's road without being sure she'd find it. He didn't have a sat phone with him, and the iffy cell reception wasn't going to cut it if she got lost and tried to call. He stopped right after he pulled onto the drive and cut the lights.

He kept his eyes on the rearview mirror, but his mind was still on Sam. She was growing more and more captivating every moment he spent with her. There was no need to avoid her now. She was an unattached adult with a great mind and a body built for pleasure. If she was feeling the same pull he was feeling, this investigation was about to get a lot more complicated on the personal side.

He wouldn't soon forget that heated look in her eyes and her matter-of-fact denial. The flush in her cheeks betrayed her as did the way she pretended to look him straight in the eye while staring at his eyebrows. He shook his head. She was an incredibly enticing combination of cute and sexy as hell.

The faint glow of headlights in the pitch darkness caught his attention. He watched as they grew brighter. As they made the turn, his cell rang and he turned on his lights.

"Yeah."

"I'm assuming that's you that just turned on your lights ahead of me." Sam's voice was smooth and warm. Feminine but not high-pitched at all.

She'd lost a lot of her Southern accent and that had made him a little sad. He did notice when she got a little riled, it tended to surface a bit.

He'd enjoy causing that to happen as much as possible.

"That would be a good assumption. The road is rough. Just follow me."

He went slow, glancing in the rearview to make sure she was behind him. She'd handled the drive up the hill just fine. Close to the end of the drive was grated, graveled, and levelled. At least there was that. Sam pulled in beside him and cut the engine.

The small log cabin above him was barely visible in the darkness, but he'd been up there enough times to know the way. Jacob kept his surroundings pristine. The contrast with his nature was a bit jarring. But then, not many got close enough to see his surroundings.

Hunter waited until Sam came around her car. Silently he took her hand and led her up the graveled path. He unlocked the door, stepped in, and quickly entered the code to disarm the security system.

"All clear, you can enter." He winked as he stepped aside.

Sam's expression was wary as she brushed past him and scanned the open area that was Jacob's living room/dining room/kitchen combo. Once the door was locked and security was back online, he filled her in.

"This is Jacob Donovan's place. He and I were in the corps together. He's ridiculously private and kinda paranoid, but he trusts me. I'm trusting you not to talk about this place with anyone. Don't come up here without me. Don't even allude over the phone with me or anyone to there being a place. Don't even say his name. Got it?"

Jacob was damned paranoid on a good day. What he was on a bad day defied description.

"Yes." She sounded a bit mocking.

"I'm serious, Sam," he warned her.

She turned and looked him in the eye. "I get it, Hunter. I'm not taking it lightly. How would he feel about you bringing me up here?"

He'd be fuckin' livid. "I'll handle it."

Her brows lifted as she turned away from him. "Hmmm. Wouldn't want to be around when you have that conversation. You can trust me."

"I know." He trusted his instincts, and those instincts wanted to wrap right around this woman in ways he'd never done before.

She glanced over her shoulder, frowning at him before turning back to study the room. "His place says a lot about him."

Indeed, it did. It was simple but organized and immaculate.

There were no décor enhancements, no photos, no wall art, nothing frivolous around. Jacob was extremely practical. If it wasn't useful, it weighed him down.

His furniture was big, heavy, overstuffed leather pieces. His dining table was small, dark, solid oak with four matching cushioned chairs.

There wasn't a whole lot Jacob wouldn't take on. His work as a private mercenary put him in some hellish situations. So, he believed in being as comfortable as possible, when possible, and he was always prepared for the worst.

The fireplace was ready to be lit, a large iron rack was filled with firewood, and there was a good-sized stack of kindling neatly piled in a metal box beside the rack. Two crystal oil-filled lamps sat on the mantle, his grandfather's memorial flag placed between them. A box of matches was near the iron fireplace, tools on the hearth.

"Have a seat. You want something to drink? I'm sure Jacob has something in here." Hunter opened the fridge and found a bottle of Moscato and a bottle of Riesling, beer, and soda.

Jacob never knew how long he'd be gone when he went on his covert trips, so he never kept much in the fridge.

Hunter was certain the pantry was stocked, as were the cabinets and the freezer. He was also pretty sure there were hidden cabinets and storage areas around the cabin stocked with all sorts of survival shit.

"No," Sam said absently, while she scanned the room. "I'm fine." Her attention shifted to her purse. "We shouldn't be here long."

Hunter glanced at the Bunn coffeemaker. "How about coffee?"

She paused, looked up, and then sighed. "Okay, you got me. I'd love coffee."

She pulled out a chair at the table and sat.

Hunter grinned as he got the beans and the grinder down from the cabinet. Yeah, he remembered Samuel and Jolene, her mom and dad, fussing over Samantha about letting her have some coffee. She always got her coffee, though. He'd heard that Sam had died. That couldn't have been easy for her. The two Sams had been so close. She was the quintessential daddy's girl. There never seemed to be an appropriate time to broach the subject and offer condolences. This wasn't it either.

His smile faltered when she laid her pistol on the table before retrieving what he assumed was a flash drive or something similar and palming it. It was still hard to see Sam as an armed officer of the law. He guessed they'd both changed a lot.

"I talked to Aunt Dottie just a few weeks ago. She was still as sharp as ever. But she seemed a bit preoccupied. The death of her friends hit her hard, but it was more than sadness. This was something else; there was an edginess in her voice," Samantha said sadly.

"Did you ask her if something was bothering her?" He poured the fresh coffee into the mugs.

"Of course. She said she was fine, that she just had a lot on her mind. I asked if she needed anything, and as usual she said no. But when I asked her if she wanted me to come for a visit, she said 'no' awfully quickly. She added that she'd like to come visit me for a week or so if I'd be willing to 'put up with her.'" Sam's shoulders slumped. "I put her off because I was involved in some time-consuming crap at work. I just knew I wouldn't be able to spend much time with her."

Aw hell, yeah, that had to eat at her. "Dwelling on 'should haves' isn't gonna help. It'll only mess with your head." Hunter walked with their mugs past her to the couch.

"I know. It's just hard to think around it."

Hunter understood completely. He also understood how unproductive it could be to let the regrets eat at you.

"Come sit in here. It's more comfortable. Show me what you found." He set her mug on the side table before he sat and took a sip from his own.

He watched as Sam left the table and walked over to sit sideways in the corner of the couch, slightly facing him, one leg folded under her. Her hair fell in loose curls past her shoulders. Her eyes were a little bloodshot. He wondered if that was from fatigue or from holding back tears.

It made his chest tighten a little at the thought of her crying. The way her lips pursed as she blew on her coffee drew his attention in less considerate ways.

"Wow, this coffee is freakin' amazing!" Surprise lit her face.

"Jacob doesn't scrimp. Sure as hell doesn't settle for mediocre coffee," he stated, still watching her closely.

Sam moaned as she took another sip. "I like this Jacob person."

Yeah, Jacob would like her too. He'd like her thoroughly and often if he had the chance. Hunter frowned at that thought. Nope, he wasn't comfortable with the thought of Jacob and Samantha meeting at all.

"So what did you find?" he asked again.

She sipped her coffee again then gave a little sigh.

"Aunt Dottie had a safety deposit box. I went to the bank today and found this." She held up the flash drive. "I didn't bring my laptop. Does your friend Jacob have a secure one?"

Hunter grinned at that. "Yep. Just don't know where it's at." He reached for his phone and sent a text to Jacob.

Need secure server.

"Not sure if we'll get access or not. Texting Jacob is hit or miss." And that was putting it mildly, Hunter thought.

"Hmm."

Unsure what the little sound meant, he watched Sam take another sip of her coffee.

"You asked about my deputies," he said, as he waited for Jacob to respond. "Two of 'em, Joe Rodgers and Ray Decker, are a problem."

"Never heard of them. Where are they from?" The way Sam pressed her lips to her mug made Hunter want to feel them pressed against any part of him.

"Decker is from Oroville. Rodgers, I believe, is from up in Oregon somewhere. They were hired by Henderson. Whether he put them there to keep tabs on me or they're in the middle of the whole thing, I don't know yet. But I don't trust them." As subtly as he could, he shifted to alleviate the strain in his jeans as a result of his growing interest in Sam's sensuous mouth.

"I see. So what's Henderson's game? Drugs?"

"Well, that's the logical answer. But I don't think so." He shook his head decisively. "We've shut down a couple of amateur meth labs. Scary shit, but nothing all that big."

The conversation he'd had with Shane came to mind, but he set it aside for the time being. He'd bring it up with Sam if it turned out to be something.

"You know my uncle and Lillian Henderson had a thing, right?" he asked her.

Sam's eyes widened. "I heard some stuff at the house after the funeral. I thought it was just gossip."

He shook his head. "Nope. I don't know if they ever

really consummated that 'thing,' didn't really wanna know. But there was a thing. A few weeks before his 'hunting trip,' Uncle Zachariah mentioned that he'd stumbled across something worrisome. Wanted to tell me about it in person."

"Didn't get the chance?" There was a soothing quality in Sam's voice.

Her warm gaze met his and held him. "No."

"I'm sorry, Hunter." She absently licked her top lip, the look in her blue-green eyes went from warm understanding to a heated invitation. Or maybe he was just seeing what he wanted to see.

"Me too." The words sounded like a groan to him, and he swallowed the last of his coffee. Back to the subject at hand, he chided himself. "I wonder if he said something to Lillian."

Sam's eyelids fluttered slightly as she looked down and cleared her throat. "That would make sense."

No, he wasn't imagining anything. "Yes and no. Uncle Zachariah was in love with Lillian. He'd never do anything that could remotely cause her harm. Two weeks later she was dead."

"So how does Aunt Dottie fit in?" Intent and intelligent, her gaze sharpened on him.

"I've got a few theories, but nothin' that sticks." That was the problem, nothing was panning out.

Hunter's phone buzzed.

Take the bottom bunk. Extra pillows in the hall closet. Pick up the steak. Don't buy the cheap stuff. Quality is expensive.

Hunter read the message a couple of times before he got it. "Be right back."

Sam nodded, holding her nearly empty cup with both hands.

It took him a moment to find the exact board under Jacob's bed that allowed him to slide the panel aside to reveal the safe underneath. He crawled out from under the bed and went to the hall closet, found four pillows stacked there. He moved them aside . . . nothing. Took them out of their cases . . . nothing. Noticed a tiny zipper on the third one and opened it just enough to get his arm inside. He felt around till he found the slim capsule. He opened the capsule and found another riddle. He knew Jacob well enough to decipher the code to open the safe. The paranoid bastard couldn't make things easy, could he?

The laptop was lying in the shallow opening. Pulling it free, he breathed out a curse, slid back, and rose to his feet to make his way back to the living room. He laid the laptop on the coffee table.

"Go ahead and boot it up. I'll be right back." Sam gave him an odd look, shrugged, and opened the laptop.

Hunter walked through the kitchen and into the pantry. He opened the freezer and shuffled through the stacks of meat neatly wrapped in butcher's paper and labelled until he found the package labelled "wagyu." He shook his head. The slip of blue paper was barely showing from under the final taped fold. On the paper Jacob had written:

In triangle ABC, the measure of angle B is 90 degrees, BC = 16, and AC = 20. Triangle DEF is similar to triangle ABC, where vertices D, E, and F correspond to vertices A, B, and C, respectively, and each side of triangle DEF is 1/3 the length of the corresponding side of triangle ABC. What is the value of sin F?

"Shit, paranoid motherfucker," he murmured through his teeth, as he slammed the lid of the freezer and walked back into the living room while he worked on the problem. He was aware that Sam was watching him.

"I'm assuming you're trying to figure out the password?"

He just nodded.

"Can I help?" He knew she was smiling without even looking up.

"Nah, I got it. Try sinFequ@ls.6."

He watched her type it in and breathed a sigh of relief when it worked. "Paranoid bastard."

Sam snickered as she slid the drive into a USB slot. "I can't wait to meet Jacob."

Hunter just grunted in response. He shook off the prickly possessiveness he felt at the thought and focused on the folder Sam opened. There were photos and a video. He sat on the couch beside her as she pressed play on the video.

"You know that guy with the mayor?" Sam's tone was all business.

Hunter squinted. "Any way to zoom in on that video?"

Sam zoomed in, but it was too pixelated. "No. I can't make him out. I wish I had more talent with this sort of thing, but that's the best I can do."

There was no audio on the video, but it was obvious Henderson was pissed. He poked the man in the chest, and the man went rigid, about to retaliate, before he lifted his hands and stepped back. Henderson turned on his heel and stalked away, and the video ended.

In addition to the video there were two photos of Henderson meeting with the man and handing him an envelope. There were also a couple of photos of Rodgers and Decker meeting with Henderson. However, they never met with the mayor at the same time.

"Well." Sam sighed. "This is a lot and nothing all at once."

"Yeah, no solid proof of anything, but hey, it gives us a direction. We need to find out about this guy. Want more coffee?"

"Mmm, I do. I'll get it, though." She stood and stretched.

He followed her into the kitchen, watching the natural sway of her hips. Working with her without touching her was gonna drive him crazy. With a soft curve of her full lips, she poured them both another cup. "I could get addicted to this coffee."

"Yep," Hunter agreed, trying to think past his growing need to feel her body pressed against him.

"Okay, so, allegedly Henderson paid this dude for something. Was he the hit man, you think?"

Hunter thought for a moment. "Could be. I got a feeling the hits were Rodgers and Decker. But they're so inept, I find it hard to believe they could pull it off."

"Technically they haven't pulled it off." She lifted her free hand palm up. "Here we are."

"Well, that's an excellent point."

"How deep are Henderson's pockets? He's certainly paying off quite a number of people."

Hunter took another sip of his coffee. "Or he has shit on a number of people."

Sam lifted a brow, pursed her lips, and nodded. After she finished her coffee, she rinsed out her cup and then turned to find him watching her. "What?" The corner of her mouth lifted.

Hunter took a step closer, trapping her against the counter with less than an inch between them. He set his empty cup on the counter behind her. "You know what." If she didn't the rasp of his voice would tell her.

Before he had a chance to make a move, she took his face in her hands, rose on her toes, and pressed her sweet little body against him. Her lips brushed his. It was just a whisper of a kiss, a feather-light touch that had the power to steal his breath. Another, just a fraction firmer, but when her tongue brushed across his bottom lip, his tenuous hold on whatever control he'd thought he had, slipped.

He wanted too much, too quickly, and at the same time he wanted to make it last. How long had he imagined tasting her, touching her? Tilting his head to deepen the coffee-flavored kiss, he sucked her lower lip just firmly enough. Her fingers combed through his hair as his tongue danced with hers in long, hungry strokes. With a low moan, she pressed her lush body tighter against him.

His hands slid down her back to grip her voluptuous ass and hold her tighter against him. Dammit, there were too many clothes between them. His cock was straining against his jeans, and he was aching to touch and taste every inch of her body. His mouth moved down her jaw to her neck. A gasp caught in her throat as his teeth grazed her neck where it met her shoulder then soothed the spot with a slow stroke of his tongue.

"Hunter." It was no more than a plea on a sigh, but it only added to his need. Every little moan and gasp just fanned the flames consuming him.

She trembled as his mouth found her collarbone, carefully walking her backward toward the couch. He unbuttoned her shirt as she unbuttoned his. The simple brush of her fingers against his chest added to his need as though he were starving for her touch. He wanted his hands on her body, to feel her heated skin against his, beneath his tongue.

Impatiently, he tossed their shirts aside, cupped her face in one hand and kissed her hard. Her hands explored his chest, his stomach, lower. God help him, he didn't want to rush this, but he didn't believe he had the strength to go slow. He reached around with one hand and unhooked her bra. He took a step back and looked into her hungry eyes before letting his gaze drop to her breasts. He wasted no time divesting her of the pretty lacy barrier.

Sam licked her kiss-swollen lips and closed her eyes. Perfect little pink nipples hardened under his intense gaze as he tossed her bra in the same direction he'd tossed her shirt. "You're beautiful, Sam," he murmured, not even sure if she heard him.

Her skin was like silk against his fingertips, her nipples like hard pebbles pressing eagerly against his palms as he kneaded her full breasts. He released them long enough to help her free him from his jeans and to help her out of hers. Her fingers curled around his shaft and squeezed gently. He groaned and yanked her against him. If she kept doing that, it would all be over too soon. He wasn't nearly ready for that.

Voraciously, she kissed him, sucking and biting at his lips. She was like a little flame in his arms, hot and out of control. Because he knew what she was about, he feigned letting her push him backward onto the couch. As she tried to straddle him, he held her still and flipped her onto her back.

"Not yet, sugar. You're back in the wild, wild west now." He could feel the moist heat from her against his knee positioned between her thighs. "We have a certain way of doing things here."

He kissed along her collarbone, down to the valley between her firm, round, luscious breasts. Her nipples, already tight with arousal, tightened even more as he drew circles around one with his thumb. Sam moaned as his tongue stroked the other. "I think you're just enjoying watching me squirm."

"No, just savoring you." He watched her as he drew her nipple into his mouth, sucking firmly as he teased the other between his fingers. Her sexy blue-green eyes widened incredulously, and she bit her plump lower lip.

"This is torture." Her long fingers fisted in his hair as she arched her back, her soft thighs pressing against his.

Unable to resist the allure of feeling her warm, supple body he moved against her, sliding his way slowly up to her long, lovely neck. Devouring her with his mouth, sucking and licking the smooth silken skin of her throat. He continued to caress her breast, gently lifting, squeezing, rasping her hard nipple against his palm. He felt the rumble of her groan against his tongue, and his mouth moved higher, along her jaw.

She arched up, pressing her body firmly against him. His cock throbbed urgently against the cushion of her stomach. He wanted her to remember this night, just as he would.

His hand moved lower along her lush abdomen. His fingers trailed through the beads of moisture, her skin growing slick, and he wasn't unaffected either. He could feel the sweat trickling down his back as he fought for restraint.

He drew back as he spread her thighs and moved between them. Urgently, he caressed her, his fingers parting her plump, slick folds. Sam gasped and pressed against his hand as he stroked her sensitive honeyed flesh. She was soaked and so hot. Her scent was so inviting. He was dying to taste her; he wouldn't be able to wait. Next time, he would take his time and have his fill. Now, he needed to be inside her.

He drew the broad head of his cock through the sodden folds of her pussy, relishing the sounds of her pleasure. He gathered the only modicum of self-control he had and gently nudged the tight entrance of her body. He didn't want to slam inside her. He wanted it to last, to take her slowly and sweetly. He slid in marginally, barely an inch, feeling her muscles pulse around him.

Son of a bitch, it felt so damn good, stroking his flesh with each harsh breath she fought for. He gripped her hips, holding her steady. The dim light gave him a clear view of her glistening, damp curls, and the burrowing of his hard length between them.

He swallowed tightly, on fire with the sensations sweeping through his body as he inched farther inside, his cock pulsing with the need to climax.

Watching her as he took her, seeing her body accept him, hearing her moan his name, it took sheer force of will not to drive into her. He withdrew and sank in again, deeper, grinding his hips into her as she lifted her body to meet his slow thrusts.

"Hunter, please." It was her tormented plea that shattered his self-control.

He fell forward, catching himself on his elbows and clasping her head in his hands. "Open your eyes." His voice was hoarse and dark. "Look at me, Sam."

When she lifted her gaze, his hips retreated. Her eyes widened before he slammed forward, driving every hard, desperate inch of his cock into the contracting depths of her vagina. A rosy flush infused her cheeks as her hips pushed against him, demanding more. Her eyes didn't leave his, but her eyelids lowered just enough to give her a mischievous, sexy look that made him crazy. "Faster . . ." The word was like a moan from deep inside her.

He braced himself, preparing to give her what she wanted. What he needed. His hips powered into her. Thrust after long, hard thrust as they both groaned and arched, drawing them both toward release.

Samantha cried out. He loved the sounds she made, all of them. But the way she moaned his name sounded somewhere between a plea and a demand and sent him over the edge. Another sharp cry issued from her throat as she began to climax. He was only a second away. Her nails bit into his arms as she rode it out with him. He clenched his teeth, as he felt the power of his ejaculation rippling through his body.

He groaned, holding himself deep and tight within her as his seed pumped hard and fast inside her pulsating flesh.

Hunter barely caught himself before he collapsed on top of her. At the last second, he twisted his body and took her into his arms, falling with her. His eyes closed in exhaustion as he fought for breath, and for sanity. Yeah, that was what he needed. Sanity.

He caressed the dip in Sam's back, feeling her tremble as he lightly stroked her damp skin. They were both fighting for breath. He felt alternately proud as hell and scared to his toenails. Sex shouldn't be that damned good; it wasn't natural.

Sam sighed deeply and wiggled against him as she let it out. He liked that a little too much. "I could fall asleep like this." Her voice was so sexy, soft, and raspy. "Don't fall asleep, I'll get my second wind here in a minute and we'll go for seconds."

Her breath caught. He heard it, felt the stillness of her body. "Oh damn. I might have to have more coffee first." She even had a sexy laugh.

"Just rest here then." He laughed, making himself untangle and move out from her. She moaned in protest and flopped onto her back as he stood. She looked incredible lying there all sprawled out. He could look at her like that for hours.

"No." She sat up and he frowned. "We really should go." There was a hint of regret in her voice as she picked up their clothes.

"Yeah," he agreed reluctantly. He'd be damned if he'd push her, and she was kinda right. "I guess so."

She gave him a half smile. Goddam, she looked cute as hell standing there naked, her hair a wreck and that sleepy, resigned look on her face. "Bathroom?"

"Down the hall, to the left." Of course she was right. It was late. They should head out for tonight. This wouldn't be the last time; they'd just gotten started. Scary thing was, Hunter wasn't sure he'd ever get enough.

She nodded and started down the hall, then stopped and turned around. "Hunter, we didn't use a condom."

Dammit all to hell. That had never happened to him before. He'd always been careful when it came to protection for both him and his lover. This was a complication neither of them needed. Being on the force, they both got checked regularly. He did anyway, he assumed she did as well. No STD worries. But shit, he hadn't even thought about using a condom. He ran his hands through his hair. "I'm sorry, Sam—"

She waved a hand. "I'm on the pill and I'm healthy. You?"

He swallowed hard and nodded. "Yeah, we get tested regularly. Still, I shouldn't have been so careless."

"Psh, neither of us should have." She took a deep breath and smiled. "I'll just be a moment."

Hunter relaxed as he watched her walk down the hall. Son of a bitch, Sam had him completely discombobulated. What was worrisome was the fact that he was loving it.

chapter five

In the country, the night could be so dark. The stars were brighter, though, and there were so many. Samantha could stare at the sky for hours. Hunter held her hand, helping her as they made their way back to their cars. Never in a million years did she think this would have happened. She willed herself not to read anything into it, steeling herself against the inevitable.

The sound of an urgent female voice came from inside his truck as they got closer. Hunter looked back at her before dropping her hand. She followed as he swung open the door and grabbed the mouthpiece of his radio.

"I'm here, Carol. What's up?"

"Hey, Sheriff." The woman sighed with relief. "I've been trying to reach someone for a while now. The Millers are at it again. Mr. Miller is armed with a shotgun. Mrs. Miller has a knife."

"Rodgers and Decker?" he questioned her, knowing the deputies were scheduled for duty that night.

"No response on here or cell," Carol reported. "According to the neighbors, this is worse than before, Sheriff. They think Mr. Miller's been on some kind of drugs in recent weeks because he's been more erratic than normal."

Drugs. Just what the hell he needed.

"Shit. Got it. On my way." Hunter put the mic back and turned to Samantha and pulled her into his arms. His kiss was quick, sweet, and warm.

"You might need backup." It didn't make sense to answer a call like that alone. Of course, Hunter knew almost everyone in the county and his charm got him far. Still, it wouldn't hurt for her to go along and help out. She had her service revolver with her.

"Oh, hell no. You're going home, Pixie. I'll call you tomorrow. Go home and get some sleep."

She'd pretty much expected him to reject that idea.

She smiled at him as she got into her car.

It wasn't a request, and yet she wasn't obeying. He had to know she wasn't about to go home and leave him to deal with two armed crazy people alone.

She followed him down the drive and waited a moment before she turned onto the main road behind him. After a second or two, she turned on her headlights. The taillights of Hunter's truck were just ahead.

The Millers lived in a little broken-down shack off of Mulholland Hill Road. It was a steep road that snaked up and around a mountain ridge. Back in the day, it was an area known for being populated by gold prospectors hoping to strike it rich. Now, it was mostly older folks stubbornly holding on to their small herds, trying to keep their run-down family ranches going, and poverty-stricken alcoholics inhabiting little shacks that were barely standing.

The neighbors probably called 911 when they heard the Millers fighting.

She could hear them before she cleared the curve. She cut her lights and slowed down, watching Hunter pull into their drive, get out, and draw his weapon.

Mrs. Miller was on the porch, ranting and raving, swinging a meat cleaver. Mr. Miller was stumbling around with a shotgun. So far the gun was pointed at the ground.

This situation could go very badly fast. She could see the neighbors down the road as they stood in their doors or on their porches, their gazes glued to the scene unfolding next door. Their porch lights were on, giving a clear view of the mad man toting a shotgun.

And they said city folks were dumb. They were on average damned smarter than this, she thought.

Samantha pulled into the neighbor's drive. Exiting the car, she pointed at the couple beginning to move into the yard.

"For your own safety, please return to the house," she told them. "I'm with Sheriff Steele. He doesn't need any distractions at the moment."

They scowled and mumbled something rude, but did as she asked. She retrieved her service revolver from the glove compartment and moved in low along the line of untended shrubs until she was directly behind the Millers.

"Bitch," Miller was screaming, his bull-like body weaving almost drunkenly. "You fucking bitch. Look what you've done. Caused the sheriff to come out here. You fuckin' waste of breath."

Mrs. Miller started sobbing and raised the cleaver to her husband. Mr. Miller grabbed her arm and twisted until she dropped the weapon, then he backhanded her and screamed for her to shut up.

"Eldon. Put the gun down. Don't make me shoot you, man. Come on now." Hunter's voice was calm and controlled, but his tone gave away his true intent.

He was serious. If he had to shoot the man, he would. He'd hate it, and he probably wouldn't sleep over it a night or two, but he wouldn't hesitate.

"This is between me and my wife!" Eldon Miller grabbed his wife by the hair and yanked her against him as she cried out in fear. "Why the fuck you gotta always bring your ass up here nosin' in my business? That uncle of yours shoulda taught you better."

Hunter didn't rise to the bait. He watched the man closely, looking for an opening to help Mrs. Miller and to neutralize Eldon without killing him.

"I'm here to help. Things have gotten out of hand this time. Let's just put the guns away and talk it out, okay?" Hunter suggested calmly.

Eldon shook his head and stumbled, almost releasing his wife. "You first."

Hunter shook his head. "That's not how this works and you know it. Put the shotgun down, and then I'll put mine away," he promised. "Then we can talk this out."

Eldon watched him closely, his broad face intent, as he watched Hunter, wide-eyed.

"Promise you won't take me in?" he bargained.

"Can't do that. But if you put the gun down now, it'll only help your case," Hunter advised him. "Come on, Eldon, you and I don't want to fight. Last time you bloodied my nose, and it hurt like a bitch for a week. But you know I'll go head-to-head with you."

Eldon nodded as though Hunter's tone wasn't faintly teasing.

"I did," he agreed, almost soberly. "But it was this bitch's fault," he snarled as he shook his wife with one hand. "She won't keep her damned screamin' down, and she's always tryin' to tell me what to do."

"Come on, Eldon, let's let her out of this. You know she's too little to fight. You wanna fight, I'll let you have first swing. Let her go," Hunter tried again.

Eldon shook Mrs. Miller by her hair. She cried out and grabbed his hands, trying to get free. He just yanked harder. "This here's my woman. Ain't none of anybody's business! It ain't none of your business."

His look dared Hunter to disagree.

"Well, you're wrong about that, Eldon. You're not allowed to beat on Vanetta whenever you get mad. We talked about this last time," Hunter reminded him, but it was obvious he was getting nowhere with Eldon.

The other man kept aiming that damned shotgun in Hunter's direction, his finger far too close to the trigger.

Samantha clenched her jaw. She was all too familiar with domestic abuse. It was clear this wasn't the first or even the second time Vanetta Miller had been beaten by her husband. Most likely Vanetta refused to press charges, every time. Eventually Vanetta would be dead.

Samantha crouched low, keeping to the shadows, as she moved closer. Hunter kept talking quietly, and finally

Eldon laid his shotgun on the ground. As he stood back up, Hunter holstered his gun. "Let her go, Eldon. I'm gonna have to cuff you."

Eldon shoved Vanetta to the ground as he reached behind him.

He'd just been waiting for Hunter to holster his gun. The pistol he pulled from the small of his back would kill Hunter as close as the two men were.

It cleared his waist, lifted.

"Gun!" Samantha shouted as she fired.

There was no time to second-guess, to try to wound rather than kill. It was Hunter or Eldon.

Eldon crumpled. Hunter and Samantha ran in together. Samantha got ahold of Vanetta as the hysterical woman went for the discarded shotgun.

"Hell of a shot, Pixie. He's dead." The expression on Hunter's face told her it wasn't a compliment.

"I know," she said flatly, as she held onto the dead man's wife. Vanetta was cussing and screaming. Her mouth was bleeding, tears streamed from her swollen eyes, leaving dirty tracks down her bruised cheeks. "But you're not."

"Fuck, Sam. Have you lost your damn mind? I told you to go the hell home!"

"If I had, all three of you would be dead!" Samantha glared up at him. Her heart was pounding loudly in her ears, and her stomach was churning. Even though it wasn't the first time she'd taken a life in the line of duty, there were always consequences. It tore at her, left her shaken to the core. But by God, she hoped it always would; it meant she still had a soul. "Vanetta, I need you to breathe."

The other woman stared back at her, dazed. "You killed my husband!"

Samantha led the woman to the porch. "Sit here, now. Take a deep breath. Slowly."

Vanetta inhaled deeply then released her breath with a shudder. "He's gone?" Hope resonated in her voice.

"He's gone," Samantha agreed softly. "You okay?"

Vanetta nodded, gripping Samantha's hand tight. "He wanted to kill Sheriff Steele. Said it was his destiny or some shit." She shuddered as she spoke. "He went crazy on me. He just went crazy . . ."

"She needs to be questioned," Samantha stated, as Hunter returned to her side. "He meant to kill you."

"So I heard," he said coldly.

Hunter had gone to his truck to get gloves and an evidence bag. He held out his hand. "Weapon, gotta bag and tag." His voice was tight, from holding back his anger she assumed.

Procedure. So much procedure.

Samantha nodded and looked at Vanetta for a moment. Shock was settling in. "I got her. Go sit in your car," Hunter said too quietly.

"I'm gonna go in and find her a blanket, and then I'll go," she promised, lips tightening at the obvious displeasure in his look.

He was acting as though he would have preferred to die. God save her from arrogant men some days. Standing, she handed over her weapon, her gaze meeting his.

Hunter sighed heavily but said nothing. His eyes were intense and angry. She scowled back before she turned and walked into the disheveled house.

It smelled of smoke, bad whiskey, and cat pee. She

breathed through her mouth as she pulled a crocheted afghan from the back of the couch. It would have to do. Samantha stepped out of the house and lay the afghan around the other woman's shoulders.

"Coroner and ambulance are on their way." Hunter spoke low and calmly. "Homicide and ID tech will be here tomorrow. Looks like you're probably gonna get that extra leave, whether you wanted it or not."

She looked up at him briefly.

His expression was hard and stoic. He was right. This was a complicated mess, and she'd be put on leave with pay until she was cleared. She'd been there before and she hated it. There was a good reason an officer was put on leave. They needed the time to recoup and heal. Even so, just as the others had, this would haunt her, but the alternative, as before, wasn't acceptable.

She wasn't sure exactly what Hunter was thinking, but she was confident that her actions were justified. He'd just have to get over his indignation.

A gentle breeze lifted her hair as she walked to her car. She shivered but the cool air against her neck felt nice, bracing.

"What happened?" the neighbor lady asked. Her face was pale in the dim light of her porchlight. "Is Eldon dead? Didja shoot him?"

"Go inside, ma'am. Everything's under control." Or was it?

"But we heard a gunshot!" the man beside her, her husband obviously, accused.

"I said go inside," she snapped, then took a deep breath. "Please. There will be some detectives that will want to interview you sometime in the next few days."

"All right then." They said it in unison and any other time that would have made her smile.

She sat in the car and watched Hunter tend to Vanetta. At some point he'd covered Eldon's body. She'd been through testing before. The reality of that was sitting there on the edge of her conscious thought, just waiting to be fully absorbed. She was sure she would play it over again many times before she would be able to let it go.

She always did.

Her history with Tom Novak and her own brush with domestic violence could possibly surface during the investigation, and she wasn't sure how much bearing that would have on the situation. To say she hadn't been affected by the events that took place before the shooting would be a lie.

Was she positive her emotions didn't guide her tonight? Her reaction had been by the book, she was certain. She played it over in her mind again, looking for some other route she could have taken, but she couldn't see how shooting Mr. Miller could have been avoided. She had followed her instinct and her training.

Finally she began to relax a little.

She'd been absolutely correct. If she hadn't followed Hunter, things may have ended so much worse than they had. A double murder and suicide wasn't beyond the realm of possibility.

A shudder went through her at the thought. The thought of losing Hunter in such a way was inconceivable.

She caught the faint, subtle scent combination of Hunter and his aftershave. On her clothes, on her skin.

An acute reminder that what had happened earlier tonight couldn't happen again. It wasn't something she
ever expected would happen in the first place, and there
was no reason to believe it would happen again regardless. There was no wisdom in letting it be a factor in
their relationship from here on. Everything was suddenly tossed in the air now.

The glow of the flashing ambulance lights caught
her attention before she heard the sirens. She watched
as they pulled into the yard and rushed out to tend
to Vanetta. They took her vitals, reported it to the hospital, then helped her onto the stretcher. It all took
maybe twenty minutes before they were pulling out, no
siren this time, but the lights were still flashing. Samantha was so focused she didn't notice Hunter walking toward her. She stiffened when he opened her door.

"You okay?" His voice was less than soothing.

"Yep." She was fine. What she didn't need was this
male attitude she was getting from him.

"That was a damn fool gamble, Sam." His tone was
one shade too close to reproving.

"One that saved your ass, Hunter." She stood her
ground, glaring back at him. "You didn't know about the
handgun, and you holstered your weapon, something
you should have never done."

"I agree." She watched him, watched the regret and
somber knowledge in his gaze. "I've dealt with these
two so many times it had become routine. I have always
been able to talk him down. This was my fault, and I'm
not backing away from it. Doesn't mean I don't hate the
hell out of the fact that you were involved."

"Hunter, he would have killed you. He meant to kill

you, according to his wife." She shook her head at that knowledge. "Something's not right in this little county of yours, and you know it."

"Fuck, Sam. I know." The knowledge in his expression was heavy with regret and concern.

People close to him, people he cared about were dying, and like her, it was starting to piss him off.

"So don't be pissy with me for showing up. It's misogynistic," she accused him, her irritation impossible to hide.

Hunter's expression hardened. "That's not why I'm pissed off."

She turned away and stared out the windshield. "You're pissed off because I'm right."

He made a sound that was much like a growl before rubbing his hands over his face. He knew she was right; he was just too bull-headed to admit it.

"God, you're stubborn." His fingers were warm as they brushed over her jaw to her chin. He lifted her face and searched her eyes. "You're not okay."

Neither was he, but she didn't want to point that out just now. She pulled away from him, even though what she wanted more than anything was to be wrapped in his arms. She cleared her throat and sat up straighter. "I'm fine. This is really gonna put a wrench in the works."

His hand dropped away as his eyes narrowed slightly. "Yeah. We'll deal with it. The coroner will be here any minute. They'll send out a team in the morning. You can go on home. Be at the office in the morning for paperwork."

"I understand police procedure." The words came out a little shakier than she'd intended.

"I know you do. Go home. I mean it, Sam. Go the fuck home. Try to get some sleep."

"Where the hell else would I go?" She wanted to scream, but her words came out low and harsh, but quiet.

"Good." He sighed. His tone had softened. "I'm gonna head back over. Hang in there, Pixie." Dammit! He had to stop it. She wasn't that silly girl he used to know. He couldn't be her soft place to fall. Not anymore.

chapter six

Anger and frustration pounded at Hunter while sat at his office desk, staring silently at the reports that lay on the desk before him. There was an air of sarcasm and mockery in each report, nothing overt, but enough to irritate his already raw disposition. It didn't help that he didn't get much sleep last night. Sam had been right. Little Pixie Pest was smart and quick. She'd saved his ass last night and that didn't sit well with him at all. He should have gone in weapon drawn. He'd slipped up, and now Sam was paying the price. She wouldn't be if she'd just listened to him. She made him crazy.

Add to that, Rodgers and Decker were becoming increasingly insubordinate. Hunter knew he was going to have to confront the mayor over them soon. The only problem was Mayor Henderson had hired both jackasses over his uncle Zachariah's head. They had been decent deputies, and for the most part they'd done their jobs.

In the past year or so, however, the two had caused more problems than they had solved.

He poured another cup of coffee and dialed Jacob's cell. Jacob knew things. It surprised him that his friend actually answered.

"Yeah."

"Hey. When you gettin' your ass back up here?"

"'Bout another week. What's up?"

Hunter filled him in without elaborating too much. Jacob was exceptional at picking up on subtle clues.

"Yeah," Jacob told him. "I know I don't know anything, but there's been some damned strange shit goin' on. Just keep your eyes open. Wouldn't hurt to ride by Sid Carter's place, check it out, make sure everything's good up there."

Jacob was referring to the camping area that was close by Sid's old place. Sid didn't live there anymore. He'd passed on and the place was abandoned. Anyone who hadn't lived here in the past twenty years probably wouldn't know who the hell Sid Carter was. The camping area Jacob was referring to was a government deal, but privately run. It was set back from the main road, the camping spots situated for privacy. Through the summer, RVs of every shape and size made use of it.

Back along the mountain, there were some hideaways easily accessible for an SUV or four-wheel drive. The caves ran for miles, could be anything going on out there.

Hunter grimaced. He probably should have been patrolling around there a long time ago.

"Have you seen anyone out that way?"

Jacob grunted. "So far, man, I don't know shit." Which was a lie if there ever was one. Meaning, they needed to have a conversation as soon as he got back.

"All right then. We'll have to have a beer when ya get back."

"You're buyin'." Jacob's good-hearted chuckle was anything but.

"Fair enough." Hunter's voice was light, but his mind was racing. Jacob was sittin' on something serious. Add to that, he hadn't bothered to let Hunter know about it before he left. That right there was not a good sign. Not good at all.

"I'll be in touch," Jacob said pointedly before he ended the call.

Son of a bitch, just what Hunter needed right now, another fucking conspiracy, or was it the same one?

Whatever was going on had him suspicious as hell. Zachariah had been killed by someone he knew. No way in hell would anyone else have been able to get close enough to make the shooting appear to be a hunting accident.

Hunter narrowed his eyes as he stared down at the files. It hadn't escaped him that Rodgers's wife was driving a new Benz, and his daughter was taking those expensive dance lessons down in Oroville. How was Rodgers payin' for all that? Sure wasn't on his deputy's salary. The possible answers that materialized in Hunter's mind made the hair on the back of his neck stand up.

The puzzle involving the three deaths? They were linked. He knew in his gut they were, but he would be damned if he could figure out where or how.

Shaking his head, Hunter rose to his feet and filed their reports. He'd have to put it on the back burner for now. Sam would be in soon to fill out her report and to meet with the lawyer, union rep, and the detectives who were apparently out at the Miller place now.

Sam was a damn good shot, a good cop. Her reaction was correct and justified, but he could tell that it had taken a toll on her. Whenever a good cop had to use lethal force, it had a lasting effect. No matter how much the perpetrator deserved it.

Vanetta was still in the hospital on a psych watch. She'd been through it. No matter how much he'd tried to get her to see reason, cajoled and begged her, she never would press charges. He honestly thought he'd end up locking Eldon up for murder one day. He lost count of how many times he'd gone up to the Millers' place to calm them down.

Eldon wasn't just drunk and mean this time, he'd been manic and unreachable. It was as though he was somewhere else. Something had him crazed. Meth was prevalent in the mountains, as was the "oxy epidemic." Really, it could have been any combination of things. Hunter should have been prepared. He'd let his guard down, assuming this call would be like all the others. He'd fucked up and that didn't sit well.

Sam. Dear God, the woman was trouble. The way it felt with her warm, soft body pressed tightly against his warred with the nagging anger that she'd followed him out on the call. It had plagued his mind all through the night.

Sex with Sam had made everything shift. It had been mindless passion, wild and out of control. Never had he experienced anything quite like that. Thinking about the fiery way she'd moaned and responded to him, the way her hot, slick body gripped his cock like an iron fist with every thrust had him hard and throbbing again.

If he hoped to get any work done he had to stop thinking about it. He couldn't get her alone right now to touch her, kiss her. The investigation would be common procedure, but it wasn't fun for any cop to have to go through. She'd be stuck in interrogations most of the day. He needed to focus on something else.

"Hey, boss," Shane called through the door, knocking sharply at the frosted glass.

"Yeah?" Hunter cleared his throat and sat back in his chair.

His brows were furrowed. "Ms. Samantha is here with her lawyer and also . . ."

Hunter waved his hand. He knew who all were there. "Could you see about getting coffee for everyone?"

"Sure. No problem." Shane's voice held none of his usual light-heartedness. He paused as if to ask something, then thought better of it. "On it."

Shane left the door open, and Hunter could see Sam standing tall and straight, looking her lawyer in the eye as he spoke to her. With a sigh, he picked up the reports and headed toward the group in the lobby.

"Looks like you're gonna be cleared." Back in his office after her lawyer departed, Hunter leaned against the edge of his desk and watched her closely. Surprisingly she'd actually sat when he told her to sit. She looked tired, not just physically but emotionally as well. "It was clean, Sam."

Her scowl was adorable, but he somehow managed not to smile. "I know it was clean. It's just been a long day."

"Yeah, it has. You okay?" he asked softly, knowing the past few days hadn't been easy on her. He hated what she'd been facing. The death of her aunt, that damned shooting, all of it. If he could have protected her from it, he would have.

"Yes." She took a deep breath and sat up a little straighter. "Just thinking."

This wasn't the Pixie Pest he was used to. It unnerved him. He wanted to touch her, make sure she was warm, whole.

"It's hard, every single time. It never gets easy," he empathized. "If it's easy, that's when you have a problem."

"I know. It was justifiable." She shook her head. "Just processing everything. You know?"

"I do know." And he did. Two tours in Afghanistan saw to that. "Come on, Sam. Let's go. You need a drink."

He stood and held out his hand, waiting for her to take it.

"No." She stood, shaking her head. "I just need to go home and try to get some sleep."

He seriously doubted she'd rest.

"Bullshit. It's only six thirty. You're gonna go back to a dark house full of old memories and brood," he accused her.

"And what if I do?" she snapped. "I'm not fragile, Hunter. I don't need coddling. I'm not that child you kept rescuing. Last night I did what I had to do; it was that simple. I'm a goddam badass, and I don't need you to watch out for me. I'm not your responsibility. We're square now, back the fuck off."

He held his tongue and his temper and watched the storm rage in her eyes.

"Okay," he finally managed through clenched teeth. "Tell me what you need from me."

To his horror, she looked up at him with golden tears swimming in those wide blue-green eyes. He took a step toward her, and she put up a hand to stop him.

"I don't need anything." Her words were just above a whisper. He handed her the box of tissues. She snatched one, wiped her eyes, and took a deep breath.

"Look." The best thing he could do for her was ignore the tears, or pretend he had. "Let's go to the Night Hawk. Have dinner and get you a good stiff drink."

"Hunter, we can't keep . . ."

He walked out of the office without giving her a chance to complain anymore. "Shane." He waved at the deputy to come in.

"Yes, sir?"

He turned to Sam. "Give me your keys."

"Why?" Sam narrowed her eyes.

"Because if you don't, Officer Warren here is gonna have to arrest you for driving under the influence."

Shane did a bad job of covering his smile.

Sam didn't even try to hide her fury. "The hell he will!"

"Aw, I don't know, ma'am." Shane squinted at her. "You're lookin' a little woozy, and if I'm not mistaken, your eyes look bloodshot to me."

Sam's cheeks flushed as Hunter looked at her with raised brows and a victorious smile.

"Really?" she snarled.

"Hey." He lifted both hands in surrender, trying hard

not to smile. "I gotta keep the streets safe, Ms. Ryder. Just doin' my job."

She kept her eyes, glittering with rage and unshed tears, trained on Hunter's. He crossed his arms, his expression indifferent, which considering how he felt, was no easy task. Relief flooded through him as she reached into her purse and retrieved her keys.

He took them from her and, without breaking eye contact, handed them to Shane. "Can you get Ms. Ryder's car home for her?"

"Sure can, Sheriff." The deputy was grinning now. He was enjoying this way too much.

"Thanks," Hunter said. "You can go. Shut the door behind you."

"Right." Shane turned on his heel and did as he was instructed.

Hunter turned to Sam and cupped her cheek.

"Stop touching me." She wrapped her fingers around his wrist lightly.

"Sam," he murmured and moved closer. He wanted to hold her. Take away the bad for a little while.

"Don't, Hunter. We can't," she whispered. Her hands slid up his arms to his shoulders.

"We can." He spoke softly, so close he could taste her coffee-flavored lips. The slight touch made him hungry for more. What they had at Jacob's cabin had only whet his appetite. "We have."

He pulled her against him, swallowing her moan as his mouth moved against hers. Her weak attempt to push him away was short-lived. Her arms went around him as she tilted her head, kissing him like she couldn't breathe without him. The way her sweet body melted against him had his cock hard and demanding attention. His hands speared through her soft hair, holding her there as his tongue brushed against hers. Like a wild cat, her teeth grazed his bottom lip as her fingers dug into his back.

What was left of his control quickly disintegrated as his hand moved to cup her full breast. Her rigid nipple pressed eagerly against his caressing palm. Fuck if his hands didn't shake while he tried to unbutton her silky shirt. Damn tiny buttons were separating him for her skin.

Finally he had her shirt unbuttoned, his fingers stroking the swells of her breasts above her lacy bra. He nipped at her collarbone and licked the spot. With one hand, he unsnapped the front clasp of her bra. Her breasts gently bounced free as he pulled away the delicate cups. The little catch in her throat as he trailed kisses down her throat drove him on. His cock was throbbing uncomfortably behind his zipper. He leaned away and took in the vision of her. Sam, aroused and needy, was a thing of beauty.

"I love how you turn pink for me," he murmured against her lips. His words sounded like a growl as he lifted her onto his desk, pushed her skirt up, and moved between her thighs.

"Oh God, Hunter, we have to stop."

He pulled back and met her gaze. "Do you really want me to stop?"

Her expression was a combination of frustration and arousal and anger. "I want it. But we can't; we have to stop."

"No, we don't." His mouth closed over one nipple, and she whimpered.

Her thighs were so soft he couldn't stop stroking them, moving ever closer to her heat. He didn't even notice she'd unbuckled and unzipped his pants until he felt her cool hand wrapping around his hard cock. He groaned against her breast as her thumb smoothed over the throbbing head. His waning control slipped past the danger zone. He needed her tight pussy gripping him like it had the night before. He needed to taste her sweet cream and feel her shatter against his tongue.

The soft plumpness of her pussy through her soaked cotton panties made him insane, so damn hot, so slick. She lifted her ass, and he pulled her panties off quickly, letting them fall to the floor. His fingers slipped inside her folds, gently stroking from her tight opening to her sweet little throbbing clit. She moved against his fingers, biting her lip to keep quiet. He needed more time, he needed more space. This was not gonna be enough to sate him. Not by a long shot.

"Hunter . . ." It was a broken whisper, a plea for release or to make it last, he wasn't sure.

A knock at the door stopped him from finding out. They froze. Sam's eyes widened with fear. Hunter let her go, holding her hot gaze that reflected the unfulfilled lust in his own. The air was thick with tension, frustration, and the warm creamy scent of her arousal. Anyone who entered the room would detect it and know exactly what it was. It had Hunter baring his teeth as he zipped his pants.

"Yeah?" He breathed deeply as she slid from his desk, quickly fastening her bra.

Hunter went to the door as she turned away to button her shirt. He stepped out into the hall and closed his office door behind him.

"Uh, Sheriff, Carol says there's a call for you. I wouldn't bother you but it's the mayor, sir," Shane said quietly. "I told her you were still meeting with Ms. Ryder, so I thought I'd better come let ya know."

"Shit. Okay, have her put it through."

"Will do." Shane paused. "She okay?"

"She's fine. She's just tired." Hunter eyed him suspiciously. The kid looked a little too concerned.

"Yeah. Ya know, I could take her home if you're busy with the mayor."

"I got this, Shane." Uh-huh. The boy was definitely crushin' on Ms. Sam.

"Right." Shane smiled a weak smile and walked toward the lobby.

Sam was standing and smoothing down her skirt when he came back into the office. "I've gotta take this call. The mayor."

Sam nodded, looking a bit shaky.

"Sam, babe, your buttons . . ." He pointed to her haphazard button-up job.

"Oh hell," she grumbled as she righted her top.

He grinned at her as the phone rang. She was so damn cute. "Sheriff Steele."

"I'm gonna need to be cc'd on all the reports involving Officer Ryder's shooting last night." Mayor Henderson spent no time on pleasantries.

"Yes, sir. You'll have them when they're done," Hunter replied succinctly.

"What was she doing with you on that call, Steele?" Henderson had a way about him that grated on Hunter's nerves. Maybe it was his voice or his pompous attitude, or just the fact that the man was everything he disliked in a person.

"It's all in the report, Mayor. It was a clean shoot. It's already been cleared."

"Just make sure I get all the reports. You hear?" Some found Mayor Henderson's emphatic drawl appealing. Hunter found it grating.

"Absolutely," Hunter said with false enthusiasm.

"Good. Hire her," the mayor commanded before disconnecting.

Hunter stared at the phone for a whole minute after hanging up, wondering which way the mayor was thinking and why he wanted Sam in the department so badly. The man could be on the right track and have worked out that Sam was here investigating. That wasn't good.

The last thing he needed was the mayor becoming more suspicious.

"Hunter, listen. This has to stop," Sam ordered him shakily, as he turned his gaze back to her.

He might actually take her seriously if her nipples weren't still hard.

"What is 'this'? There's a lot going on right now, Sam," he interjected.

"This . . . this . . . thing between us needs to be over. I will not risk your career. Also, it complicates things, adds stress to an already ridiculously stressful situation. If and when people around here discover—*this*—you know it will get messy."

Messy didn't bother him much, but her continued objections were going to dent his ego a bit.

"Sam, you've had a rough day . . ."

She scowled. "My name is Samantha, and do not patronize me, Hunter. I'm serious." Her voice sounded deep, hoarse, shaky with residual passion. Her heart was pounding so hard he could see her pulse at her throat.

"I'm not patronizing, but I have to admit to a bit of confusion," he said. "What kind of 'messy' are we talking about?"

Her lips thinned in irritation. "Messy," she snapped. "The kind were someone ends up getting hurt."

His brow raised slowly as he began to understand exactly what she was implying. By damn, she thought he was just playing with her? It stunned him a bit. "You don't trust me."

"Hell no, I don't trust you! Hunter, I don't really even know you. You sure as hell don't know me," she said with an edge of anger.

A slow smile curled his lips, and he nodded. "You're right. We'll fix that, but you don't get to call all the shots, babe."

She tilted her head to the side, and her mouth parted in surprise. "Yes, yes I do, Hunter. I said no, and no means no."

"You didn't say 'no' to 'this.'" He knew he was irritating her. "You've said 'please,' and I believe I've even heard you say 'yes' a time or two." She was adorable when she was incensed and sexy as all hell when she was aroused. The combination was a heady mixture he couldn't resist baiting.

"I'm saying 'no' now," she said through her teeth.

"Absolutely. Understood." He nodded, still smiling. "I've never wanted to force you, Sam. No is absolute." He could almost read her mind by watching her changing expressions. He knew her a lot better than she realized, but she didn't need to know that. "As far as this investigation we're doing, you're working with me, and you'll do things my way." He pushed away from the desk and walked toward her. He didn't touch her, he merely waited until she tilted her head up to meet his gaze. "As far as 'this' between you and I? I'll take your 'no' very seriously." He watched her swollen lips part on a shaky sigh. "Make sure you mean it."

chapter seven

Damn if Hunter didn't have her feeling discombobulated. She walked around the square, window-shopping,
trying to clear her head. Baffled was not something
Samantha was used to being. She prided herself on
knowing exactly what she wanted, how she wanted it,
and how to go about making it happen. Hunter saw
right through her bravado. Even when she didn't see it
herself. Trust him? She wasn't sure she trusted herself.

She went into the drugstore for old time's sake. It
brought back so many memories. When she was little,
her daddy gave her money to spend there while he went
to the hardware store on the corner.

The familiar bell on the door rang as she entered, and
she felt the present fade away. The shop hadn't changed
much at all. It even smelled the same, like vanilla and
lemons. Samantha stood still for a moment and let the
memories and emotions cycle through her mind.

"Well, will you look here at who just came through

the door, John?" Clara's bright smile hadn't faded in the least. John Abernathy, the pharmacist, and his wife, Clara Abernathy, were still running the neat little drugstore.

"Little Samantha girl!" John came in from the back of the store wearing his white lab shirt with his name and his profession embroidered on the left side pocket. She couldn't help but smile. "We were wonderin' if you'd forgotten us."

"Never!" Samantha laughed as she returned Clara's embrace. "I just haven't had a moment to stop by yet."

"Of course. We understand. I'm so sorry for your loss, honey. Losin' Dottie like that was a terrible shock," John said softly. Clara nodded in agreement.

"Thank you." She wasn't sure what else to say. It was a shock, and it was going to take some time before just hearing her aunt's name didn't cause her heart to hurt.

"I still can't understand how it happened. Dottie was never one to take too many pain pills. Besides, I filled that prescription over a month ago when she twisted her ankle real bad."

"Oh?" Why hadn't she thought to ask about that sooner? "She'd mentioned spraining her ankle, but she said it was nothing and it was already better."

Mr. John rubbed his chin. "Well, it weren't nothin', but that sounds like Dottie. She was healthy as a horse, always on the go, that one. Maybe it was givin' her fits and she took too many on accident." His brows were furrowed, and his voice was soft and reverent. "Sadly, it has been known to happen."

Samantha nodded in agreement, but she didn't agree at all. She was pretty sure Mr. John didn't either by his expression. None of it made sense to anyone who knew her aunt.

"Sit over here at the counter and I'll fix you something to eat. Are you eatin' right?" Clara's concern was sincere.

Lord these well-meaning Southern women would make sure she was plump as a Christmas turkey if she wasn't careful. "I'm eating just fine, Mrs. Clara. Thank you."

"Well, at least let me fix you a dish of ice cream. I heard about what happened with the Millers. You must be all shook up."

Samantha opened her mouth to protest, but John interjected. "Now, Clara," he chided his wife, who glanced back at him sheepishly. "We know you cain't talk about such things, darlin'. We're just glad you're all right." He patted Samantha on the shoulder and sat on the stool beside her.

"Thank you, Mr. John. I'm just fine." She was feeling a bit overwhelmed by all the attention, but it wasn't unpleasant. The couple had always been a stable presence in Deerhaven and in her life. At least until her family moved away.

Clara put the dish of ice cream in front of Samantha with a smile and then folded her hands. No frills, just two ample scoops of vanilla in an antique glass dish. Yet there was nothing ordinary about it. No use in balking, even if she thought it would do any good. The last thing she wanted to do was disappoint Mrs. Clara, and to be honest, the ice cream looked really good.

"Oh wow, this is delicious," Samantha said after one bite.

John beamed proudly.

"John makes it himself in the back with fresh cream," Clara said, grinning.

"Well done, Mr. John." Samantha took another bite and let it melt in her mouth.

"Now." Clara leaned on her elbows. "Tell us all about you and the sheriff."

Samantha nearly choked on her third bite. "What do you mean?" she asked, trying to keep her expression blank as she wiped her mouth.

Clara patted her hand. "Samantha dear, the whole town knows you and our handsome sheriff are sweet on each other. I, for one, think it's just marvelous. Little Hunter needs someone to love after all he's been through."

Samantha nearly choked again, trying not to laugh at Clara calling Hunter "Little Hunter." There was nothing little about Hunter. Somehow she managed an "Oh?"

"That wife of his did him so dirty," John added, without bothering to hide his disgust.

"Oh my, yes." Clara's expression changed from pleasant and happy as usual, to distressed. "Oh! You didn't know?"

Samantha shook her head, waiting for the whole story, which might or might not be embellished. Hunter would most likely not want her to know or he would have told her himself. But then there was a lot about Hunter's past that he hadn't shared with her.

"Well, let me just tell you," Clara said with determined indignation. "When Hunter was sent off to war the first time, he hadn't been gone six months before she started spendin' her weekends up in Reno. She met up with some wealthy man outta Las Vegas and started messin' around. She knew better than to bring him to the ranch, I think. Hunter's ranch hands wouldn't have let that fly. Talk was she'd spend her weekends away from home, sometimes even weeks at a time. Finally, she sent Hunter a letter tellin' him she didn't want him no more. Bless his heart." She shook her head. "He was just destroyed."

"That's why he went and signed up for another tour," John added sadly. "She'd always been kinda highfalutin' and prissy. Never understood what the boy saw in her anyway."

"Well now, John, she could be sweet when she wanted to. She was right pretty, and she certainly knew how to present that big bosom of hers." Clara's voice dripped with disdain.

John grunted with distaste. "Psh . . . pretty is as pretty does, Clara. Besides, I don't think Hunter was that simple. Wasn't there somethin' about a baby?"

"Oh! That's right! That's why Hunter married her in the first place. He got her in trouble and was doin' right by her. Some say she trapped him. But, ya know, I think he really did love her then."

Samantha sat stunned, listening intently, her heart breaking for Hunter. In her mind, there was nothing worse a woman could do to a man than betray him while he's risking his life for their country.

"That's right," John said. "Said she had a miscarriage, but the rumor is she never was pregnant."

No. Hunter wasn't gullible. Samantha was willing to bet real money there'd been a baby. "That's awful," was all she could think to say. It was awful. "Where is Kelly now?" There was an edge to her voice that had Clara looking at her with wide eyes and John smirking.

"She divorced Hunter and married that rich Vegas man," John informed her. "Don't know what happened with her after that. Heard they had a big fancy wedding in Las Vegas." John scoffed again. "What a waste of money."

Well, it was a damn good thing Samantha wouldn't have to come in contact with the wench. She'd have to snatch her bald headed. She didn't know Kelly, but there was a very real animosity brewing inside Samantha for the woman.

Samantha let the new information sink in and the rage dissipate as she browsed the store. The Abernathys gave local crafters a shelf or two on consignment for little or nothing, always had. It was one of the many reasons she loved the couple, and Samantha believed their generosity was one reason their little shop did so well.

She bought a couple of candles that Mrs. Hickman had made. She thanked the Abernathys for the ice cream and hugged them both, promising to visit again soon. She headed home; her head was spinning with all the information, all the new revelations. Things just kept getting more and more involved and convoluted. Add to that the unexpected emotions flooding through her, and well, it was giving her one hell of a headache.

Hunter was struggling with his own tangle of thoughts and emotions. What he needed was some fresh air. He walked out to the pasture thinking of Sam. Stubborn little thing was still a pest, but God, he was enjoying every minute of it. He had to be realistic. He had some demons, not like some of his army brothers had, not even close, but he had them just the same.

Then there was Kelly. He hadn't told Sam about her yet. He wondered if she'd heard. When she found out, or he finally told her about it, how would she react? He clenched his jaw at the thought. It was the past, but it was part of him and Sam had a right to know.

Too much time, energy, and emotion was spent on that particular mistake. The same question nagged him whenever Kelly's name materialized in his mind. Did she miscarry or did she terminate the pregnancy? The rumor was she lied about the pregnancy, but that wasn't true. He'd been there when she took the test. He'd driven her to the doctor's appointment. There'd been a baby. There was no child now, and it didn't matter at this point what happened. At least that's what he kept telling himself. He just desperately wanted to put it away.

Riding helped. With all that had been going on, Hunter had neglected to spend any time with the two mustangs in over a week. Buck and Shiloh both came to the fence to greet him as he approached. Buck snorted indignantly and nodded his big head. Shiloh nuzzled his arm, looking for her apple. Hunter laughed, presented them both with their snack, and rubbed their noses. "All right, let's go see if those boys got anything done."

Levi and Ethan were checking trails and mending fences as needed up on the northeast side of the pasture. Hunter decided to ride Buck up to check on them, ask them some questions. They might have seen something and didn't think anything of it at the time.

The twins were good kids; they liked to party when they weren't working their asses off for Hunter on the ranch. They'd been wild as bucks all over the country-side. But hell, they were twenty-one and popular with the young single ladies of Deerhaven. Rumor had it, they were popular with some of the not-so-young single ladies as well. Hunter shook his head, those two liked to play rough and loose. One of these days they may end up snagged by one of those hot little cougar's claws.

The twins were nearly done mending a post as Hunter rode up. They were identical and few could tell them apart. Both had black hair and ice-blue eyes, both were about six feet tall and built like linebackers.

To their wicked advantage, not many noticed that Levi had a thin sliver scar at his left temple that barely peaked out of his hairline. He got that when the rope broke while swinging over Sutter's Creek and he cracked his hard head on a jagged rock.

Ethan had a few more subtle freckles around his eyes than Levi did. He also had a scar on the right ass cheek from thinking it'd be fun to mess with Uncle Zack's Charbray bull. That bovine was a beast, and Ethan was lucky as hell he came out alive. Kids always think they're invincible. Ethan and Levi still believed they were.

"Hey, Uncle Hunter," Ethan greeted him, taking off his hat to wipe the sweat away.

Hunter nodded in return. "How's it lookin'?"

"Myrtle is about to calve soon," Levi answered, as he gathered tools, loaded them on the back of the utility vehicle and started securing them.

"Yeah," Ethan agreed. "Gonna move her to the barn tomorrow. She's two to three weeks out, I'd say."

Calving could be the easiest, most natural thing in the world for a momma cow. Or it could be a lot of work that required intervention. "This is her first. She doin' okay?" Hunter asked.

Ethan smiled. "Yeah, she's lookin' good. Eatin' and lounging around like a pregnant lady oughta. I think she's gonna do fine."

"All right. If for some reason I'm not reachable when it's time and anything goes wrong, you have the okay to call Doc Mosley."

Both nodded. Ethan grinned. "Heard you been hangin' out with Miss Samantha."

"That so?" Hunter tilted his head in amusement.

"Yeah! She's hot too." Levi raised a brow. "Girl's got curves in all the right places. Mmm, mmm, mmm."

"Right?" Ethan interjected, leaning against the newly planted post. "Good Lord, the woman can fill out some jeans. And the way she walks . . ." Ethan sucked in air through his teeth.

Hunter narrowed his eyes, not that the twins were easily deterred. Obviously, they were trying to push his buttons, and he'd be lying if he said it wasn't working a little, but hell, they weren't wrong. Buck danced to the side a step, sensing Hunter's tension elevate slightly. Hunter patted Buck's neck to calm him. "She does, indeed." Hunter spoke quietly, his voice low. "Miss Samantha is way out of your league."

Levi's grin widened. "I don't know, Uncle Hunter. The two of us together could rock her world. Hey, ya never know, maybe she could teach us a thing or two."

"You go sniffin' around Sam, and I'll teach you a whole hell of a lot." Hunter's smile turned feral.

Ethan laughed and Levi raised his hands in surrender. "Okay, okay, we get it." Levi was still grinning.

"Absolutely, Uncle Hunter. Miss Samantha is off limits." Ethan smirked knowingly.

"Uh-huh. Still got my eye on the two of you." Hunter chuckled. "Maybe I should call y'all's momma."

"Aww, damn, that's cold." Levi sobered.

Ethan stood straighter, his smile fading. "You wouldn't."

"The hell I wouldn't," Hunter said. "All's fair in love and war, boys."

They looked at each other and smiled. It was like they communicated telepathically sometimes.

"Listen, you guys see anyone or anything unusual lately? Maybe around the lake or out around the campgrounds?" Hunter asked, changing the subject.

They looked at each other again, then back at Hunter. "No," they answered in stereo.

"We haven't been out too much the last couple of weeks. There's been a lot of work around here." Levi took off his hat and combed his fingers through his hair before replacing it. "We're planning to go out to the lake this weekend. We'll keep our eyes open."

"I'd appreciate it." Hunter patted Buck's neck.

"Anything particular we're supposed to be lookin' for?" Ethan asked.

Hunter thought for a moment about how much to tell them. He decided to be vague. "Anything out of the ordinary, that's all."

"This have to do with Uncle Zack's death?" Ethan's voice was hard.

"Just keep your eyes open. And y'all stay out of

trouble. By the way, I heard about you and Jenny Talbert, Levi."

Levi's eyes widened, feigning righteous indignation. A grin pulled at the corner of his mouth, ruining the effect. "Mrs. Talbert is divorced. She is a fine, respectable woman, Uncle Hunter."

"Yeah. I know. However, Mr. Talbert is a jealous man, and he's none too happy about that newly signed divorce decree. The ink ain't even good and dry yet," Hunter warned.

"Aw, come on now, Uncle Hunter. The woman has needs." Levi grinned.

"Psh, he ain't lyin'," Ethan interjected. "And she's loud! Can't get any sleep when she's over."

Levi smirked. "Ladies love cowboys. I just do what I can. What can I say?"

"Good God," Hunter muttered, shaking his head at them as he turned Buck around to head back to the stables. "Y'all keep your eyes open and your noses clean."

"Uh, ya see, Uncle Hunter," Ethan explained with a stoic expression, "if we do that, then the ladies will be sad because it's near impossible to do it well if we don't get our noses all up—"

"Stop!" Hunter raised a hand and interrupted Ethan. He didn't need the mental image. "Just . . . try to stay of trouble. Okay?"

"Yes, sir," they answered in unison, chuckling.

chapter eight

Samantha's mind was too busy to relax. She'd taken a hot bath and lit her new candles, but nothing helped much. When she found herself pacing, she decided enough was enough. She got dressed in a pair of jeans and a T-shirt, brushed her hair out, and checked her reflection in the mirror. She quickly reapplied her lipstick before grabbing her keys and heading out.

The Night Hawk was pretty busy for a weeknight. The food was always really good comfort food. Samantha had to admit it was just what she needed. The warm amber liquid in her glass was blurring all the sharp edges just right.

Hunter sauntered in and shattered what little alcohol-induced peace she'd been able to achieve. He walked straight to her booth and slid in across from her. Now, he watched her as he leaned back, making himself comfortable. "Feelin' better?"

"Yep." She lifted her eyes to gaze at him without

raising her head. "Don't let this go to your head, but you were right. I needed a drink."

A feral grin curved those very talented lips of his. "One may have been your limit, Pixie."

"I'm fine." The truth was she was starting to feel a bit too loose. It was her second and her last if she wanted to make it out of there on her own feet. She slid the glass with the remainder of her drink toward him. "But I've had enough."

Hunter picked up the glass and threw back the last of the whiskey. She bit her lip as she watched him lick his lips.

"Damn, girl. Sadie brought you the good stuff." He grinned.

"Mmm-hmmm, that's what I asked for." The whiskey wasn't the only thing making her warm and tingly.

It was, however, weakening her resolve to behave when it came to Sheriff Sexy Face. She chuckled at her assessment of Hunter as she slipped her feet out of her sandals. She watched his eyes widen as she gently moved her toes up his inner calf to his inner thigh.

"So, what happened to your 'no'?" he asked then, a brow lifting in playful mockery as she found the iron-hard length of his erection.

"I've reassessed." She shrugged.

And she had. It had nothing to do with what the Abernathys had told her either. "No" wasn't going to work because she wanted him too damned much. Protecting her heart from him wouldn't be easy. He'd been hurt, and he was protecting his heart as well. No doubt she'd end up hurt, but as she watched him from across the table, she knew it was a risk she had no choice but to take.

His lips tilted at the corner as he reached under the table and grasped her foot and began massaging it. He applied just the right pressure in just the right places.

An involuntary moan escaped her lips as his hand moved to the top of her foot and then to her ankle. She slowly inched forward. She could feel the heat before she felt the bulge. Hunter narrowed his eyes, and she couldn't help but grin. Her foot trailed up and down his thickening erection, pressing against the denim. He was long and thick and very hard.

"Unzip your jeans," she mouthed. She watched his eyes darken. His hand stilled on her leg.

"Let's dance." It wasn't a request and his words sounded more like a growl.

He gave her no time to put her sandals back on before he was pulling her toward the dance floor. "But I don't know any line dances."

"S'okay, it's a slow song," he answered hoarsely.

He yanked her against his hard body, and for a moment her world tilted. If he hadn't been holding her so close, she probably would have fallen over. She lay her head against his chest, closed her eyes, and breathed in the scent of him. Oh, this was nice. A small annoying little voice in her brain was screaming for her to be sensible. She ignored it and looked up at Hunter. "What are we doing?"

"We're dancing, Pixie," he murmured against her cheek.

"You know what I mean, Hunter."

A soft chuckle rumbled low in his chest. "What do you wanna do?"

His hand moved down her back and sat just above her ass, then he pulled her closer. She could feel how hard he was, and she remembered what he felt like moving inside her. She shivered as the memory flooded her mind. Her body reacted instinctively.

She raised up until her lips were against his ear. "I want to make you lose control."

Her words were barely above a whisper, but he heard her. She knew he heard her because his big body tensed in her arms and his fingers flexed against her hips. "Let's go." His breath was a harsh rasp against her ear.

The cool spring breeze made her shiver as they stepped out of the saloon. It did a lot to clear the fog from her mind but it did nothing to cool her arousal. Hunter led her to his truck and helped her up into the passenger seat. She rolled down the window as he pulled out of the parking lot. The wind in her face felt good and cleared her mind. It didn't take long to get home. She didn't wait for Hunter to open her door for her. Hunter's arm snaked around her middle to steady her as she hopped down. On the porch, Hunter pulled her back against him as he took the key from her. The heat of his hard body was as intoxicating as the whiskey.

Hunter guided her into the house and quickly locked up. With a sigh, she turned in his arms. His mouth found hers, his tongue stroking, igniting her blood. It felt so good, so incredibly good, even better than before. His kiss was skillful, yet insistent, like he couldn't get enough. Samantha was just as hungry. She unfastened the button on his jeans and then lowered his zipper. His rigid cock was thick, hot, and pulsing in her palm.

He groaned as his hands slid down her body to grip her ass and pull her close against him. Her pussy throbbed, sensitive and slick. Moaning, she bit down gently on his bottom lip and laved it with the tip of her tongue.

The sound that rumbled low in his chest sounded more animal than human as he walked her backward. The room spun as he twirled her around and bent her over Aunt Dottie's floral upholstered sofa and flipped her skirt up. She gasped, her hands gripping the cushions as she braced herself, anxious for what she knew was coming. The sudden caress of cool air against the backs of her thighs and her rear made her shiver as Hunter moved away briefly to push her panties down. They fell to her ankles and she stepped out of them.

"You're so wet and ready." His voice sounded raw and predatory, his fingers lightly stroking her sensitive flesh. "Spread your legs," he demanded even as he guided her legs apart with his hand.

It felt like her whole body was throbbing as he slid the wide head of his cock up and down between the slick, swollen folds of her pussy. "Please . . ." Whimpering, she pushed against him as she arched her back.

"Fuck," he growled through clenched teeth.

An orgasm gripped her, taking her breath as he pushed deep inside her. He didn't stop and he didn't go slowly, thank God. Her legs trembled as waves of pleasure rippled through her body. Her cries were muffled by the sound of her blood pounding in her ears to the rhythm of Hunter's thrusts.

Hunter's groan punctuated hers as he drove deep inside and held her tight against him. She could feel the hard, hot pulses as he filled her.

As the pleasure subsided she stood straight, his hands at her waist as she turned to face him.

"You okay?" He trailed kisses, warm and gentle, over her jaw to her ear.

"Mm-hmm."

"Bedroom." She didn't bother with the lights as she led him through the small living room down the hall to the bedroom.

In the bedroom, he pulled her into his arms and kissed her possessively as they helped each other get out of their clothes. Once naked he smoothed his hand over her butt and up her back. She trembled at his urgent touch. She pressed hungrily against him, wanting him closer. His hands were just rough enough, just hot enough to make every inch of her throb with need all over again.

His kisses dominated her senses. She didn't even notice that he'd moved them to the bed until she felt herself falling. He massaged her breast as he kissed and nibbled along her collarbone. A shaky breath escaped her lips on a moan as his mouth left a burning trail down her breastbone. Finally his mouth closed over a nipple and she arched to give him better access as he sucked, nibbled, and kissed, torturing her slowly. He squeezed it lightly between his lips, flicking it with his tongue.

"I love your nipples," he murmured against her sensitive skin. That gorgeous male mouth was definitely well-versed in the female body.

It was so easy for him to make her crazy, drive her

wild. Little tremors gripped her with every pull of his mouth on her nipple. Every flick of his tongue made her want to scream.

She was already on the edge of another climax from what he was doing with his mouth alone. Sensations coiled inside her tighter, building her arousal. Her fingers bit into his well-shaped ass, loving the feel of his hard muscles flexing under smooth skin.

Reaching between them, she trailed her fingers over his silky, steel-hard shaft before wrapping them around it. She felt the blood pump into his thick flesh as she stroked over the flared ridge at the base of the head.

"Not yet, baby." His hands restrained her, his big body controlling her effortlessly.

Her body trembled with the intense sensations coursing through her as he continued to trail kisses down her body, his tongue torturing her. He circled her navel with his tongue and bit the tender flesh there, sucked it, then soothed it with slow, moist strokes. He stroked her inner thighs, spreading her wide. He kissed and nibbled his way down her body to the top of her cunt.

His tongue stroked over her soft tender lips, slid between her moistened cleft, then laved her heated flesh with long and firm upward strokes. She was so close, so close. Hunter's lips closed over her clit and sucked hard. Her breath caught in her lungs, and she bucked up as she climaxed hard and fast. He gripped her hips, unrelentingly torturing her with his talented tongue as she ground against him with each crashing wave of her orgasm.

Hunter rose above her as she slid bonelessly back to earth. She was breathless, gasping, her body humming with pleasure. Without giving her time to fully recover, he slowly slid his fingers into her, the walls of her vagina gripping them as it spasmed with the aftershocks of her orgasm. Then he slid them up through the slick folds of her flesh, driving her toward climax again as he found the firm, rippled flesh of her G-spot. He took her nipple into his mouth, nibbling, flicking his tongue over it, making it harden further, and she pushed forward for more. God, someone should patent his fucking tongue, she thought as she groaned with growing need.

She ran her hands up his muscled back and fisted them in his hair. She pulled him up to her and kissed his mouth. Her hands moved down his stomach and caressed his balls, letting her fingers trail up his steel-hard, thick shaft. He pulled away from her and met her gaze. His eyes had gone dark and heavy-lidded. Her thumb rubbed across the hot, smooth head of his cock.

The deep, hoarse whisper surprised her, made her feel sexy. "I want to feel it in my mouth." She licked her swollen lips.

"God, you know how to tease a man." He moved his fingers inside her and gently pressed his thumb against her clit. "Later, if you still want to. Right now, I want to feel your sweet pussy gripping my cock again."

She inhaled sharply as pleasure shot through her, pushing her upward. He moved his hand from her and positioned himself over her. Moving the full head of his thick shaft through her slickness, up and down through her swollen folds. He rubbed slow circles around her clit. She clutched at his shoulders.

She moaned as he slowly slid inside her. He took her arms and lifted them over her head, then leaned down and kissed her, sucking her bottom lip. He moved deeper into her, then rose, lifting her thighs. He draped each ankle over his shoulders. He grabbed a pillow and braced it under her as he grasped her hips and filled her to the hilt. She moaned harshly, arching into the strong thrust. She clenched her muscles around his cock, and he closed his eyes, hissing air through his teeth.

He slowly withdrew till he was almost free then plunged back in. She felt the tension building. She was almost there, almost ready to come. She fought against it, wanting it to never end. Samantha moaned harshly, panting.

He kissed the inside of her ankle while he began pumping in and out of her in a slow, rhythmic motion. Waves of sensation washed over her like honey. It was driving her up, higher and higher, the feeling growing stronger and sharper until she thought she'd go mad.

She looked up at him and met his gaze. He looked hungry. She ran her hand down his hard, rippling stomach to where their bodies met. She closed her eyes and tilted her head back as her fingers felt his hot cock slide in and out of her, felt his balls slap against her.

His hand closed over hers, and she opened her eyes again, watching him as he directed her fingers to the little swollen nub nestled in the slick folds of her female flesh. He was thrusting into her faster and faster. She sucked in a breath as their fingers rubbed over her clit together, taking her up until she exploded, ecstasy radiating through her.

She cried out and flung her head back. Hunter drove into her, tenderly circling her clit. She bucked against him as the next orgasm hit, even stronger, until she thought she'd splinter and disintegrate. His lips parted on a groan and his eyes narrowed, focusing on hers, plunging into her one last time as he came and shuddered against her, his hot cum filling her.

She lay panting as he lowered her legs and rested on top of her, his semi-hard flesh still seated inside her. It felt good to have the weight of this man on her, better than any of her fantasies. She had this irksome fear that no one else would ever measure up.

chapter nine

Hunter figured he was screwed, and not just literally, as he rolled to his side and brought Samantha's body close against his chest. Damn, if that hadn't been the best fuck of his life. The fiery heat and melting passion he found in her was more than amazing, it was downright scary. No woman should be so tight, so hot and wet, her inner muscles sucking every drop of semen from his taut balls until he was gasping.

He remembered his little Pixie Pest and the way she used to look up to him with eyes sparkling with hero worship. She wasn't so much a pixie anymore, though. Hell if she wasn't still a pest, even if she had been his hero this time.

From scrawny little troublemaker into full-grown warrior woman, she was a wild flame in his arms. He couldn't believe how hot and hard that made him now. From the moment her eyes had stared into his at that damned bar, he had been ready to explode. It wasn't normal, he warned himself. If he were listening, maybe it would help.

Even now, he was semi-hard; his sensitive flesh achingly aware of the slick, hot portal awaiting it inches away. He could feel the smooth satin of her thigh against the sensitive head of his cock. He knew within minutes he would be hard and ready again. She didn't need this. Holy shit, he didn't need this. She was a wildcat that sapped his strength and made him want to howl at the moon in male satisfaction.

Looking like an innocent angel, snuggled against him, her breathing slowly evening out. Well, appearances were deceiving; all that sweetness was infused with red-hot spice.

Shower. That was all he needed to clear his head, he thought. A shower. He could get up right now and walk right out that door. Hell, his house wasn't far away, and the water was nice and cold there. He knew that for a fact.

He shifted to move away from her. He had everything figured out until his betraying flesh slid across slick, silky skin. He closed his eyes on a groan and settled between her thighs once again, instead. Okay, so the cold shower could wait.

He rubbed his face against her full, hard-tipped breasts. They were gorgeous. Round and firm, with little pink nipples that tempted him as surely as anything could. Like pretty raspberries, all prime and ripe and ready to pluck. His tongue stroked one softly.

"Again?" There was surprise in her voice. That crisp, stern Yankee accent was shocked, but growing husky with the return of heat.

Who would have thought his Pixie would come home with that upright starch in her voice that made her sound so damned untouchable? It made his libido stand up and howl in hunger.

"Aw now, sugar," he whispered with a smile, allowing his country twang to deepen to a slow drawl. "If it's worth doin', it's worth doin' right."

"I believe you did it pretty damn right the first time," she gasped, as his lips pulled at one little berry with a teasing caress.

"Aw, there's always room for improvement." He smiled against her flesh.

"Improvement?" Her sexy blue-green eyes widened incredulously, and she bit her plump lower lip. "God help me," she murmured, her long fingers fisting in the sheets at her sides as she arched her head back against the pillow, pushing her breasts closer to his mouth.

Damn, she was responsive. Her breath hitched, suspended, then released on a low moan of pleasure as he transferred his attention to her other nipple.

"Oh, that feels good." She seemed surprised as he drew on just the tight bud of nerves tempting his lips and tongue. He went no further. He just let his tongue stroke over her nipple, grazing it gently between his teeth, listening to the strangled gasps that issued from her throat.

"Someone was in a hurry earlier," he teased her as he kissed the darkening flesh. "We take things slow here, darlin'. Nice and easy, so we can savor every experience. Remember?"

She arched languidly in his arms, a small, whimpering moan escaping her lips as his tongue rasped over her again, then he drew her nipple into his mouth, suckling at it slow and easy. The hard little point throbbed beneath his lips, tightening and stabbing at his tongue in needy greed.

"This is savoring?" she asked in breathless amazement. "God, Hunter, this is torture."

But she struggled to lie still beneath him, her hands gripping his shoulders as he sipped and sucked at her breasts, loving the taste of the berry firmness as she arched against him.

"Torture?" he asked her gently, smiling when her nails bit into the tough skin of his upper arms, and her thighs shifted against his, her hips grinding against the thigh he pressed to her hot center. Damn, the woman was like fire in his arms. Like pure lava, melting and flowing from her core, dampening his thigh with a liquid plea.

"Hunter, I don't know if I can stand this," she panted harshly, her hands reaching to spear into his hair as he licked from her nipple to her neck.

His let his teeth rasp the sensitive skin at her collarbone, then lick at it with a slow swipe as he tasted the smooth sweetness he found there. She tossed her head, groaning as he pressed his thigh against her drenched mound, allowing her to ride it as her hips rose and fell in demand. Unable to resist that long, lovely neck flushed with heat from her arousal, his mouth devoured her, sucking and licking the warm silky skin of her throat. His hand caressed her breast, gently lifting, squeezing, rasping her hard nipple against his palm. He felt the rumble of her groan against his tongue, and his mouth moved higher, along her jaw.

"Sure you can, sugar," he whispered, his tongue outlining her ear with a slow sweep. "You're a badass."

He raised his head and found her mouth open, soft and yielding. He tasted that full, hot lower lip she kept nibbling on and drew it into his mouth. He tilted his head and deepened the kiss, their breath blending as he moved his tongue against hers in long, slow strokes.

He felt her shiver against him, and his cock throbbed in its own demand. Damn, where had his self-control gone? She made him want to thrust hard and deep and drown in the heat pouring from her. He had to force himself to let his hand move slow and sure from her waist to her breast. There, he cupped the mound of heaving flesh, moving his head to rub the erect nipple against his cheek.

She cried out harshly, her hot cunt thrusting against his thigh as he pushed it harder against her. And still he didn't hurry. He wanted her to remember this night, just as he knew he would. He rubbed his lips over the stiff point, licked it tenderly, then moved back to her neck as one hand moved lower along her smooth, flat abdomen. His fingers trailed through the beads of moisture forming there. Her skin was almost as slick as the hot folds of flesh between her thighs. And he wasn't unaffected either. He could feel the sweat pouring from his body, drenching them both as he fought for breath.

He moved then, drawing his thigh back from the heat of her pussy as he spread her legs wide, moving between them slowly.

"Hunter, please." She shivered, whimpering in her female need as he nudged the slick entrance of her body with the broad head of his cock.

Control. He fought for it. He didn't want to slam inside her. He wanted it to last forever. He wanted to take her gentle and sweet, and show her how damned good it could be. He slid in marginally, barely an inch, feeling her muscles clamp onto that small invasion in desperation.

He fought for breath. Son of a bitch, it was good. So damned hot and silky, clenching, stroking his flesh with each harsh breath she fought for. He gripped her hips, holding her steady, watching the point where their two bodies met. The dim light of the moon's glow spilling onto the bed gave him a clear view of her glistening, silky curls and the burrowing of his hard length between them.

He swallowed tightly, on fire with the sensations sweeping through his body as he inched farther inside her, his eyes riveted by the sight of her female lips widening, drawing him in as her vagina milked his cock, keeping him pulsing with the need to climax.

He wasn't going to rush this. Damn, if it wasn't the best he had ever known. Watching her as he took her, seeing her body accept him, hearing her cries for more. He gave her more, spreading her inch by inch as her keening cry was lost in his male groan of triumph, as his darker, intimate hair meshed with her wet curls, soaking both.

He shook his head, grinding his hips into her as he resisted his body's demand that he take her hard. Fast. "Now, Hunter. Now." It was her tormented voice pleading for release he couldn't resist. It shattered his self-control.

He fell forward, catching himself on his elbows and clasping her head in his hands.

"Open your eyes," he growled. "Look at me, Samantha. Look at me while I make you scream."

His hips retreated. Her eyes widened in protest. He slammed forward, driving every hard, desperate inch of his cock as deep as it would go inside the sucking depths of her vagina. Her mouth opened, a gasping cry issuing from it. Her pupils dilated in further pleasure, a harsh flush mounting her cheekbones as her hips pushed against him, demanding more.

"Faster. Please, Hunter. Faster." Her eyes didn't leave his; they glazed over, her eyelids lowering just enough to give her a mysterious, sexy look that made him crazy.

He felt his muscles bunch, braced himself with knees and elbows, and with a quick prayer that she would come quickly, he gave her what she wanted. What he needed. His hips powered into her. Thrust after long, hard thrust, as they both groaned, arched, slamming their bodies into each other, fighting for the ultimate high while their blood thundered, rushed.

Samantha screamed for him. He relished the sound, thrusting deeper inside her as he felt her clench, gush. Another sharp scream issued from her throat as she began to climax harshly. He was only a second away. He gritted his teeth, fought a shout, and lost his control as he felt the rippling power of his ejaculation tearing through his body.

He cried out her name, holding himself deep and tight within her as his seed pumped hard and fast inside her gripping, spasming flesh.

Damn, if he had to die, this was the way to go. Hunter barely caught himself before he collapsed on top of her. At the last second, he twisted his body, falling beside her, his eyes closing in exhaustion as he fought for breath, and for sanity. Yeah, that was what he needed. Sanity. Sex like this should be outlawed, though he'd hate to have to arrest himself.

He grinned at that. His hand fell to Samantha's stomach, feeling the sharp rise and fall of it as she fought for her own breath. They were both gasping, fighting for control. He felt alternately proud as hell and scared to his toenails. He wanted to beat on his chest, he wanted to slink away and hide from her. Sex shouldn't be that damned good.

"Amazing, you're absolutely amazing, but I think perhaps I've died." Her voice, so proper and well-cultured, made him smile. Deerhaven, California, didn't boast many Yankees. He was pretty damned sure they wouldn't brag about any, if they were there. Fact was, Sam wasn't a real Yankee, and he intended to remind her of just that. Right now, he had a soft, vibrant, incredibly lusty she-cat on his hands, and he loved it.

"Sure 'bout that?" he whispered against her ear, feeling the involuntary shiver that raced over skin. "Just let me catch my breath, sugar, and we'll try for another round. See if I can bring you back to life."

"Uh, slow down now, cowboy. Give a girl a moment to recharge," she said with a soft sexy laugh.

There was a faint protest there. Real faint. Hunter wished he had the strength for the chuckle he wanted to release. Damn, it was all he could do to breathe.

"All right then, better get some rest." He took a deep

breath, making himself rise and reach to the foot of the bed where the comforter had been tossed.

Damned A/C was hell on damp skin, he thought, feeling her shiver again. He covered them both, then settled back beside her with an exhausted sigh.

"We have to get up early." She cuddled into his arms, her head against his chest as a last sigh whispered over his chest. "Don't ignore the alarm."

He glanced over at the red digital display on her side of the bed. Alarm was set, at least. He would have hated to have to go to the trouble.

"Sure thing, sugar." He yawned, pulling her tighter in his arms, his chin resting against the top of her head as he closed his eyes.

Damn, a sudden thought struck him. She wasn't going to run him off before dawn? He frowned, wondering how long it had been since he had spent the night with a woman, instead of sneaking out of her house before daylight. Neighbors and gossip—they turned normally intelligent women into gibbering masses of nervousness. They wanted to play, but damned if they wanted anyone to know it.

He had always been amused by the same shy, sweet, parlor room ladies gasping and moaning in the dead of night, then pushing their lovers swiftly from the back door before dawn. Not this one, though. He ran his hand along her back, finally allowing it to rest at the top of her buttock as he sighed in satisfaction. Maybe he'd try for more the next morning.

chapter ten

Samantha woke up with a smile on her face. She stretched languidly, kicking the covers from her naked body. Her muscles ached, a pleasant reminder of the night before. A hot shower would loosen them up just fine.

She curled her toes, and her sigh was more of a moan. Sex had never been this good nor this fun. She'd imagined being with Hunter so many times, she'd almost been afraid it wouldn't live up to her fantasies. A low chuckle left her throat. This time reality surpassed fantasy. She felt like an overindulged feline and nearly purred with smug satisfaction.

Opening one eye, she noticed the time on the clock and pouted. She had too much to do to lay in bed all morning but the cool sheets felt so good. Hunter had apparently already left, so she best just get up and get busy.

She rolled onto her back and brushed the hair out of

her face. She placed her other hand on her stomach. Hunter . . . the mere thought of him had her body humming. She closed her eyes and breathed deeply, remembering his lips on her mouth, her neck. Her fingers trailed lightly between the valley of her breasts. She would have to talk to him about cooling this off some if they were going to continue working together. Otherwise they'd be spending all their time in bed, or wherever.

"Now see, that image is gonna haunt me all day long."

Samantha sat straight up and scowled. "Dammit, Hunter."

Hunter stood leaning against the doorframe with a wicked glint in his eye. He grinned and walked toward her, his voice low and seductive. "Sorry, sugar, didn't mean to startle ya." He sat at the end of the bed and lifted one of her feet to rest against his shoulder and gently began massaging her calf.

"I thought you had left already." Her voice was a bit breathy, her eyes fluttered closed as his hands moved higher, kneading the tight muscles there. He lifted her foot, and she felt his teeth graze over the arch. Her breath caught in her throat as what should have only tickled sent pleasure feathering through her. "Don't you need to be at work?" she croaked softly.

He chuckled, that low sexy rumble. Was everything about this man hot? "I do."

He was tempting, dressed in those low-slung jeans and beige button-down shirt. His sleeves were rolled up again, revealing his tight, tan skin over thick, corded muscles. She wanted him naked, covering her; she wanted that mouth all over her body again. Her body clenched at the thought, the slick sliding between her thighs only adding to her need. She couldn't get enough of him. Samantha lifted a single brow and gave him a sly, hungry smile. "And yet, here you are."

"Temptress," he growled at her, and she nearly shivered. He moved over her and she reached up and ran her fingers through his shower-dampened hair.

His hand cupped her breast. The heat of his palm, the roughness, sent delightful shivers racing over her skin. Her nipples contracted, aching for more attention, and he obliged them, rubbing his thumb across their hardened peaks as he kissed her, swallowing her moan, his tongue playing with hers. He broke away too soon and nipped at her full bottom lip then licked it before moving away from her.

"Get up, sugar." Hunter's voice was husky, and she thought he growled again when he bent and nibbled then kissed her shoulder. "We gotta talk."

She moaned seductively, watching Hunter's strong handsome face. He was right. They both had work to do, but this might be the last time she got to touch him like this. His lids were lowered, and with her free hand she cupped the growing bulge in his jeans.

"There's all kinds of ways to communicate." Her hand moved over the outline of his thick shaft that pressed against the rough material.

His hand closed over hers as she started to unzip his pants.

"Sam, baby, you're killin' me." He cupped her cheek and kissed her. "I'd love nothing better than to stay in bed all day with you," he whispered. He kissed her mouth once more, then her nose. "We need to have a serious talk, and I can't think straight if you're lyin' there all naked."

With an exaggerated sigh, she sat up again, pulling the sheet up and dreading what he had on his mind. "All right. What specific thing do we need to seriously talk about?"

"I want you to transfer to Deerhaven and work for me."

That shook her for a moment. He said it like it was suddenly a given, like she wouldn't think of declining his "offer." Did he think he could be in control now that he had rocked her world sexually? Well, he was in for a huge disappointment. Maybe he was joking, maybe she misinterpreted his tone. She looked up at him, searching his eyes for the humor and finding none at all. "Hunter, I told you—"

"Yeah, I know, you have a better paying job up north." He moved away from her to the dresser, picked up his wallet and his gun. "Just think about it a little longer, for me. This is and has always been your home. I think if you're honest with yourself, you'd admit that's true. You know you belong here."

Did he realize how condescending he was being? It wasn't all about the pay, and it was irritating that he seemed to think that's all there was to it. Her eyes narrowed. "You don't know me as well as you think you do."

That slow, arrogant smile that always pissed her off curved his mouth. "Yeah, right. Sugar, you're all grown up now, but I can still read you like a book. Look, it makes good sense. You're gonna need more than a couple of weeks here to help me uncover this mess. We still have no lead on the mystery guy. Besides, Henderson wants you here. Why is that, Sam? Don't you wanna find out?"

Hunter had a way of manipulating people to get them to do what he wanted while feeling privileged for the chance. Or better yet, making them think it was their idea in the first place. Well, she knew that condescending tone all too well. She'd fought too hard to move up the ranks. Hell if she'd let Hunter come in and belittle everything she'd worked for.

She kept her voice calm and steady, unlike the emotions rioting through her. "In spite of what you may think, I'm not your silly little Pixie Pest anymore. I'm highly trained and educated, and I worked hard for my position with Detroit PD. It isn't disposable, neither am I." Hunter opened his mouth to speak, but she held up her hand. "Don't you dare underestimate me or my ability. I'm not gonna follow along behind you like some meek little thing. I will not be Henderson's pawn, nor will I be yours."

His smile became a firm straight line as he met her gaze. "Do you honestly believe that's what I think?" He paused a moment, the muscle in his jaw pulsing. His voice was hoarse with the effort to keep it even. "Fuck that, Samantha. I'm not that simple. I would have thought you'd think more of me than that." His hands on his hips, he shook his head, then met her gaze again. "You have a job if you want it. I hope you'll take it because frankly, I need your help. I don't need a pawn. I need an officer I can trust, but playing 'the pawn' with Henderson could give us an upper hand." His voice was low and dangerously quiet. "If you want to go back to De-

troit, fine. I have work to do. I don't have time to defend
myself against all your bullshit, and I won't beg you.
You can probably come by and pick up your weapon by
the end of the week." With that, he turned and walked
away.

She jumped at the sound of the front door slamming
so hard it rattled the windows. Had he ever been mad at
her before? Really mad? Damn. That realization settled
heavy in her stomach. She'd always been prepared for
misogyny to rear its ugly head, and she'd battled it long
and hard. She'd just automatically assumed that's how
Hunter was thinking. She heaved a heavy sigh and
rubbed her hands over her face. Didn't make any differ-
ence at this point. She'd made a mess of things. It stung
to admit to herself that she was wrong; it was gonna
sting a lot worse to admit it to him.

Since she was in the frame of mind to be honest with
herself, she had to concede that Hunter had made a lot
of sense. Her mom was in Florida with her new husband.
Her friends were more acquaintances and fellow officers. Yeah, she had open cases up in Detroit, but the
hard truth was that someone else could pick them up and
close them just as efficiently as she could. Detroit was a
big city, and the reality of her situation was that she was
very expendable. Here she had a chance to make a dif-
ference.

Hunter said he needed her.

She looked at herself in the steamy mirror. "Don't go
there, Samantha," she murmured. Hunter needed someone on his side in Deerhaven; he didn't mean he needed
her personally.

All right then, eating crow wasn't gonna be fun. The

sex had to stop, it had to. Once she was his deputy, it would be beyond inappropriate. It's wasn't forbidden, there's "Freedom of Association," but she'd seen officers ruin their lives and careers by "dipping their pen in the company inkwell."

Just wouldn't work out well for either of them.

She tucked her green, cotton, button-up shirt into her jeans and fastened the button and then the belt. They were a little snug from eating at the Night Hawk too much. She'd better keep all the good home cooking in check or she'd outgrow her clothes. Maybe there was a gym in town, or at the station. She'd have to be sure and ask. But first, she had to face Hunter and apologize. Perhaps he wasn't still mad, and hopefully the job offer was still open.

chapter eleven

Hunter had driven through town, pretending to patrol while he simmered over the conversation with Sam. She inflamed him in every way, and this was not his favorite way. Stepping out of his cruiser into the heat of a California summer, he inhaled deeply and attempted to tamp down his irritation. It didn't help that he had an impromptu meeting with the mayor. The man delighted in making Hunter's life as difficult as possible. It was best not to let Henderson know just how bad his mood was. Oh, there was always the pretense, the big smile and the hard slap on the back, but they both knew it was an act.

"Afternoon, Sheriff," Margie Reynolds greeted him as he entered the mayor's outer office. "You're lookin' good. How've you been doin'?"

Margie was a bleached blond, forty-something soccer mom with delusions of regaining her high school days. She wore the makeup heavy—especially the bronze blush, blue eye shadow, and mascara—and she had thick, heavily permed hair. She was a good woman, though, and damned near always had a smile for everyone. How she put up with Mayor Henderson's sour attitude and still kept herself pleasant, Hunter had never figured out.

"Morning, Margie, you're lookin' mighty fine yourself. How's the mayor's mood this morning?" he asked her in a near whisper, smiling down at her slow and easy.

She rolled her eyes at the question.

"Figures." He grimaced, pretending to shudder. "Is he ready for me, or do I need to cool my heels a little longer?"

"He's ready, but he has company." She glanced toward the office to be certain of privacy and lifted her finely penciled brows. "Some slicked-up city boy out of Detroit." She frowned.

Detroit? This had to do with Sam. Hunter kept his expression bland. "So do I just go in or wait on my summons?"

Margie fought her snicker and lost.

"Go on in, you gorgeous thing." She waved to the door. "Just knock first. He yelled at his daughter for ten minutes for not knocking first."

Hunter shook his head. He strode to the door and rapped on the wood panel, perhaps a bit hard.

"What?" Henderson barked, obviously startled by the sound.

Hiding his smile, Hunter opened the door and stepped in. He kept his expression casual as he faced the mayor's curiously smug demeanor and the oily superiority of the man with him.

The fella from Detroit was a pretty boy, there was no doubt about it. With his thick, sandy-blond hair just a bit long and brushed perfectly back from his long, arrogant face, thick light lashes, and baby face, he likely turned a few female heads. He was built along the lines of a bodybuilder, gym-created through power lifting, rather than a man whose body was honed from actual hard work.

Oh, he was strong, but how long could he last? It was apparent by the way he carried himself he was very proud of himself and felt all he surveyed should feel the same.

"Hunter, this is Tom Novak." The mayor introduced him with the same officious pride of a man showing off his particular bright boy. "Tom, this is Sheriff Steele." The mayor wasn't skilled at hiding what he was thinking. For a man who was forever boasting about his business acumen, he had the worst poker face Hunter had ever seen.

"Novak." Hunter nodded as the man stood silently beside the mayor's desk. Hell, he wasn't about to offer to shake that snake-faced bastard's hand. They were staring at him like he had just crawled out from under some slimy rock.

"Tom's in from Detroit; he works with the chief information officer for the Detroit city government. He's here to see about a friend of his. He stopped by after he learned some disturbing news while having breakfast at the diner." Henderson frowned in obvious disapproval.

He might have actually pulled it off too, if Hunter didn't see the smug sneer lurking in his expression.

Something was fishy as three-day-old bass about this whole thing. "And that was?" Hunter arched a brow, playing it cool, as he tucked his hands in his jeans pockets and regarded the newcomer.

"Seems there's some question of sexual impropriety in your office." Henderson crossed his hands on top of his desk and assumed his most pious expression. "This is greatly disturbin' to me, Hunter."

Hunter lifted his brows. "Me too." First he had heard of it. "Who's being sexually improper?"

"Novak heard tell it was you, with that pretty little Samantha Ryder, the officer I told you to hire. First, she went on a call with you, discharged her weapon, but was cleared of all that." He waved his hand in dismissal. "Not a problem since I'd already approved her hire. But sexual harassment is a mighty dirty way for a man to try and get a gal to come work for him."

Hunter didn't even bother to hide his surprise. "Just whom did Novak learn this from?" Hunter asked darkly. "Assuming I'm allowed to know."

Novak stepped forward. "I overheard the rumors, as Mayor Henderson told you, at the diner this morning and was disturbed. But I'm aware of how small-town gossip can be. I immediately contacted Samantha, and she confirmed that you'd put her in a compromising situation. She's very upset over this, Steele."

Now Hunter was hard-pressed to hide his incredulity. "When did you talk to Ms. Ryder?"

Novak cleared his throat and looked at his very pricy

watch. Hunter could almost see the gears turning as he calculated his lie. "I'd say about three hours ago."

He knew that was a damned lie. Not three hours ago Sam was all curled up next to him, warm and snoring softly. He wasn't about to tell them that.

"You will, of course, not harass Miss Ryder any more than you already have. We want to minimize her discomfort and embarrassment." Mayor Henderson frowned at him heavily.

Hunter watched them both carefully, kept his expression stoic, and waited.

"I think a resignation would be in order at least, Mayor," Novak suggested. "Samantha has been through enough, so I don't think we should bring her into this—"

"Oh, I think maybe we should." Hunter stiffened his shoulders. He gave Henderson a hard look. "I don't know what the hell this is all about, Mayor, but you didn't put me in that office, and you can't take me out. I'll be damned if you'll run me out of it on some trumped-up, bullshit charge. Call Ms. Ryder in here and see what she has to say." Especially considering he knew damned well they hadn't talked to her.

"Samantha of course wants to cause no waves. She assures me she will press no charges if you leave quietly—"

"Mayor, do I look like a dumb redneck to you?" Hunter asked him coldly, staring into the man's surprised face. "Let me assure you, I am not. And I doubt very much Ms. Ryder told Novak here shit. I'll be more than happy to stand aside and let you ask her about it yourselves, but I have every right to face my accuser."

Novak and the mayor exchanged a telling look. Of course they didn't want him checking into this.

"There's no need to be so profane," Henderson objected with acute distaste.

"There's no need to be a liar either, but someone in this room is, and I assure you it's not me." He gave Novak a chilling stare. "Now you two better get your stories straight and stop playing footsie here. I know damned good and well you haven't talked to Samantha. I've known her near all her life; Samantha's not one to bold-faced lie. So, I'd like to know what the hell is going on here."

"Tom?" The mayor feigned surprise, obviously uncertain how to proceed.

"Perhaps I haven't spoken to Samantha," he bit out, "but I have spoken to your officers, Steele, and I know how you've harassed—"

Hunter turned on his heel and stalked to the door.

"Steele, you have not been given leave to walk from this office." The mayor's voice rose in anger. "I have not dismissed you, young man."

Hunter gripped the doorknob, glancing back at them, anger churning in his stomach now—anger and a suspicion that ate at his sense of pride in his job.

"I don't need your permission." His voice was harsh, cold. "You want my job so damned bad"—he sneered at Novak—"then come and take it, if you can."

He jerked the door open and then slammed it as he stalked out. Son of a bitch. He ignored Margie's look of shock as his boot heels thundered across the hardwood floor and the outer office door was given the same treatment as the mayor's.

Damn, if he wasn't getting good at door slamming. Best it was the door being slammed and not Novak's overdeveloped body. He knew Henderson had been trying to get him out of office ever since he took the position, but he hadn't expected this. This one had been more than a surprise. That the man would come at him with lies didn't shock him. It was how ridiculously flimsy the lie was.

On the other hand, if his relationship with Sam hadn't progressed to the point it had, he likely would have been willing to believe it. His fists clenched at the thought. His cool cynicism had become well known. Maybe that's why Sam was all too willing to believe he'd been using her.

Hunter was laid-back, affable, but always silently suspicious. His trust in Samantha shocked him for a minute, though. She'd been right: He didn't really know her; she could have been there to play traitor, but he knew to his soul she wasn't. He hadn't been using her, but Novak and the mayor sure as hell were, which made him madder than hell.

Hunter growled under his breath as he unlocked the car and got inside it. One sure way to find your opponent's weakness was to arm yourself with knowledge. Besides Jacob, the best person to talk to for info was his brother-in-law. Mark Ferguson, an officer with the California State Police force, could get the answers he needed. It seemed Mark had connections all over. When he got back to the office he'd call Mark. He needed this Detroit bigwig checked out now. At this rate, he was going to owe Mark a whole week away from his sister, Hannah, and damn if that wouldn't suck. Hannah was pure mean when Mark dropped her off for one of his hunting weekends. So mean that Hunter refused to let her stay last year. Damn, he hoped his ole buddy was in a gracious frame of mind when he called.

chapter twelve

At exactly twelve forty-five Samantha swung open the station door, hiding her trepidation behind a stoic expression, and gathered every ounce of self-confidence she had. The station was only marginally cooler than outside and just as humid. Big metal fans blew dust around the small, dim area. A coffee pot sat half-full on an old metal cart huddled in the corner. Apparently Shane Warren made the best coffee, and he always kept it fresh when he wasn't on patrol. If for no other reason, Samantha thought, her transfer was worth that coffee. Shane smiled cautiously up at her from behind the large metal desk facing the doors. It was as neat and orderly as Officer Warren himself.

"Hey, Samantha." He grinned. "Uh, Sheriff's in his office. Go on in."

Samantha grinned back. "Okay, thanks."

He blushed a little, his blond brows pulled together over those curious pale blue eyes of his. "I think he's expecting you. He said to just send you back. I'd still knock first if I were you."

"Thanks, Shane," she said without glancing back at him.

"Samantha, I don't reckon it's anything to worry about. I can't imagine he'd be pissed at you for anything," Shane called out. "But Sheriff seemed to be in a pretty ugly mood."

"That's okay." *I'm sure he is.* Samantha sighed.

She stood at Hunter's office door for a moment, gathering inner strength. She didn't knock; she just turned the knob and sauntered into the office, shutting the door behind her.

Hunter looked up at Samantha standing there, her hands on her hips. She hoped her face conveyed the determination she felt inside.

"Uh, I'll call ya back. Yeah, uh-huh. Bye." He hung up and stared at her.

He opened his mouth to say something, but she held a hand up and stopped him. "I'm sorry. I was out of line this morning."

Hunter nodded, the corner of his mouth lifting. "Me too."

That crooked smile of his sent her mind straight into the gutter. Why did every cell in her body want to merge with his so badly? "That being said, I've thought about it and agree that transferring to this department might be a good move for me."

His eyes narrowed slightly and his head tilted. "Why do I feel like there's something about this I'm not gonna like?"

"No, I don't imagine you will. I don't like it either.

However, you know we have to end this thing between us." She frowned at him. Frustration and arousal were making her snippy.

"If you want to end this thing, then you're gonna have to stop coming into my office with plump nipples all firm and ripe, ready to be sucked." Her scowl only prompted a grin from him. "Hey, you could try those padded bras. They may work." She crossed her arms over her breasts. "Don't know what you're gonna do about the blush that creeps up your throat and the way your eyes get darker when you're turned on." Even his laugh was sultry.

"Hunter, if I'm gonna work under you . . ." He lifted his brows at her choice of words. "Dammit!" The word was forced through her clenched teeth. "You know what I mean! There have to be boundaries."

He sighed. "Relax, Sam, I get what you're saying. But people already know we're having . . . a thing."

Samantha didn't have to ask what that meant. With a sigh, she sat in the chair opposite Hunter's desk. "Oh well."

"Just means we'll have to be more discreet is all." Hunter's eyes were like molten steel, they didn't match his nonchalant smile nor his indifferent shrug.

Samantha narrowed her eyes. "Be realistic, Hunter. If I'm working . . . for you, it's inappropriate to continue a sexual relationship."

"We'll see." He held her gaze.

"You are so arrogant," she snarled at him as she stood. The man had a way of bringing to life nearly every emotion she harbored all at once with very little effort. At the moment, however, anger was leading the pack.

He stood as well and took a step toward her, his gaze still locked on hers. "So are you."

She retreated a step involuntarily and frowned. "Me?" she snapped, her temper boiling just barely under the surface. "You're the one who has to act all superior, in every aspect, I might add. You think you're calling all the shots, but you're not."

He took another step toward her. "Yes, you. I'm not acting superior at all. But, Sam sugar, I am calling the shots."

She shifted from one foot to another, fighting the urge to take another step back. He challenged her balance, kept her off center, hot, irritated. "Well, that's not going to work for me."

"No?" Slowly he stalked toward her. "We want the same things." His voice was a near purr, pulling at her, making her want contact. The memory of the feel of his hot skin against hers flashed in her mind and she nearly gasped.

"Yes. We do. But we can't always have what we want." She took a step toward him in spite of her attempt at being stalwart and stoic.

He pulled her into his arms. "We can have this. Do you really want to pretend this doesn't exist between us? Do you really believe we can ignore it and it will just go away?"

"Hunter," she said softly, shaking her head.

He walked her back until she felt her body pressed between the wall and him. His hands were braced on either side of her head as he moved against her, pressing his thigh between her legs against her mound. A flood of pleasure flowed through her. How could she be so aroused so quickly? She closed her eyes and bit her lip against the hungry moan clawing from deep inside her.

The knock at the door sounded like a gunshot and had almost the same effect on Hunter. He jumped away from Samantha, his hand going to the weapon at his hip.

The door opened and Officer Warren popped in. "S'cuse me, Sheriff . . . uh . . ." His eyes scanned the room from the desk to the bookshelves to his left. He blinked twice when he found them. Samantha moved, her arms crossed over her chest again, to stand in front of Hunter, afraid Shane would notice the bulge pressing aggressively against the sheriff's fly. Hunter glared at Shane, his hands on his hips. "Oh, hey, Sheriff, sorry to barge in . . . I didn't mean to interrupt . . . I mean."

"No big deal, Warren." Hunter's voice was husky with arousal. "Just going over some things with Officer Ryder. She'll be transferring here."

Warren smiled, looking from one to the other and nodded "Cool!" He fidgeted, with a hand still on the doorknob, and cleared his throat. "Anyway, shouldn't have barged in . . . Sam . . . Officer Ryder, you have a call. I explained that you were in a meeting with the sheriff and offered to take a message. But the dude was kinda insistent that he talk to you immediately."

Samantha knew before she asked. "Who is it?"

"Tom Novak. He said he's a friend from Detroit." Shane's brows knit together as he watched her.

Samantha stilled; her blood seemed to freeze in her veins. That asshole was never going to leave her alone. She gritted her teeth and nodded once. "I'll come take it." Before she could take a step, she felt Hunter's firm hand on her shoulder.

"Just put it through to my phone, Warren. You can take it in here, Sam."

"No, I think it would be best if . . ." Samantha began.

"You can take it in here." His tone left no room for negotiation. Shane frowned and backed out of the room.

Samantha frantically tried to think of a way out as Hunter strode across the room to his desk. The short, shrill rings began just as he turned the phone toward her then sat in his chair, leaned back, and folded his hands together over his stomach. She could feel Hunter watching her as she stared at the phone. She moved mechanically to the desk and picked up the receiver as she lowered herself to perch on the edge of the big overstuffed chair.

"Hello."

"Samantha, sweetheart, it's so good to hear your voice."

Nausea swept through her, and she clenched her teeth against her desire to scream. If she could reclaim the two years she'd wasted with him, she would. The man wouldn't take "no" for an answer. Being that he worked closely with the chief information officer for the City of Detroit's government offices, he'd been able to get around any official action she'd tried to take against him.

Feeling defeated, she sat there, avoiding Hunter's perceptive gaze as she listened to Tom's saccharine-sweet endearments, all the while trying to lead with her mind and not her emotions. Yet the image of Tom's face contorted in disgust, the threats, and the bruises he left on the surface as well as deep inside her were all still fresh in her mind.

"What do you want?" A myriad of emotions co-alesced into red-hot anger, and yet she kept her voice steady and calm. It was a testament to her control that she didn't hang up on him.

"Still so cold." He sounded as if she'd wounded him. "I heard about the shooting and investigation. I was concerned. I wanted to make sure you're okay."

God, he was infuriating. "I'm fine. I was cleared."

"Of course. I knew you were cleared. Samantha. Enough of this now, I need to see you. We have to talk." There was that edgy tone in his voice that made her shudder.

"No." It was simple, firm, clear.

"Samantha, we will work through this. I've given you space, you've had plenty of time to think things through."

Dear God, was he stalking her now? "There's no reason for you to be in Deerhaven. Calling me here is wildly inappropriate. How did you know where I was?"

"You weren't answering your cell, babe. I took a guess."

Tom didn't guess. He was too precise, too calculating.

"I didn't answer your call because I blocked your number. There's no reason for you and me to talk."

"You aren't alone, are you?"

"Of course not. You know that, you called me at the police station." She was shaking, starting to lose her temper. She needed to get him off the phone.

"Samantha, listen to me. I've heard things about the sheriff. Has he been harassing you?"

"Are you serious? No."

"He has, hasn't he?"

Samantha's eyes widened. In any other circumstance, she would have laughed at Tom's asinine question.

"Sheriff Steele has been a complete gentleman." She swallowed her disgust. Why was she even talking to Tom? "If I need to file a restraining order against you, I will."

His chuckle bordered on maniacal. "You and I both know that's not necessary, Samantha. What would be the point?"

She knew what he meant by that. He had so many connections in the Detroit government he'd get past anything she attempted, unscathed.

She glanced up at Hunter, his eyes were cold and hard. She had to defuse this. Besides it being humiliating, it wasn't something in which she wanted Hunter involved. She was moving away from Detroit. Eventually, Tom would move on. Wouldn't he?

"Samantha, baby, listen to me. I love you. I'm worried about you." He had softened his voice and injected just enough faux emotion to make her temper boil.

"Well, you can relax. I am perfectly fine. As you well know, I can hold my own. Go home, Tom." She slammed the receiver onto the cradle and took a deep, steadying breath.

"You want to explain that?" Hunter didn't bother to hide the anger in his voice.

"How does he know about you?" Uneasy suspicion had her brows knitted over her narrowed eyes. "What's going on, Hunter?"

Hunter leaned back in his chair and watched her

thoughtfully. "I was called into the mayor's office this morning. I met your 'pretty boy' there."

Samantha clenched her teeth. "He's not my 'pretty boy,' Hunter. Don't pull that shit with me now." He lifted a brow and held her gaze. If he was trying to intimidate her, he was gonna fail. "What did he want?"

"He tried to convince me he had talked to you this morning and you were accusing me of sexual harassment." His statement was matter of fact, calm, and didn't match what she saw in his eyes.

Though she wasn't shocked at all, she was still feeling incredulous that this was happening. "I can't believe this."

"And in the next breath he demanded the mayor insist that I resign from office."

Samantha stared at him, unable to form words. The audacity! "That son of a bitch. I actually thought he was smarter than that."

Hunter rubbed his chin. "Well, honey, to be honest, if I wasn't curled up nice and tight with you about the time Novak said he talked to you, I might have been pissed enough to doubt your word. I'm not a real trusting type."

She glared at him. "Are you telling me you wouldn't have at least asked me about this?"

"Eventually." He shrugged. "Thing is, people know about the night we left together at the Night Hawk. There's already talk, and the mayor has heard it."

"This isn't happening." Samantha groaned as she rubbed her temples.

"Oh, but it is, sugar." Hunter was smiling now, but

his eyes were still cold, hard steel, which wasn't necessarily a good sign. "Hey, I can understand his desire to get you back in his bed, can't fault him for that. The problem is, it's clear you aren't interested, and he's being pushy about it. That's bad enough. Add to that, he's here now, and it didn't sound like he's going to leave any time soon. Unless I miss my guess, he and our self-important mayor are just a little too tight to suit me."

"This doesn't make sense." She shook her head. "Why would he want to lie, or even care if you resigned?"

Hunter shrugged. "Tryin' to get you back, evidently."

Samantha made a disgruntled sound in response. There was more to it than that. Why did he go to the mayor, and how did he even know the mayor?

"How well did you know him?"

It was her turn to shrug. "We were lovers for two years. We got engaged. I lived with him. It was a volatile breakup. Tom's not easy to get along with and even harder to get away from."

"Did he hit you?" Hunter's voice took on a harsh tone. She glanced up at him and did a double take. She wasn't sure how she felt about his fierce expression.

"Yes," she answered cautiously, her voice softer than she'd wanted it to be. She cleared her throat and paused for a moment, trying to decide if she wanted to trust him not to judge her. With a nod, she continued, "There are worse ways to hurt a woman, Hunter. He was dogmatic and demeaning. He was very charming and manipulative. He was demanding, critical, and controlling. But yes, there were a few times that he became physically violent."

She watched the muscle in his jaw pulse, "Oh. Just a

few times," he said sardonically. "How did you deal with it?" Maybe she shouldn't have told him Tom hit her. Hunter looked like he wanted to break something.

"I reported it. Tried pressing charges . . ." She really didn't want to go into all of that with Hunter. Not right now. "I just wanted to be free of him."

After a moment Hunter nodded in understanding and didn't press. "First things first. We need to get you set up as an employee. Paperwork is a bitch."

Samantha felt the tension begin to leave her muscles. "I'm well aware."

chapter thirteen

Focusing on the tasks at hand were difficult the rest of the day for Hunter.

Novak was gonna be a big problem; the bastard wasn't gonna leave Sam alone. There was a lot more going on there. She'd told him more with her expressive eyes than she had verbally. Novak had hurt her and then he'd hit her.

If Hunter wanted to get anything productive accomplished, he couldn't be thinking about that. It made his blood boil, every muscle in his body coiled up ready for attack. That wasn't going to help anything and especially not Sam.

Back in his office he picked up the phone and punched Mark's number.

"Ferguson," the burly trooper answered on the first ring.

"Hey, Mark, it's Hunter. How's my sister doing?" Hunter didn't even try to smother his laughter.

"Damn you, Hunter, that woman's making me crazy. Do you know she painted the front room purple? Freaking purple. What drives that woman?"

Hunter held the phone away from his mouth. He couldn't control his laughter on that one.

"Laugh it up. You'll be laughing when I cart her ass back up that mountain to you," Mark threatened good-naturedly. "She's been fretting over you anyway. Talking about how you're all pitiful and lonely now, probably not eating right and all that crap. Let her paint your living room purple. Now why the hell are you calling? If you wanted to check on Hannah, you could have called her yourself."

Hunter chuckled. "You know some people in Michigan, right?

"Some," Mark answered cautiously.

"I need to know all you know about the City of Detroit's CIO's right-hand man."

Mark was one of the few people aware that Hunter was investigating the three deaths on the down low. There was silence across the line for a long moment.

"Fucking Tom Novak?"

"Yep, that's the one." Hunter's brows lifted at the edge in Mark's tone. "Showed up in town this morning all buddy-buddy with Henderson."

Mark paused. "I've heard some pretty shady things about him. What do you think is going on?"

"Don't know. That's what I'm tryin' to figure out. Look, Samantha Ryder's here to handle Dottie's estate, and Henderson was pushin' hard for me to talk her into taking a position on the force here. Come to find out she and Novak had a relationship that ended badly about a year ago."

"You think she's involved?" Mark asked, his voice low.

Hunter frowned. "I don't think she is. But hell if I know for sure. I knew her way back, Mark, when she was just a little thing. I can't see her being part of her aunt's murder."

"Right. Okay, I'll see what I can find. In the meantime, I heard an interesting rumor the other day that I wanted to run by you. We uncovered a human trafficking ring up here a few weeks ago. One of the women we rescued, an illegal Latina who could speak a little English, says they spent some time in what sounds like a cave system down there. Aren't there some old gold mines and tunnels in your area?"

Hunter frowned. "Yeah, especially up close to Feather Falls."

Mark sighed. "Look, Hunter, there could be something very ugly going on down there. Just keep your eyes open, let me know if you come across anything."

Hunter shook his head. Deerhaven was pretty laid-back and off the beaten track. Made sense to use old mines and the caves for something like that. "I'll keep you updated as much as I can."

"You do that, and I'll hold Hannah off from that visit she wants to make home," Mark laughingly promised.

Hunter winced. He didn't need Hannah here right now.

"Seriously, Mark. Promise me for sure." Hunter shook his head. Damn, Hannah could throw a monkey wrench in his plans right fast.

The last thing he needed was his baby sister finding

out he was working with a woman, much less that he was attracted to her.

Attracted . . . ha, that was a gross understatement.

Mark chuckled. "All right, good plan then. I'll call if I get any new info," Mark said decisively. "Later there, bro."

Bro. Hunter swallowed his laughter. Mark only called him bro when he was put out with Hannah, his little Southern honey.

Hunter disconnected, frowning thoughtfully.

He was pretty certain the caves in Deerhaven would be a good place to hide without someone hearing about it. Newcomers stood out like a sore thumb, so hiding out would be smart. He could put out a few feelers, check things out. Until then, he had to get Sam set up and get her working.

It was gonna be imperative that he get back into that woman's bed right soon. Just the thought of her had his cock swelling. He shifted in his chair, hoping to ease the pressure. Damn, if he wasn't pantin' over her like a dog over a bone. Sam was extremely warm, soft, and so damn juicy. Holy hell, he was a hungry man. This was not gonna be an easy job if he didn't exert some strong will power. He wasn't sure he had it where Sam was concerned. Keeping his mind on work was his only hope. He couldn't walk around the station dick first. Good time as any to formally introduce Sam to Rodgers and Decker. Yep, that would help him curb his libido.

Sam was smiling at whatever Warren was telling her. She was so pretty, her smile was perfect, her lips full, and kissing her was like breathing fresh air when you didn't know you were suffocating. Nope, couldn't be thinking about that. He cleared his throat. "All right back to work, Warren." He turned his attention to Sam. "Did you get your uniform ordered?"

"Yes. I have my own vest, belt, and weapons. Speaking of which, may I have my weapon back?"

"Yep. Warren, get Sam her weapon." He shot Shane a firm look.

"On it, Sheriff."

"You hear from Decker or Rodgers?" he asked the deputy, wondering where the other men were.

"Out on patrol," Warren called back to him as he turned down the hall toward the evidence room.

Patrol, right.

Hunter got on the radio and called for an update. Decker said he was up at the Coopers' place to take a report on a possible bovine theft. Rodgers was wrapping up yet another traffic citation with the Lafollette boy. Kid had a lead foot and a death wish.

Maybe introductions would be best if they were done in the morning; it was getting late.

"How you doin', Pixie?"

She scowled at him.

"Samantha." Attempting to hide her smile, she tilted her head. "I suppose you should call me Officer Ryder now."

He grinned, lifting his eyes to hers. "Mm-hmm, might be hot. You got handcuffs, Officer Sam?"

She lifted one brow and pursed those sexy, rose, bow lips. "I do, and I know how to use them. I also have plenty of zip ties."

"Well damn, girl, sounds like you're well equipped for a good time," he murmured, watching the flush that bloomed on her cheeks.

"Shut up." She laughed.

God, he was beginning to love that laugh way too much. He couldn't wait to kiss her again, feel her skin under his hands. Warren came back as if on cue.

"Here ya go, Samantha . . . I mean, Officer Ryder." He grinned at her like an adoring puppy.

"Thanks, Warren." She exaggerated a serious expression as she took her weapon from him.

"So, Ryder." Hunter winked. "We'll see you in the morning. Introduce you to everybody, give you the formal tour, and get you started. Good?"

"Works for me. See you guys in the morning then." She turned and walked toward the door.

"Seven, Officer, don't be late."

"Yeah, yeah." She waved her hand without turning around. Her chuckle made him wanna go after her and turn her over his knee. Yeah, she was gonna test him, push him. She knew exactly what kind of effect she had on him.

Damn woman.

chapter fourteen

Samantha slumped down on the sofa with a sigh. She'd been on the phone for hours. She still needed to call her mother and let her know what was going on. That would be a lot easier to deal with than the others. She'd expected some disappointment from her chief, but he hadn't been happy about her leaving the Detroit force at all. Still, he'd wished her well and promised to transfer her files. She'd have to somehow get all her things moved.

She'd worry about that later. First things first, she needed some groceries and supplies. The nearest Walmart was about twenty minutes away, and she didn't want to fool with it. She decided to get absolute necessities at the Safeway and go to Oroville to shop on the weekend.

Yep, she was back in the hills for sure. It was exciting, she had to admit.

Then there was Hunter.

Thoughts of him and that damned talented mouth of his were constant. Working with him was gonna test her self-control to the extreme. His voice made her warm all over, his touch made her shiver. Hell, she was a basket case. Samantha shook her head. No, she had too much to do to get caught up in all her erotic thoughts of Hunter.

Driving into town, she thought about all the work ahead of her. She needed to make a list. A list would definitely help. When she got back home, she'd fix herself some dinner and take care of that.

The store was busy for a Tuesday afternoon. Even so, everything was a bit outdated. She gave the old cart one final energetic jerk, freeing it from the others, and headed to produce. Groceries, right now she needed to focus on groceries. Just what she needed to get through the rest of the week.

Man, the store was sadly lacking when it came to fresh produce, but she managed to find what she needed and moved on.

Her first week with the sheriff's department would be interesting at best. Tension at work was gonna be tough enough with Hunter. Just a look from him had her body reacting, but maybe that would subside in time. She hoped so because she wasn't so sure her fellow officers would deal with her being there. She had a feeling Rodgers and Decker wouldn't be very happy about it. Shane was okay. Such a nice guy, eager to be helpful and so very amenable.

"Whoa there, Sam." Hunter caught her cart before she ran into him.

"Oh jeez. Sorry."

He leaned over a bit, pretending to whisper. "Maybe you shouldn't fantasize about me while operating any kind of vehicle." He frowned and shook his head. "Dangerous, way too dangerous."

"Ha ha ha." She made a face. "It appears you're following me."

Hunter stepped up next to her, scanning the contents of her cart. Her stomach did little flips. Why did he have to smell so good?

"Small town, sugar. Although I wouldn't mind following you." He leaned back to check out her ass.

Damn, she didn't need this. She was trying to organize her thoughts and be productive. Why was he here, now, at the Safeway of all places? She didn't remember that behemoth he called a truck in the parking lot, and that thing was hard to miss. Now all she was thinking about was taking him home with her, running her hands over his chest, and . . . damn.

She narrowed her eyes. "What are you doing here?" He was invading her space, stealing her air, making her too warm.

His sly smile was slow and easy. Fine laugh lines fanned out from eyes that glittered with mischief. His teeth were straight and white, and there seemed to be so many of them. Was that an ever-so-slight hint of a dimple in his left cheek? Yeah, yeah it was. Holy Moses, the man was a wet dream walking and that smile was pure sin. As fine as he looked in uniform he looked like sex walking in his jeans and black AC/DC tee. He stepped closer, pursing his lips as he perused the contents of her cart. He picked up the small cucumber she had selected for her salad and met her gaze. "Aw, Sam, this will never do, sugar."

"Huh?" she mumbled, momentarily distracted by thoughts of tasting his neck. "What?"

He lifted a brow. "This." He lifted the little cucumber. She stared at it, frowning, shaking her head. "Sam, this will never satisfy you, baby, not now anyway, not since the other night." Samantha's mouth fell open, and she stared at him, dumbfounded. He looked at it, pressing his lips together, and shook his head. "Nope, this won't do at all." He strode past her to the produce department and started searching through the sparse selection of cucumbers.

Samantha shut her mouth with a snap and followed behind him "Hunter! That's so wrong!"

He grinned. "Aww, but sugar." He held up a long, round, smooth cucumber. "This one here is damn near perfect."

Her eyes widened. He couldn't be serious. Her cheeks felt flaming hot as she quickly looked around, hoping no one was witnessing her humiliation.

"Yeah, beautiful, isn't it?" He pushed it toward her at an obscene angle, and she leaned away. "Feel how smooth . . . hard to find 'em that smooth, and firm too."

"I need it for a salad." She started shaking her head "You're crazy, you know that?"

He looked at her pointedly. "You're not the least bit curious?"

"Oh my God, you're ten kinds of wrong."

"I'm just playin'." He put the larger cucumber back and left the little one in her cart. "I just love it when you turn all pink." He ran a finger down her neck to the hollow at her throat. "I'd be willing to bet my truck that you're just a little bit turned on. I'm not above trying some adventurous naughtiness."

"Sheriff Hunter," she said through her teeth. "This is not the way to go about being discreet. Tone it down."

"Can't." He sounded almost regretful.

"Well, why the hell not?" She all but stamped her foot.

He gave her a sideways look. "Do you really want me to explain it? Here? In the middle of the grocery store?"

She pressed her lips together, turned around, and attempted to stalk off. "Ugh."

Oh, the arrogance, the audacity of the man made her crazy. What appalled her most, what really pissed her off, was the fact that he was right. It did kinda turn her on.

No "kinda" about it, the creamy hot slide of moisture between her thighs reminded her that he had power over her. It only took his presence to heighten her senses. Then he'd teased her, filling her mind with hot and sweaty images. *No. Memories.* Yeah, she had to admit, he had her body aching for him with little effort at all. No one had ever had this instant, vicious effect on her.

In the dairy aisle, he reappeared. His arm brushed her breast as he reached for a carton of milk, sending an electric shock of sensation singing through her.

"I'm coming over tonight, Sam," he whispered close to her ear. "And we're gonna have a good time."

Samantha held her breath, trying to rein in the urge to jump him. "You think?"

He gave her a wry smile. Leaning down, he lightly

kissed her mouth, lingering there for a moment. He flicked his tongue over her bottom lip before he moved away.

"I know." He winked at her and walked away.

Samantha shook her head and tried to focus on finishing up her shopping. All the way home she tried reasoning with herself about Hunter. Too reasonable, too much logic when she knew she'd never be able to resist him. She carried her groceries in, set the sacks on the kitchen counter, and began putting then away. Two sharp raps on the door alerted her before Hunter opened the door. "Hey, Pixie."

She scowled up at him as he stepped into the kitchen and leaned against the doorframe. "You're supposed to wait to be invited in. It's polite."

The man always seemed so confident, she thought, as he walked toward her and caged her in between the counter and his body. "I've been invited in, and sometimes polite is just boring."

She stifled a sigh. He was right, and so damn intoxicating. He made her want and feel things she'd never even thought to fantasize about. So why the hell was she fighting it? Their lips met gently at first, then that flash fire of need he always caused surged through her. She pressed closer, relishing the hardness of his body. She loved the taste of him, the way his fingers flexed against her hips. As much as she wanted him, she knew this wouldn't end well.

With no small amount of will power, she put her hands on his chest and pushed him away. "Okay, Hunter, we have to stop. We can't."

"Mm-hmm, we can, Sam. We did. Remember?" He

crushed her against him again and kissed along her jaw, taking his time, giving each inch his full attention. "Let me refresh your memory."

"No. Listen, we need to be serious, just for a moment." It was more of a murmur as she pushed him away again.

His hands gripped her waist and pulled her to him. He nuzzled the sensitive skin right under her ear.

"I am serious, I'm fuckin' religious about this." He nipped at her neck and shoulder. "You're invading my dreams, Sam, and my nightmares. My dick hasn't been at ease since you walked those legs into the Night Hawk, swinging that fine ass of yours." At some point, she wasn't sure when, he unbuttoned her shorts. His hands slid inside the waistband of her panties to cup her bottom. "So soft, round, firm. Fits in my hands like it was made for 'em," he murmured, pulling her hard against him.

"Hunter, we have to stop," she whimpered weakly.

He pulled back and searched her face. "If you really want me to stop, I will, Sam." He held her gaze, his eyes were molten steel. "Do you want me to stop? Do you?"

"No," she whispered harshly, pulling his shirt from his jeans, desperate to touch his skin. "To hell with it."

"Thank God," he said, grinning at her fervent struggle to get closer to him. He let her go long enough to pull his shirt over his head. She couldn't wait, her hands glided over his warm body, the crisp chest hair tickled her palms, his nipples hardened at her fingertips, and she sighed.

His erection was unmistakable, and her body craved the feel of him inside her, stroking the very core of her.

She fumbled with the button fly of his jeans. Her knuckles grazed his hard shaft, her frustration mounting.

"Hunter." Her strained voice seemed to come from far away; the sound of her blood pounding through her veins was so loud.

"Yeah, sugar?" His mouth was like a brand on her ultrasensitive skin, and she momentarily forgot what she was doing. Her shorts and panties slid to the floor. His hands cupped her ass and continued to squeeze and rub as he pulled her closer. Waves of sensation unfurled from her core and feathered through her entire body. His fingers stroked the cleft of her bottom cheeks. His leg spread her thighs apart enough so that his fingers delved lower, slipping into her hot, dewy channel then slowly circling the entrance with just enough pressure to have her moan breathlessly. Her blood surged hot through her veins, to collect in her nipples and clit, causing them to swell and ache with the need to be touched.

"You're burning me alive," she whispered. Finally unbuttoning the last button, she trailed her fingertips along the underside of his cock. Their mouths met again in a fiery tango of tongues and gasps. Samantha pushed his jeans down, freeing him. Wrapping her hand around his shaft, she passed her thumb over the ridge at the base of its pulsing plum-like tip. Breath hissed through his teeth, and she kissed his chest, nipping at his collarbone and licking the hollow at his shoulder.

"Well then, I'm goin' up in flames with you." He pulled her tank top over her head and had her bra unfastened and on the floor before she could acknowledge what he was doing. Her breasts filled his palms; he lifted them, his fingers caressed them and squeezed her nipples. Pleasure sizzled along her nerve endings. He bent and took one hard peak between his lips and gently rasped his tongue over it.

Aching heat speared through Samantha, her legs buckled and she wrapped them around his waist as the thick head of his cock probed at the sensitive wet folds of her heated cunt. She fisted her hands in his hair and rocked against him. He braced her body, trying to hold her still. She met his gaze. "Hurry." Her voice was low and sultry. She wrapped her arms around his neck and bit his shoulder then flicked her tongue over the spot.

"Wild cat," he growled, carrying her to the bedroom. "I'm going to teach you the value of taking it slow if it kills me." He set her on the bed, leaned down, and kissed her quick on the mouth as he untangled her arms. "And it just might."

He stood and stripped off his jeans. She looked up at him, her body vibrating, anticipating his touch. She couldn't help but smile at his hot survey of her body. This man made her feel like a goddess. She wanted to be the one torturing him this time. She wanted to see his eyes glaze over with the force of his climax. She shifted to her hands and knees and crawled down the bed to where he stood.

She gripped his cock firmly when he tried to push her back.

"Not this time, cowboy. You've gotten your way. It's my turn now," she said and trailed her tongue over the crease that led to the tiny opening. With a slow grin, she watched him swallow hard.

"Wait, I . . ."

"Shhh, sit and lie back." She moved over him as he

did her bidding and urged him to slide higher up the bed. She continued lightly massaging his incredibly stiff erection but couldn't resist tasting the taut skin of his stomach. Warm spasms against her tongue tempted her lower. She heard his breathing accelerate as she scooted down to nestle his hot cock between her breasts. His breath caught and his hips pressed him closer. "Sam, baby, you're so soft."

She wished she had some oil on hand or something, she thought. Oh well, sometimes a girl had to improvise. She shifted and in one smooth stroke took him into her mouth as far as she could, making him as wet as she could. Then she secured the thick glistening shaft between her breasts again.

"Good God," he muttered as his hips rocked back and forth. Samantha pushed her breasts together and bent her head to suck the tip as he slid smoothly between them. Heat infused her body, her inner walls clenched, and erotic waves danced through her. "Oh yes, Sam, tighter, baby." She pressed her breasts tighter against his steel-hard cock.

Her mouth closed over the round head and drew him deeper till she felt him throbbing against the back of her throat. She swallowed, then moaned, the sound vibrating along Hunter's shaft.

"Ah, yes," he said through clenched teeth. She milked the thick ridge that pulsed along the underside with her tongue, pressing firmly as she sucked. His hands fisted in her hair, and she thought she heard him growl. She caressed him with her lips as she glided up to lick and kiss the silky tip.

With one hand, she cupped his balls and traced firm

little circles on the patch of flesh behind them. Her tongue delved into the crease, and she closed her lips over the tip, sipping at the pearl of arousal that collected there, and then she surged over him again. He began thrusting into her mouth, his breath coming in pants. His muscles tensed as he gently rubbed his thumb over her cheek. "I can't hold back anymore, Sam."

She sucked harder. His balls tightened.

"Sam . . . Oh Jesus!" She took him even deeper and swallowed as his climax splintered and his hot seed spurted into her mouth. Her mouth pulled and milked him until he lay still, gasping for breath, his body coated with a sheen of sweat as she took her time licking his cock clean.

He reached for her and pulled her into his arms. "You okay, sugar?" he murmured against her hair. His hand moved over her breast, and she closed her eyes, drinking in the spirals of pleasure.

"Mm-hmm." She laid her hand over his as it stroked her breast, teasing her nipple.

She loved it when he did that.

He slid one leg between hers, his hands caressing her as he kissed her neck. He knew just how to touch her and just how to kiss her to make her yearn for more. His lips found hers, and she let herself get caught up in the pleasure, the intensity of his kiss. Slowly sliding against him, damp with sweat and arousal, she rode his thigh and enjoyed the way his body felt under her fingertips.

When she felt his hard cock press against her hip, she gasped. "You're hard? Again? Already?"

He tilted his head, deepening his kiss.

"It seems . . ." He kissed down her jaw, ". . . that I

can't . . ." nibbled her neck, licked her collarbone, ". . . get enough of you."

He adjusted his body till he was lying over her, nuzzling his face between her plump breasts, inflaming her skin with each flick of his tongue, each scrape of his teeth. The weight of him only added to her arousal. She raised a leg and thrust her hips forward, pressing against his hard thigh as his lips finally closed over one eager nipple. She cried out, her hands clutching his shoulders.

"Sweet Sam," he said against her aching flesh.

She arched up, giving him better access. His hand slowly moved down her stomach to comb through the soft curls of her mound. She shuddered as he cupped her and dipped his fingers into the drenched folds.

"Hunter, please." She moved her body against his hand; the feel of his rough skin against her slick tender flesh almost sent her over.

Suddenly he took her wrists and placed her arms above her head, then kissed her mouth. "Be still or I'll handcuff you."

"You wouldn't . . ." Her denial was cut off by the dark expression on his face. The air left her lungs and her eyes fluttered closed as his finger slipped inside of her and found her G-spot. She couldn't help moving against his fingers.

"Oh . . . I can't," she cried out. "I can't be still."

"Look at me," he murmured huskily as he withdrew his hand.

Opening her eyes, she looked up into his stormy eyes. He slid his cock into her as he licked her juices from his fingers. So slowly, making her feel every inch. She arched her back, bringing him deeper inside. She felt so filled, so engulfed, and still she wanted more of him.

"I said, be still." He let his full weight press her into the mattress.

She was effectively pinned under him, and his mouth took possession of hers as he began to move. Deliberately drawing out every measured thrust, every gradual retreat, making her feel him. Anytime she tried to tilt her hips, he seated himself deep inside her and stopped. The pulse of his thick cock had her flexing the walls of her vagina, gripping him.

"Hunter." His name was barely a whisper against his lips.

"Fuck." He rose above her, watching her face as his hands glided over her breasts, her stomach. He grasped her hips. "Hold on to me, baby."

He fucked her rhythmically, with a slow, burning passion that made her feel like she may burst into flames. It began as soft waves of pleasure pouring over her. She gripped his back as the climax tore through her. Hunter surged in and out of her body relentlessly, pushing her higher.

Her climax exploded with an intensity of ecstasy that took her breath away. Her senses were filled with only Hunter and the pleasure he gave her.

Just as the power of her orgasm decreased to a soft ripple of pleasure, Hunter reached between them, his finger rasped over her clit firmly. "Come with me, Sam." Hunter groaned. Her nails dug into him as another orgasm crested and surged through her. Sharper this time and just as mind-blowing.

chapter fifteen

The clock radio woke Samantha from a sound sleep. Hunter must have set it for her. It appeared she'd met her match; his stamina and energy seemed limitless. The man had worn her out and that just would not do. Nope. Not at all.

The hot shower did wonders for her sore muscles so she took her time. Keeping it easy and simple would be best for her first day. She applied minimal makeup and pulled her hair up in a ponytail. Jeans and a tank top should be fine. It was gonna be a hot day. Maybe they'd have an extra uniform shirt to borrow until hers came in. If not, oh well. She wasn't even sure how Hunter planned to assign her work.

The drive to the station gave her time to organize her thoughts. So far she'd been too distracted by Hunter and all the incredible things he could do with his mouth to get any solid work done. That was going to have to change. They had to focus on the investigation and stay alert.

"Hey, Ryder, you're with me today," Shane called out as she walked into the building. "On patrol."

Samantha took off her sunglasses and squinted, waiting for her vision to adjust to the florescent lighting. How in the hell was she going to get anything done riding around the county with Warren? Not like she could stick with Hunter. That would be a red flag to anyone who might be paying attention, and there was a very real probability that someone was paying attention.

She plastered on a grin for Shane. "Cool." He was really good looking in a sweet, adorable way.

"This here's the locker room." He gestured to the room off the hallway. "Just pick out one that doesn't have a lock on it. I think we have a spare lock, I'll go check."

Turning into the locker room, she noticed, judging by the nameplate on his locker, Officer Joe Rodgers. She walked past him and stuffed her purse into an empty locker at the end of the row.

Ignoring the scowl on his face, she held out her hand. "You're Rodgers, right? I'm Samantha Ryder. Just starting today."

"Yeah. I know who you are," Rodgers all but spat and ignored her hand.

"Problem?" Might as well meet the flack head-on and get it out of the way.

"I was just wonderin' if you was plannin' on puttin' on some clothes."

"Hey, I'd vote for tank tops on a day like today."

Shane returned and handed her the spare lock he'd found. "Anyway, her uniform is on order. So, she's got a good excuse."

Rodgers just shook his head with a derisive harrumph. "Yeah, I know what she's up to."

Samantha shut her locker and locked it before turning her attention to Rodgers.

"All right, Rodgers, let's hear it. What am I up to?" She stood with her hands on her hips, waiting for an answer. She could feel the anger rising, but she kept her expression stoic. This could be a good thing. Give him the rope with which to hang himself.

Too easy.

He jutted out his jaw and glared at her. "All's you need to know is, I know. Decker knows too. Hell, we all see through you."

Samantha tilted her head and narrowed her eyes, looking at him like he'd just spoken Greek. "Rodgers, have you been drinking? What the hell are you talking about?"

"Hell no, I ain't been drinking. I don't disrespect my uniform." His gaze ran the length of her body and he smirked. "You just need to know we ain't gonna put up with it."

What exactly was "it"? *Come on, Rodgers, get really mad.* "Oh yeah?"

"Yeah, and we ain't a bunch of idjits you can just come in here and handle with a swing of your ass either."

Samantha hoped she was pulling off her smile. It felt more like a scowl. "Look, Rodgers, if your libido can't handle working with a woman, then that's your problem . . ."

"My libido ain't interested in anything a little slut like you has got!"

"Hey! Officer, that was inappropriate—" Shane started forward, but Samantha put up a hand to stop him.

Her smile faded. There were so many things she could say. She wanted to get in his face and cut him to shreds. Instead, she walked away with a wave of her hand.

"Whatever." She walked out, punching Shane lightly on the arm as she passed him. "You eat breakfast yet?"

"Nope, there's coffee. Hey, you okay?" he asked as he followed her out, concern filling his voice.

"Warren, it would take more than a crotchety, old, insecure man to ruin my mood today. You want to run by the Sonic when I get done with the sheriff?" she suggested as though the locker room confrontation was forgotten.

"That sounds good, sure." Shane nodded, gave her a smile then started back to the front.

So Rodgers is a big mouth, Samantha mused. Good to know. His inability to keep his thoughts and temper in check may come in handy. She knocked on Hunter's office door and waited.

"Come," he snapped.

Hmm . . . what happened to that good mood, she thought as she stepped in. "You know I can't do that on command."

His expression softened as he lifted his gaze to hers. "You did last night." He smirked. Well, damn, he had a point. "I have your new badge and a shirt for you."

"Already?"

"Yep. I've got skills." Hunter winked.

Samantha narrowed her eyes but couldn't hide her smile. "Indeed."

Hunter chuckled as he handed her a new shirt. "This is a men's medium. I think it will fit."

She unwrapped the shirt and put it on. It fit just fine, a little lose around the middle but perfect across her chest. "So, I met Rodgers. He's a hothead."

Hunter's expression was unreadable. "Yeah?"

"Yeah. You know, that could be an advantage for us." She buttoned up and tucked the shirt into her jeans. "He does not like me at all. It'd be easy to get him flustered and shootin' off about things he doesn't mean to blurt out."

"Not a bad tactic," he mused, though neither agreeing nor disagreeing with her using it.

"He seems to think that I'm up to something. Now that could be very innocuous, or he could be aware that I'm investigating my aunt's death."

Hunter rubbed his jaw. "Nah, I got a feelin' Rodgers just might be in over his head. He's been jumpier than a rattlesnake in a pickle barrel lately."

A smile pulled at the corner of Samantha's mouth at the colloquialism. "Well, I'll be sure and keep my ears and eyes open around him."

Without looking at her, Hunter nodded. "Good deal. Let's just lay low today. You go on ahead and ride with Warren. He'll get you up to speed pretty quickly."

"I bet he will." Samantha resisted smiling.

"Oh yeah?" Hunter met her gaze then and lifted a brow.

"Oh. Yeah. He's a sweetheart and one hell of a sexy man." She managed to sound completely serious.

"He's no man, he's a boy," Hunter scoffed.

"But he has dimples, a nice ass and, mmm, so much potential."

His smile faltered, his voice lowered. "He's green and too young for you."

Samantha kept her expression as blank as she could. "I bet he's willing and eager to learn." Samantha lowered her lids seductively on the word "eager" and Hunter's frown deepened.

"Oh, I see." Hunter narrowed his eyes. "You gonna raise him the way you want him, huh?"

Samantha shrugged. "That's the best way." She picked at a nail, trying to hide her smile.

"Problem with that, Sam baby, is you don't know what you want." He pushed away from the desk and sauntered to where she stood, looming over her. "So, see, after all that training and raisin' up, all you'd have is a worn-out, confused, little boy and an unsatisfied Officer Sam."

Samantha lost her resolve and laughed. "You think so? I don't know. That's the thing about getting them young." She sucked in air through her teeth. "So much stamina. That's a really good attribute in a man. I think I want stamina, Hunter."

She knew Hunter was aware she was teasing. It had something to do with that grin that almost curved his lips before he jerked her against his hard body and kissed her breath away.

"I got your stamina, Sam," he whispered low, his breath warm against her lips as he squeezed her ass. "Get to work," he grumbled.

She chuckled low and rubbed against him seductively before taking a step away, turning on her heel, and heading for the door.

"And stop looking at Officer Warren's ass."

She grinned over her shoulder and waggled her brows at him. It was so much fun seeing him fight with himself.

"I mean it. That's sexual harassment, Officer Ryder." He grinned.

She waved a hand in dismissal. "Yeah, yeah. I'll behave." She laughed.

Hunter . . . What was she going to do about that man? She loved getting him riled and that was no easy task. She was well aware of the fact that he could easily turn the tables on her. A sly smile flitted across her lips as she rebuckled her belt around her waist.

Everything in her wanted to sink into him and make him her world, but that was so damn dangerous, not to mention stupid. She had to keep her head clear and he fogged it up. The really scary thing about it was that honestly, she wanted more than anything to just surrender and let herself fall in love with him. If she did that, he would consume her. She couldn't let that happen. She couldn't give herself over like some wide-eyed, fantasy-driven child.

"Hey." Warren gave her a questioning glance as she got into the patrol car and sighed with disgust. "You okay?"

"Hmm? Oh yeah, fine." Samantha leaned down and turned the air up. "This heat is oppressive."

"It's the humidity. I'm sure being on patrol in Detroit is a lot more exciting than this is gonna be, huh?" he asked.

"I don't know if I'd call it exciting. It can get boring too, in a different way." Detroit seemed a world away now. A world she was not missing.

They pulled into Sonic and ordered. Warren filled her in on the day-to-day expectations. He told her all about the usual troublemakers between bites of their Breakfast Toasters.

"I'm sorry about what Rodgers said earlier. He and Decker are hot-headed rednecks." There was a hint of worry in Shane's gaze.

"You have nothing to apologize for. I can handle them," she assured him.

"Yeah, I'm sure you can. They're in tight with the mayor. They think that gives them some power. I just do my job and ignore 'em as best I can. Let the sheriff handle it. Ya know?"

"That's the best thing to do," she agreed.

"Yeah." He nodded, wiped his mouth, and gathered the empty wrappers. "You want anything else?"

"Nah, I'm good." There was some shady stuff going on and if it was that obvious that it was going on, then why had it been allowed to go on?

"Hey, you know your way around, don't you?"

Samantha glanced at him. "Yeah, somewhat."

"You wanna drive?"

"Sure."

"Figured you might." He chuckled. "You don't seem like the ride-along type."

That was the sincere truth.

Samantha hated being a passenger. She preferred being behind the wheel, in control. They changed seats, and after tossing their trash in the trashcan, Samantha pulled out.

"Probably gonna be a real slow day. I hope so. Gonna try to get the sheriff to let me off a little early." He rubbed his hands together.

"Hot date?" She grinned, keeping her eyes on the road.

"Man, I hope so," he said, smiling back sheepishly.

Samantha laughed, taking the curves smoothly. She missed these backwoods roads. The lush green that framed the two-lane road.

As suspected, the day had been slow. Just a couple of speeding tickets, lunch at the café on the square, one fender bender, nothing too exciting. Warren was fun to ride with. They talked about his upcoming date and joked around. He really was great as the "good cop" to her "bad cop" thing with some kids that were trespassing at the quarry.

"Hey, turn up here, and we'll work our way around and back to the station," Warren suggested.

"All right, that'll get us back early. I can file the reports if you want to head on home to get ready for your date."

"Yes! You're the best, Ryder."

"Yeah, yeah. You owe me one." She laughed and then her smile faded as the camper in front of them weaved a bit. "How long have we been following this rickety camper?" she asked, getting frustrated with the ten miles under the speed limit she was forced to drive.

"Not too long. They probably noticed us and they're bein' cautious." He shrugged.

Samantha's brows knit together. "A bit too cautious," she murmured and straightened in her seat.

"Aw, you know how people get when a cruiser is behind 'em." He smirked, cutting his eyes to her.

"Yeah, but I get a bad feeling about this one." Samantha's frown deepened.

This was definitely not good.

It wasn't too much longer before the camper began to weave again. Maybe the driver was just tired, but she had a feeling either they were drunk or worse, nervous.

"I'm gonna pull them over and check them out," Samantha said, hitting the lights.

"Okay, wouldn't hurt." He shrugged again, watching the camper closer.

The driver in the camper seemed to ignore her for a while. She doubted they didn't see her. She hit the siren in short bursts twice, then again. Finally, they pulled over.

"Now look, don't go in with a ball-bustin' attitude. This could be a bona fide redneck. Rednecks tend to rebel for the fun of rebellin'. Hell, maybe I should go deal with it?" He was clearly nervous now.

Samantha gave him a sideways glance. "I've been a cop for a while. I've dealt with worse." There was a little bite in her sarcasm.

"Yeah." He looked at her dubiously. "All right then."

"Warren, don't forget, I'm from here. I grew up with rednecks." She was sick to death of being second-guessed.

"Hey, don't get mad, I'm just . . ."

"It's all good." Her voice softened a bit as she reached

for her ticket book. "Don't stress. I got it. Just call in the tags."

She rose from the car, keeping her hand on her gun, and walked up to the cab cautiously. The driver rolled down the window. "Is there a problem, Officer?"

"License and registration, please." She kept her voice firm and authoritative as she leaned down and took stock of the driver and his passenger.

Both were Caucasian males, clean-cut in jeans, clean shirts, and baseball caps. The driver was a bit larger than the passenger. She guessed he might be six feet, tough, muscular.

Something about him looked familiar. The passenger was a bit over six feet and wiry. She didn't smell any alcohol on the man's breath or in the cab, and he seemed to be coherent. However, his movements were jerky, his shaky smile and a nervous chuckle alerted her that something wasn't right. The passenger fidgeted and wouldn't look at her.

"What'd we do, Officer? I was under the speed limit," he said, reaching for his wallet.

"I noticed you were weaving quite a bit . . ." A muffled cry had Samantha stopping mid-sentence. She tilted her head to the side and raised a hand for the driver to keep quiet. "What was that?"

The driver looked up at her with narrowed eyes, his lips stretched into a tight smile. "What?"

Again, she heard a whimper coming from the back of the camper. The sound was one of distress, fear. Was that a child? It had the tiny hairs on the back of Samantha's neck prickling. She turned to the driver in time to see his passive expression turn into a pinched, hateful snarl of a man desperate for escape. Samantha had no time to react. The man swung open the car door, smashing the metal window frame against the side of her head.

White light exploded in her brain, and she stumbled back. The camper wheels spewed dust and gravel as they sped away. Samantha got up as fast as she could and ran back to the cruiser. Her head hurt and her stomach roiled as she jumped in and took off after the camper.

"I called for backup!" Shane shouted as Samantha slid into the driver's seat. "You need to let me drive."

"I've got this," Samantha bit out. She blinked twice, the winding road in front her stopped undulating, but it didn't help that it kept on curving up and around, as though it had been carved through the mountain by a snake.

"Ryder, pull over, we need to get you checked out. You got hit in the head hard." Samantha kept driving. She knew on some level Shane was right, but she couldn't let them out of her sight. They'd get away. "I got the tags! Let 'em go!" he said through his teeth.

Samantha's eyes narrowed as she struggled to keep the road in front of her in focus. "Shit. Probably stolen plates. Damn, Shane, you really that green?"

"I know enough not to risk my own life or a fellow officer's!" he shouted as the tires squealed in protest. Samantha made the next curve just a little too sharp. Shane sucked in his breath and grabbed the dashboard. "At least pull over, and let me drive. I know these roads better."

She clenched her teeth. "I thought you said this road takes us back to town."

"It does if you take that left at Melvin's Food and Gas back there." A mix of fear and anger had his voice sounding more like a growl.

"Shit, where the fuck is backup? Where does this road take us?" She sped up and clenched her teeth against the pain clawing at her brain.

"Eventually into Nevada." Shane's voice was thin and breathy.

"Shit!" she yelled.

"Samantha, stop. You're not gonna catch them! Listen to me . . ."

Samantha took the next curve and growled, her voice low and menacing. "Officer Shane, either shut the fuck up or I'm slowing down and shoving you out! Do you understand me?"

Shane cursed under his breath and buckled his seat belt tighter as he grabbed the mic and called for backup once again.

Samantha concentrated on her driving. Thankfully, her eyesight was steady and sharp again, although the siren only intensified the pain throbbing in her head.

She heard Shane's uneasy voice as he spoke with the dispatcher, but his words didn't register. She kept her eyes focused on the curve of the road and the vehicle ahead. The camper shimmied and swayed all over the road. So far there had been little to no traffic. But there was a child back there. Was he kidnapped? Was he hurt? How could she back down? She just had to stay with them until her backup showed.

She saw the sunlight glint off the barrel of the rifle

just in time. "Shit! Duck!" she yelled and pushed Shane down in the seat just as a bullet punched through the windshield over Shane's head.

"Holy shit, back off!" Shane pleaded with her frantically.

"Just stay the fuck down!" Samantha was pissed now—no, past pissed, she was livid. No way would she let the bastard go now. Shane just barely missed catching the bullet with his face. She pushed the thought aside; she'd deal with that later. She had to catch these assholes. Shane was speaking frantically into the mic again. She slammed her foot down on the accelerator and yelled in rage as a bullet hit her radiator.

"Samantha!" Hunter's voice was clear and strong through the radio, and it wasn't missed that he'd said her name correctly. She grimaced, surprised that she didn't like it. "Backup is on its way. Can you maintain pursuit?"

She snatched the mic from a wide-eyed Shane. "Affirmative, Sheriff. Too close to back off now. I think there's a minor involved," she replied, strangely calm, even though she could feel her heart in her throat.

The danger was very real. Her life, Shane's life, also her career, was on the line, but it was the life of this unknown child that drove her.

There was a pause before the radio crackled again. "Don't get headstrong and careless, Sam. Keep a safe distance."

A bullet shattered her side-view mirror with a loud metallic ping. "No, sir, we can't lose them. I'm staying on them until I get backup."

If she let them escape, they may never find them again. She'd been on the force long enough to know that, and Hunter knew it too. Grotesque scenes of what they might do with the child kept playing over and over in her mind, scenes of molestation, mutilation. She couldn't let them go, she couldn't.

"Dammit, Officer Ryder, was that gunfire? I heard gunfire." Hunter's growl crackled from the speaker.

She didn't have time to argue. "Just get me my backup, Sheriff." Gritting her teeth against the need to heave, she dropped the mic. Shane grabbed the mic and started to sit up. "No, Shane, stay down. Just stay down. One less target."

Panic rose in her and clawed at her throat as she leaned into the steering wheel. White billows of steam were pouring out from under the hood and the car was losing momentum. She could barely see through the web of cracks in her windshield, and bullets still popped and pinged against her cruiser. God, she didn't want to lose them. There sounded like an explosion, and for a moment she thought they'd go up in flames before she realized her right tire was shot out. She braked slowly, but the car was going too fast. It shook hard and bore to the right. She swerved, fighting for control, sliding to a halt precariously close to the edge of the ravine.

It all seemed to happen in slow motion. A minute or two passed before her mind caught up. She looked over at Shane. "You good?"

Shane nodded, but he looked shaken as he unbuckled his seat belt.

Her head was pounding. She looked him over. "Not shot or anything, are you?"

"Naw, I'm okay. You okay?" he questioned her, his gaze direct, assessing despite the nervousness in his voice.

"Sam!" It was Hunter's voice, only it sounded tight and deeper than usual.

"Yeah," she muttered to Shane as she picked up the mic. "I lost them."

"Are you okay?" He sounded mad, and something else.

"Yeah, car is shot up, though."

"Fuck," Hunter growled. "Shane?"

"We're both fine. Just a little shaken."

"God. Sam." Hunter's voice shook, with anger? With fear? Samantha wasn't sure.

Shane had managed to get out of the car and around to the front without falling into the ravine. He stood looking at the bullet-riddled grill while he rubbed the back of his neck. Wouldn't hurt for him to get checked out.

"Shane might have whiplash. Hunter . . . the kid," she said through her teeth. The possible pain and horror awaiting that child plagued her mind.

"We'll find the truck, Sam. Stay put. I'm almost there," he ordered.

"Understood." She put the mic down and got out of the car. She was about to ask Shane about his neck when another cruiser pulled in behind them. Decker and Rodgers got out and walked up to them.

"Boy, y'all really fucked it up this time." Decker

smirked at them. Shane's expression changed, his jaw clenched as he took a step toward Decker.

She stepped in front of him. "The sheriff is on his way."

"Bet he is." Rodgers's lip quivered in disgust.

Samantha narrowed her eyes at him but said nothing.

"What were you thinkin' anyway, drivin' like a crazy person over these roads? Hell, you're trained for city drivin' . . ."

"She handled these roads like a pro. She would have caught them if they hadn't started shootin'," Shane defended her. "Or maybe if we'd had the backup we called for sooner. But I reckon y'all two were just takin' it safe, huh?"

Hunter arrived before the verbal war could continue.

"Rodgers, Decker, what are y'all doin? You two get the hell out of here and see if you can find that truck. The California Highway Patrol can assist me here."

"CHiPs?" Decker jerked alert then. "Hell, Hunter, since when do we want troopers in our business?"

"Since the bastards who opened fire on two of my officers got away and the other two are standin' around mouthin' off with their thumbs up their ass." Hunter gave the men a fierce, level stare. "Now get to it or you and Decker both can take a leave of absence while I find someone willing to follow orders."

Decker's lips tightened. Carefully, as though he were more than aware that Hunter was just looking for an excuse to tear him apart, he headed back to his vehicle.

"This is a mistake, Sheriff," Rodgers muttered, his eyes narrowing on Hunter.

"Then it's my mistake, isn't it? Now get the hell out of here." He turned toward his deputy, preparing to back up the order with action if need be.

Rodgers's fists clenched, he shook his head with a short, rough movement then stalked away. Hunter kept his eyes on Rodgers and Decker. After a brief, furious discussion, the two men got into their cruiser and peeled out, headed up the mountain.

Hunter jerked his cell phone from his hip, watching Sam check on Shane. He hit speed dial, then waited impatiently as the phone rang.

"What do you need?" Jacob's voice came across the line, quiet and controlled.

"You heard?" Hunter knew the other man kept a police scanner on hand, and there was no way in hell to block him from transmissions.

"I heard." There was a low throb of anger in the other man's voice.

Hunter knew if there were two things Jacob hated, it was flesh runners and drug runners, and from all appearances, the ones operating in Deerhaven were more dangerous than most.

"Check your end, but don't get into trouble. They were headed that way. I sent Rodgers and Decker out after them, so be on guard," Hunter warned his friend.

Jacob grunted sarcastically. He was a man of few words when the situation warranted it.

"Keep your cell on hand," he finally growled. "I'll be back with you later."

"You do that," Hunter bit out. "And watch your ass. I don't have time to haul you out of trouble."

He disconnected the line as two California Highway

Patrol officers roared into the area, sirens blasting. A tight, cold smile shaped his lips as he identified the officers.

Mark had come through for him. Hunter may be short on loyal deputies, but by God, Mark had just pulled two of the meanest damned troopers to ever ride a California highway in to help him after his earlier phone call.

His brother-in-law evidently wasn't taking any chances. These men were troopers with a grudge, and the power to back up any investigation they undertook. Gabriel Sloan and Logan Grant.

He caught Gabriel's hawkish gaze. Tall, controlled, a man of few words, Hunter guessed. A brief nod was all the answer he needed. Assuming expressions of arrogant intent, the two officers strolled his way.

Let the games begin, Hunter thought, because shit was about to get real.

"Sheriff Steele." Gabriel tipped his hat back on his head and surveyed the scene with predatory interest.

He was as tall as Hunter, lean and muscular, with a square jawline, and piercing hazel eyes. He had once been more laid-back and easygoing than he was now, but circumstances had changed that over the years.

Hunter didn't look back as Sam and Shane moved closer to them. He needed to get them to the hospital to be checked out. Probably should have called the paramedics.

"We got a line on your tags and your boys," Sloan told him quietly, as he eyed Sam and Shane.

"They're safe," Hunter assured him.

Sloan lifted a brow and studied the two for a moment before nodding. "Truck was stolen 'bout two weeks ago. The witness described Jasper Michaels, a small-time illegals dealer, as the thief. Jasper was seen not long before that with Wago Darney, an illegals flesh peddler of the worse sort. If you've tagged him and your officer saw him"—he titled his head, indicating Sam—"then she best watch her ass. Wago doesn't like witnesses of any kind."

Hunter's jaw clenched. This was getting deeper than he could have ever suspected.

At the hospital, Hunter stood watching the ER doc examine Sam. She shot daggers at him a few times, pissed because he insisted she get checked out. Shane had some neck strain and was having an MRI to assess the scope of the damage.

It looked as though Sam may have a mild concussion but that was all. Both officers had been surprisingly lucky; the bastards in that truck had meant to kill them both. What had Hunter on edge more than anything was the fact that the two officers could be targeted now.

He stepped outside with the doctor while Sam dressed. The doctor explained that she would be sore, and though her concussion was mild, she might need a day off to rest and heal. Getting her to do that was another story. They were all immersed fully in this conspiracy now, and he knew Sam well enough to know that the child she encountered would haunt her until she uncovered the whole ring. It didn't help a damned bit finding out that Tom Novak was involved. Hunter reluctantly filled her in on what Mark had discovered. She'd taken it all in and was still processing. She couldn't let her experience with Tom dominate. It was a matter of compartmentalizing. She could do this.

"I'm ready." Samantha walked from her room, dressed in the soft, gray sweat pants he had brought, and a loose, light-gray T-shirt. She looked tired and worried, and he didn't blame her. "Were you able to get anything on that vehicle?"

He tossed her a sideways glance. "Sam, we aren't going to discuss this tonight. You're going to go home, take your meds, and go to sleep."

Hunter took her arm as they walked toward the exit to the waiting room at the end of the hall.

"Hunter, the longer we wait . . ."

"You're taking tomorrow off. I need you at one hundred percent." He almost winced at the controlled violence in his voice. "I'm on it."

Dammit to hell, he could have lost her. He almost shuddered at the thought. He was doing better, though; he had been shaking from the first sound of gunfire until he pulled up to the scene.

"Hunter, you weren't the one who heard that child cry out," Samantha said in a harsh whisper, as they waited for the receptionist to press the door lock so they could leave. "I was." She continued as she lowered herself into an uncomfortable waiting room chair, "That was a child in pain, and I won't forget about that sound."

"I'm not asking you to forget about it," he told her, fighting to keep calm. "But you can't do anyone any good until you're pain-free, Sam. Especially that child. Take a day. It's just a day, for God's sake. By then I should have a lead on what's going on."

He meant what he said. He was on it for damned sure. It was not lost on him the problems he was potentially facing. He obviously couldn't trust Rodgers and Decker.

With Sam and Shane out of commission, at least for a day or so, that left no one on his immediate force to back him. He had phone calls and plans to make, because he would be damned if he would see his county used for what he was suspecting it was being used for, especially by men who had sworn to protect it.

Silence lay between them then, thick and heavy, as he sat beside her, waiting for word on Shane. Nothing moved quickly in an ER waiting room.

A couple of hours passed before Shane came shuffling out into the waiting room with his discharge papers in hand.

"Hey." His voice was soft, pained.

Hunter stood. Sam followed as he walked toward his deputy. "Hey, what did the doc say?"

"Not really whiplash, just some strained muscles. No serious damage." Hunter's sigh of relieve was audible. Shane gave him a sideways smile. "Said I should be good to go in a day or two. I'll be fine once I get rid of this headache."

"Yeah, you'll take tomorrow off too. I'll pick up your prescription and get you home."

"Naw, Sheriff, thanks. I wish. But my sister insisted on pickin' me up. She's about to lose her damn mind. It'll be easier just to let her have her way. Trust me. Ryder, you okay?" he asked Sam then, his look probing.

"I'm good. Thanks." She nodded.

Shane started to nod and then winced. "Good, that's good. Y'all go on. Brandy'll be here any minute. I'll see y'all tomorrow."

"No, you won't. You're off tomorrow."

Shane started to debate, but the look on Hunter's face

had him shutting his mouth quickly. "Yeah, okay. I'll check in tomorrow."

"Okay. Get some rest." Hunter patted Shane lightly on the shoulder then led Sam from the hospital entrance to the cool comfort of his pickup. He helped her in, then locked her seat belt in place and closed the door.

As he walked to his side of the truck, he kept a careful eye on the cream-colored sedan that had followed him to the hospital earlier in the day. He would have been worried, except the two men who watched him did very little to hide their presence and screamed Feds. Now why the hell would Feds be on his tail?

"I want to take you to the ranch," he finally told her, as he pulled out of the hospital parking lot and headed back to Deerhaven. "We'll pick up your prescription, swing by your place, and pack what you need, then head to the house. I don't want you alone right now. Especially with Mr. Slick roaming around town."

"Who?" Her exclamation of surprise had him tossing her an irritated glance.

"Novak," he bit out. "He's been by your house this afternoon, according to one of your neighbors. She called it in, thought he looked 'wily' and suspicious. I don't know what the hell is up with him, Sam, but I don't like the games he and Henderson are playing. Our best bet right now is to keep you away from him until we know what's going on."

He glanced over at Sam, watching as she licked her dry lips nervously. His cock twitched. Dammit, he really liked the sight of that. He wished he were the one licking those tempting curves instead, though. Lord, she had a strong effect on him.

"I really do not want to deal with this." She sighed, leaning her head back against the seat.

She was pale, a bruise was blooming on her forehead just above her temple, and she was in no condition to do anything but sleep. She would definitely rest, and he'd keep his hands off her if it killed him.

He took a deep breath. It just might kill him.

chapter sixteen

"Dammit, Hunter, I'm not going to bed." She stood stiffly in his great room. She scowled at him and sat on the sofa, her arms crossed, trying to hide the weakness she felt. "I just wanna sit here for a while." She nearly sighed; the big overstuffed sofa was plush, the leather, butter-soft and so comfortable, she just wanted to sink into it.

She looked up into Hunter's eyes and resisted her desire to cringe.

They were hard and cold as granite. The muscle in his jaw flexed.

"Samantha. You fought me at the drugstore when I asked you to take your meds, but you took them. You fought me at your house when I told you to stay in the car. You stayed in the car. You fought me outside when I wouldn't let you carry anything in. We already know I'm gonna win. Stop being so damned bull-headed," he snapped.

He was mad and struggling not to yell. She could tell, but she couldn't seem to care.

"I'm not the bull-headed one. I don't wanna go to sleep right now. I wanna think. I'm gonna sit right here until this blasted pill wears off and I can think straight, and then I'm gonna kick your damn fine ass." As soon as she got rid of the headache. Damn, it was irritating. Nearly as irritating as the way these meds made her head feel full of cotton.

"When you're up to it, my ass is yours. Until then, you'll damn well do what I say." His voice was low and menacing.

He picked up the bags he'd packed and walked down the hallway.

Damn man, she thought. She ran her hands through her hair and took a deep breath. She was starting to feel better. The pain wasn't as sharp, and she was feeling fuzzy, warm, and mellow. It was the fuzzy part that she hated.

She scowled in frustration and defiance as she glanced around, taking in her new surroundings.

The décor was the typical old west, cowboy fare but with a few updates. There was no sign of anything feminine, but Hunter's Uncle Zack never married so it stood to reason. Besides, it suited him. The furniture, however, was new. Rugged, heavy, masculine, and built for comfort. Over the stone fireplace was mounted a wide-screen television. Samantha was willing to bet it was equipped with state-of-the-art surround sound as well. Two recliners sat across from a loveseat that divided the living area from the kitchen and dining areas. A newspaper, two remotes, and a *Sports Illustrated* decorated the rustic wood coffee table.

Hunter returned with a pillow and blanket. Samantha watched him warily as he dropped his bundle on the floor beside the sofa. He stood over her, his long muscular legs straddling her knees. Her eyes dropped to his hips, the evidence of his arousal clearly straining against tough denim, just at her eye level. She raised her gaze to his and lifted a brow.

Hunter's eyes narrowed. "Don't look at me like that," he growled and began pulling her shirt up. The corners of her lips tilted upward as she cupped that hard bulge in his jeans. He held his breath and grabbed her hand. "Sam. You need rest."

She shook her head; it felt so heavy that she leaned it back against the sofa. She didn't fight him as he undressed her and pulled her nightshirt over her head.

"I don't need rest," she murmured, frowning. Her voice sounded weird. "I need sexual healing."

"Sam, baby." Hunter's voice sounded far away and so gentle.

"Hmm?" She reached for him. His mouth, she wanted that wonderful hot mouth of his on her.

"Go to sleep." He lifted her a bit to lay her down.

"I'm not lying down, Hunter. I don't wanna lie . . . around." She fought it, but her eyes drifted close.

He kissed her forehead, her nose, her mouth. Just a tender kiss, lingering for only a few seconds. "Okay, Pixie, whatever you say."

* * *

Samantha woke the next morning with a pounding headache. She opened her eyes slowly, and then squinted against the sunlight, hissing as she struggled to sit up.

She scanned the room, remembering where she was. Another blanket was thrown over the recliner. Coffee, she smelled coffee. Hunter stood in the kitchen making coffee. Follow the coffee, she told herself.

Standing took more effort than she thought it should have. She had expected to be sore, but tomorrow it would be better. Lifting her chin, she took a deep breath. She could take a little stiffness. No big deal.

Hunter saw her hobbling toward the bar dividing the kitchen from the living area. He cursed under his breath, wiped his hands on a kitchen towel, and helped her onto a bar stool.

"Sam, you needed to sleep in a bed. If you weren't so damn stubborn, you wouldn't be as stiff," he growled.

She scowled at him. She knew he was right, but she wasn't about to let him know that.

"Bullshit," she grumbled, thankful for his hard body to lean against.

"You're gonna fall off the stool. Let's move you to the table." His voice was gentle, but it was still too bossy for her liking.

"I'm fine. Please, Hunter, I just need coffee and ibuprofen."

The man was fast and efficient. She held her mug with both hands, inhaling the mouthwatering aroma of freshly brewed coffee. He set a glass of water in front of her and held a large white pill out to her in his wide palm.

"Take this," he said in an adamant tone.

She looked at the pill. "That's not an ibuprofen."

"No, the doc didn't give you ibuprofen," he said firmly, lifting a brow. His lips were pressed together in a determined line.

"That will make me goofy. I need my mind to be clear. I'll stay here, but I can still help figure things out."

"Samantha." He was warning her, and it only made her more determined.

"I don't need it." She turned her head, careful not to grimace in pain, and met his gaze. "Quit treating me like a child."

"You're acting like a child," he bit out. "You take everything as a challenge."

"Whatever." Now he'd gone and pissed her off.

She turned away and sipped at her coffee.

"Samantha, take the damn pill. You still have some of the medication from last night in your bloodstream. When it wears off completely, you're gonna be in pain." His voice was low, uneasy.

There was no way she was taking it. She didn't like feeling out of control, and she disliked being told what to do even less.

"No." She glanced at him from the corner of her eye and continued to drink her coffee. He walked back around to the kitchen, shaking his head.

He brought her eggs and toast and sat in the chair next to her. "How bad is the pain?"

"It's just a little headache. No worries. Thank you for breakfast." She downplayed it as she nibbled at the toast and managed a few bites of the eggs. "Any news?"

"Not yet. I'm gonna head out in a bit if you're okay. Gonna meet with a contact," he told her.

"I feel okay; you should let me go." Hunter set his cup down heavily and waited until she met his gaze. He looked tired and worried. She frowned at that. When was Hunter ever worried? "Okay, okay. I'll stay here," she acquiesced before he could say no again.

After he left she washed the dishes, dried them, and put them away. A hot shower left her feeling limp and tired, her body ached, and her head pounded. Reluctantly, she took half of the pain pill and crawled into Hunter's bed. The cool gray cotton sheets and heavy quilt felt wonderful and it smelled like him.

She inhaled deeply and let herself drift.

Hunter pulled into a well-kept driveway, grated, gravelled and levelled, and shook his head in exasperation. The small log cabin sat on a slope above him, the windows dark, the door tightly closed.

Hunter got out of the Jeep and strode quickly to the front door. Pausing, he was ready to pound on the window when the first sounds penetrated his focus. The hungry, gasping, female moan was almost a shock.

Hell, he thought Jacob was a monk of some kind. The sounds of pleasure rose as Hunter turned and walked to the back of the cabin.

He stopped at the side of the house, shaking his head, as he pulled his sunglasses from his eyes and stared in shock at the scene before him.

Jacob had a pretty, little, black-haired business type stretched over the picnic table, her narrow skirt around her waist, her white silk blouse opened. Hell, it looked like he'd cut her bra open rather than unhooking it from the back.

The woman's deep black hair had escaped the knot that struggled to stay secure on the top of her head. Stray wisps clung in damp strands along her cheek and neck. A fine film of perspiration glazed the woman's pale skin and Jacob's broad naked back.

The woman's legs were splayed wide, giving Hunter an unimpeded view of the soft flesh into which the mountain man was vigorously plowing. The soft sounds of wet pussy and hard cock filled the air. Slapping flesh overlaid it, and adding to the arousing mix was the woman's ever-increasing cries as Jacob drove her closer to climax.

Her hands were gripping powerful arms, nails pressing into flesh. Her body arched, her full breasts, tipped with hard nipples and flushed with lust, were a damned tempting sight. Almost as pretty as Sam's berry-tipped breasts.

He felt a shade of discomfort at his voyeurism. But damn, it was just one of those sights he couldn't look away from. He couldn't believe that Jacob had allowed himself a moment of vulnerability.

The first had been nearly fatal. Hunter assured himself that he just wanted to be certain Jacob stayed safe while immersed in his pleasure.

As Hunter watched, Jacob's thrusts increased. The sound of balls slapping against a rounded ass filled the air. The woman jerked, arched, her head was thrown back as she began to beg in desperation for release. Then she was crying out, her body stiffening as Jacob drove into her hard, deep. The sounds of their mingled climaxes had Hunter shifting uncomfortably.

Damn, if he hadn't wished he had gone back to the

Jeep instead. The woman's cries were much too reminiscent of Sam, reminding him how tight and hot her cunt was around his flesh. He sure hoped she got over her mad soon.

"Dammit, Hunter, this isn't a peep show." Jacob was breathing hard as he moved away from the woman, jerking her skirt over her exposed flesh, then fastening his jeans quickly. "What the hell are you doing here?"

Jacob helped the woman from the table, shielding her face with his big body as she fought to fix her clothes. He whispered something to her; Hunter couldn't make out the words. But there was a surprising edge of tenderness as Jacob touched her cheek and kissed her brow quickly.

"Taking notes." Hunter grinned. "That's some fine form you got going there, my friend. I say you should give lessons."

The brawny ex-ranger frowned back at him, his brown eyes narrowing dangerously as he stood in front of the woman. Then he turned back to her, tucked a strand of hair back from her face and sighed heavily.

"Go on inside." He nodded at the open back door. "I'll be there as soon as I shove this bastard off my mountain."

The woman flushed, tugging her blouse closed and rushing away from Hunter's curious gaze.

"You used to have better manners," Jacob grunted angrily as he sprawled out in one of the large, wooden chairs beneath the shade of a nearby tree. "What the hell happened?"

Hunter flushed, but fought to ignore it.

"And you used to hear better." Hunter shrugged.

"Must have been a while for you if you didn't hear me cursing you as I came up this mountain."

"I heard your Jeep. You need a tuneup," Jacob snarled. "Now what the hell are you doing here?"

Hunter walked over to a matching chair and sat down heavily. He needed Jacob's help; he couldn't afford to alienate him right now.

"You owe me," Hunter said simply. "You're keeping shit from me again, Jacob, and I need to know. What the hell's going on in my county?"

Jacob breathed out heavily as the sound of a vehicle could be heard starting up, then pulling out from the side of the house. Evidently the woman had decided not to stick around.

"Fuck." The other man sighed. "Took me six months to get her here, and you just ran her off." He shook his head and rose from his chair. "Come on into the house. We can talk there now."

Following, Hunter paused at the kitchen doorway as Jacob began pulling maps and reports from a hidden panel in the wall and spreading them out on the kitchen table. That done, he all but stomped to the coffeemaker as he gestured toward them.

"What have you heard?" Jacob asked.

Moving to the table, Hunter sat down, his gaze going over the maps.

"I heard a report there's illegals hiding somewhere in my county." If anyone knew, it would be Jacob.

Jacob grunted sarcastically. "Lot of things go on in these mountains."

That was the damned truth. It was becoming danger-ous to even attempt hunting anymore.

"Yep, and you seem to know who's doing the better part of it and where they can be found," Hunter said, watching his friend thoughtfully.

Jacob turned back to him.

"From what I've managed to find, we have some major players involved with this," Jacob informed him, as he placed two steaming cups of coffee on the table and sat across from Hunter. "Everything I've pulled together suggests they're using the mountain roads, paved and unpaved, to transport their cargo, both human as well as drugs."

Satellite and ground-based maps were laid out between them, marked with Jacob's distinctive shorthand to pinpoint areas suspected as drop-off points. One was suspiciously close to an area where Hunter knew the mayor kept his hunting cabin.

"I suspect Henderson's involved, as well as your two deputies, Decker and Rodgers. And I'd say he wanted Officer Ryder on the force to keep an eye on her. She's known in Detroit for being a little too obstinate and a whole lot too meddlesome when it comes to minding her own business and ignoring certain things."

Hunter grunted at the information. "She resembles that remark," he murmured, ignoring Jacob's surprised chuckle.

"Now, here's what I think," the other man continued. "The mayor's wife, Lillian Henderson, somehow found out what her husband was involved in, or he was afraid she heard or saw too much. They tried to make her death look like an accident, but Zack was crazy in love with that woman and didn't buy it. So they killed him too. Then, somehow, Ms. Coulter became a risk as well."

"She, Zachariah, and Lillian were all childhood friends," Hunter stated. "They stayed close." He slid the flash drive Samantha had slipped him across the papers as Jacob narrowed his eyes on it. "She found that in Dottie's safe deposit box. Pictures of Henderson with several men, but there's also other pictures. Men I've never seen but they were obviously in town at some point because I recognize the locations."

Jacob took the slender drive from him and tucked it into his shirt pocket with a nod. "I'll get back to you on these."

"So, you think we're looking at illegals and drugs?" Hunter asked.

"Not alone." Jacob sighed. "There's murmurings they could be transporting known terrorists as well. And they've been highly successful doing it. A Libyan Homeland Security picked up about six months back finally broke a few weeks ago. He was taken through Deerhaven and thought he heard one of the men mention Henderson."

Hunter's head jerked up in shock. "Terrorists?" Son of a bitch. They were using his county to transport terrorists. They'd killed his uncle and two friends to further destabilize their own fucking country?

"'Fraid so." Jacob nodded, his expression deadly still as he stared back at Hunter. "This is going to blow to hell and back if we're not careful. They won't care if they kill your deputy, your sister, or you to keep their little pipeline going. You need to watch yourself. And your woman, Hunter. Every time we get close, someone dies. And it's starting to piss me off."

chapter seventeen

Several hours later Samantha woke and raised up on her elbows. The clock on the nightstand said one forty-five. Her headache was still there but not nearly as sharp as it had been, just a dull throb remained. Her stomach growled, reminding her that she hadn't eaten much for breakfast.

She sat up on the edge of the bed and waited to see if her headache grew worse. When it didn't, she stood and ran her fingers through her tangled hair, yawning as she padded sleepily to the kitchen. She cursed the stupid drugs under her breath for her foggy brain.

"Oh hey, Miss Samantha." The deep male voice that wasn't Hunter's startled her.

She stared at the two men standing in the kitchen and tried to clear her mind enough to decide her next move.

"So sorry, we didn't know you were here. Um . . . I'm Ethan, this is my brother, Levi. We work for Uncle Hunter."

"Uncle Hunter?" Samantha repeated. Both men nodded. "Hannah's?" She frowned at them.

"No, Aunt Hannah married our uncle Mark, our momma's brother."

Samantha nodded slowly. "You're twins."

"Yes, ma'am." Levi nodded.

"Do you live here?" she asked, putting the pieces together finally.

"No, ma'am," Levi answered sheepishly. "We live in the cabin up the hill a piece. But Uncle Hunter has better food, and we were closer to the ranch house so we decided to raid his fridge."

"Yeah," Ethan added, "we kinda do that a lot."

Samantha smiled "Gotcha."

Hunter walked through the front door then, and she turned her head to catch his eyes darkening as he looked from her to the twins. It was then she realized she was standing there in her nightshirt and panties and that was it.

"Hi, Hunter, met your nephews." Her voice was a bit higher pitched than she meant for it to be. "Yeah, so, I'm gonna go put clothes on now."

Hunter was glaring at them now. "No need. They're leaving. Aren't you, boys?"

Samantha stood still, worried for the young men.

"Uh, yes! Absolutely," Ethan said as he reached for his beer.

"Leave it," Hunter snapped.

"Right, okay," Ethan answered as he headed for the door.

"Yes, sir. Thanks for lunch!" Levi shouted as he headed out the door.

Hunter waited until they closed the sliding glass door behind them, he turned to her and grinned. "Go back to bed, Sami Jo. I'll bring you something to eat."

He called her that just to piss her off. She scowled at him. "What if I don't wanna?"

"Then I'll put you back to bed," he said with a lifted brow.

She narrowed her eyes. "You and what army?"

He dropped the loaf of bread and advanced on her. Before she had a chance to turn and run, he had scooped her up into his arms.

"Ugh! No fair!" she groused.

Hunter laughed softly, impervious to her struggles, as he carried her to his bedroom and put her to bed. If she were honest, she'd have to admit that she really wanted to go back to bed. Hunter's he-man show of dominance kinda turned her on too. But she wasn't going to be honest and admit anything of the sort.

Hunter sat on the bed beside her, smoothed her hair back from her face, and spoke softly. "How are you feeling?"

She scowled up at him. His concerned expression made her feel bad for fighting him. "Better."

He kissed her lightly. "Good."

She lay back, feeling exhausted, closed her eyes again, and felt the bed sag as Hunter slipped in beside her and gathered her to him. The badass cop part of her gave way to the woman in need. She turned toward him. He kissed the top of her head, and she sighed. For the first time in fifteen years, she felt at home. "I've slept too much already."

"Nah, just rest. The more you rest, the sooner you'll be back to harassing me."

She laughed softly and snuggled closer.

Samantha woke early the next morning feeling much better. Still a little stiff but no real pain. She heard Hunter turn on the shower, and a wicked thought whispered through her mind. With a determined smile, she walked down the hall and opened the door to the bathroom. Steam billowed out as she stepped in, trying to be as quiet as possible. She could see the silhouette of Hunter's well-defined body through the translucent shower curtain.

She bit her lip and pulled her nighty over her head, letting it drop to the ground, her panties following. Already her body was tingling with anticipation, her nipples tightened, moisture gathered between her thighs. Hunter spun around when she pulled the curtain back. He stood there, water sluicing over his tan muscular planes as his gaze traveled over her naked body.

She watched his cock respond, and she couldn't help but reach out and caress the velvety tip as she stepped into the tub. Her fingers glided up his thickening shaft as her free hand slid over his chest to his neck. She pulled him closer, and her lips slid over his, slick by the water. She teased him with slow strokes of her tongue as her hand closed around his now rock-hard cock.

Hunter grasped her hips and pulled her close. She pressed tighter against him as his hands slid over her ass, squeezing her flesh. He lifted one leg to his hip, and his fingers delved deeper, sliding through the slick honey collecting between the swelling sensitive lips of her pussy. He pulled away, his breath labored. "Sam . . . ?"

There was a question there. "No pain, just need you," she murmured against his jaw, kissing her way down to his neck. She bit and licked his collarbone. He groaned as he lifted her easily and braced her back against the shower wall. Her vagina contracted as he slid inside her slowly, drawing him deeper. He felt so good filling her, stretching her. Soft moans whispered from her lips as her fingers sifted through his hair. His body moving against hers with slick friction drove her wild.

His mouth devoured hers. With one hand, he held her while the other cupped and kneaded her breast, his fingers skillfully circling, pinching her aching nipple. She trembled in his arms as he picked up the pace. Was that ringing in her head?

Hunter paused, cursing. Samantha whimpered, then managed to form words. "Maybe you should get it." The phone stopped ringing and Hunter growled as he thrust into her, kissing her hard. Then it started ringing again. "You have to get it."

A string of profanity left Hunter's lips as he eased out of her and made sure she had her balance. He kissed her again and stepped out of the shower, still cursing.

"Well, hell." She stepped into the shower spray, her whole body pulsing. With resolve, she finished her shower and turned off the water. She grabbed a towel from the rack and stepped out of the tub, wrapping it around her. She found another towel in the closet and dried her hair with it.

In the living room she found Hunter was still on the phone, holding a towel around his waist. Might as well put on the coffee. She ran her fingertips over his flat stomach as she passed him, not missing the way the towel tented just a little lower.

"No, Shane, you did the right thing. You should have called." Hunter winked at her, but she could tell something was up. She leaned back against the counter and waited.

"Right." He nodded, his frown deepening. "Well, that's normal for them. Tell me exactly what they asked."

She wished she could hear the other side of the conversation. It was driving her nuts watching Hunter clench his teeth and that muscle in his jaw jump.

"Uh-huh. Yep. Nope, don't worry about it. Take today off too." He paused, shifting from one leg to the other. "Good, good. Yeah." He looked up at her, and his expression softened. "She's good." He chuckled and Samantha frowned. "Exactly. Okay, you bet. If you need anything, call. Don't hesitate. I'll check in with you later."

"What was that all about?" Samantha asked, watching Hunter closely. He stalked toward her. Bracing his hands on the counter on either side of her, he leaned down and sucked at her neck. Her eyes drifted closed as she tilted her head to give him better access.

"Shane." He lifted her, setting her on the counter, and kissed the top swells of her breasts. "Decker and Rodgers were asking him questions they shouldn't care about. I'm sorry, babe, but I have to go deal with this."

"I'll go with you."

Hunter laid his hands on her shoulders. "No headache?"

"I'm fine." She looked him in the eye.

"You promise?"

"I promise." Samantha scowled then winced as she jumped down.

"You're not one hundred percent yet."

"Oh my God. Didn't I feel one hundred percent about twenty minutes ago?"

Hunter leaned down and kissed her. "Oh, hell yes. But that is not the same thing. It won't hurt you to rest one more day."

"Ugh," Samantha muttered. "I can't stand feeling so useless, Hunter."

"You're far from useless. One more day, please?" He kissed her forehead. "For me?" Damn him and his forehead kisses.

"You don't play fair." Samantha scowled.

Hunter kissed her lips. "When I get back, we'll pick up where we left off."

"Uh-huh," Samantha muttered, going to the fridge. "You got any cucumbers in here?"

chapter eighteen

Samantha sat on the edge of the couch with the remote in her hand, flipping channels without really paying attention to what she saw. There was nothing on anyway. Hunter only had basic cable and the sports package. Neither of them had Netflix. Just soaps, court TV, and Maury, nothing on which Samantha wanted to waste her time. As if she didn't have all kinds of time to waste. She clicked off the television and set the remote on the coffee table, sighing heavily, strumming her fingers on her knee.

What was Hunter doing? Had he found the camper? The waiting, the inactivity, made her stir-crazy, which made her irritable. The memory of the child's cry gnawed at her. She was well enough to do some investigating of her own. Why in the hell did she give Hunter one more day? If he had a home computer, she could at least check some things out on that. She took a deep breath and blew it out.

She had to find something to occupy her mind or she'd lose it. She got dressed in denim shorts and one of Hunter's blue cotton T-shirts and tied the long hem in a knot at her hip. Braiding her hair took a little longer because her shoulders were still sore, but she got it done.

She was sick to death of puttering around the house. She carried the freshly washed laundry she'd spent all of ten minutes folding, into Hunter's bedroom. She put hers in her bag and laid his neatly on his bed. She almost wished Hunter were a slob. As much as she hated cleaning up, it would at least give her something to do.

With a sigh, she wandered into the kitchen to refill her coffee mug then crossed to the sliding glass doors in the dining area. She pulled back the drapes to let more light in. The wraparound porch opened up onto a nice-size deck complete with a BBQ pit and sturdy furniture that Samantha was willing to bet Hunter had hand crafted with wood from his land. The deck was new. Possibly added on when Hunter moved in. It was perfect for entertaining or just relaxing.

Reading too. Getting absorbed into a book could possibly occupy her mind until Hunter got back and she could find out what in the hell was going on. She went to the entertainment center and scanned Hunter's small collection of books. Tom Clancy, figures; Stephen King, a definite maybe. She curled her lip at the one Louis L'Amour. Oh well, it wasn't like she expected he'd have J. D. Robb or Linda Howard. She continued browsing and lifted a brow when she came across *The Complete Works of William Shakespeare*. Poor Bill, he thought he knew so much about women. She smiled and shook her head.

She selected a Stephen King novel and tucked it under her arm as she grabbed her cell phone and her coffee mug. With some effort, she got the sliding glass doors unlocked and the security bar removed. She stepped into the warm, California June, closing the door behind her. She walked to the edge of the deck and looked out over the pasture. The cattle were grazing far away, closer to the edge of the woods.

Setting the mug on the little table beside the Adirondack chair, she dropped her book.

"Crap." She set the phone down and bent to pick up the novel when she heard a pop and the glass door behind her shattered. Samantha jerked her head around without lifting it and caught the slightest glimmer of sunlight on metal. Her training kicked in and the cop in her took over. She clenched her teeth and snatched her phone from the table. She stayed as low as she could and ran for the house. Another shot hit and splintered the wood frame inches from her head.

Adrenaline flooded her bloodstream as she picked away shards of glass and pried the door open. She quickly crawled through the doorway into the house. It wasn't until she was in the hallway that she stood again and ran to the bedroom. She grabbed her gun belt off the hook inside the closet door, unholstered it, and ran back to see if she could catch sight of the shooter.

She crouched low and held the gun steady. With one hand, she called Hunter's cell phone. She figured the shooter could have already gone, or he could be heading her way. The twins didn't seem to be around. She scanned the tree line for signs of movement anyway.

"Answer, dammit," she hissed impatiently.

"Yeah," Hunter answered tersely.

"Had an attempted hit, just now. Shots fired. Might need some backup." Samantha kept her voice even.

"What?" Hunter's deep voice took on an uneasy edge.

"A sniper took out your sliding glass door." Her reply was low-pitched and deceptively dispassionate.

"Fuck!" Hunter growled and disconnected.

Samantha dropped the phone and used both hands to aim her gun. Assholes. Evidently they wanted to finish the job. Well, fuck them. They'd underestimated her. She moved to the edge of the doors and carefully nudged the drapes aside. Her gaze shifted from the woods to the surrounding area. The cattle had fled out of sight. Her eyes sharp, she focused on taking steady breaths, keeping her cool. She struggled to rein in her fury.

She doubted the sniper would give up that quickly. Especially since most likely they knew she was alone. She snarled, hoping they did try to come for her. She'd take their sorry ass out, maybe take out both kneecaps and torture them till they told her who had that kid. Her mind went back to the child she'd failed to rescue. Did they still have him? Was he safe? Fuck! She had to do something. To hell with this convalescence shit. It wasn't like her, but she would have to break that promise. She had wasted too much time lying around. The bastards were still shooting at her and that just pissed her off.

It had only been minutes when she heard the spray of gravel and then car doors slamming shut outside. She moved to the hallway and trained her revolver on the door with perfect aim, as the deadbolts were swiftly unlocked.

Hunter burst through the door with his gun raised and his teeth set. He met Samantha's gaze and advanced on her as he holstered his weapon. "Goddammit," he bit out, his eyes cold and dark.

Samantha lowered her gun with a sigh. "We need to check along the tree line. The barn too. And the stables."

"You're bleeding," he snapped.

She looked down at the blood that flowed down her shins and shrugged. She hadn't felt anything. They were probably just nicks. Before she could take a step toward the door, Hunter scooped her up and carried her into the bathroom. She fought him, but he held her firmly.

"Be still. Did you get a shot at him?"

"No, I didn't want him to know I had a gun until he was eating a bullet. Damn it to hell, Hunter, this is ridiculous." He sat her on the closed lid of the toilet and knelt in front of her. "We need to canvas the area. He was in the woods, but he may be hiding closer to the house. Are you listening to me?" she asked, trying to slap his hands away.

He wet a washcloth in the sink beside them and wrung it out. "Gabriel Sloan and Logan Grant are taking care of it, now shut up," he replied sharply without looking at her.

"Shut up? Shut up?" she yelled, eyeing him incredulously, ignoring the sting as he carefully washed away the blood and picked out shards of glass. "Who are those guys?"

He glanced up at her curiously. "CHP, remember?"

It came back to her then. "Oh yeah. I remember."

"You may need stitches . . ." he said, his voice hoarse with rage.

"Too fuckin' bad." she snapped. "I'm not going back to the hospital. I'm sick of you babying me. I'm not fragile—"

Hunter took her face in his hand and kissed her hard, fast, silencing her tirade. It wasn't tender; it was a kiss that meant to stake claim. When he pulled away, she was panting. Her lips felt swollen and bruised. It pissed her off even more that her body so readily responded to him. His expression had her swallowing her biting retort. She shuddered at the warning, the fury, and the fear she saw in his eyes.

His thumb caressed her jaw; his gaze searched her face. Her heart pounded against her ribs. Again his mouth closed over hers. His lips moved with aching gentleness, sending ripples of need curling through her.

"We found the casings, Hunter. Checked all the out buildings. Looks like he cleared out . . . oh, sorry." Logan stood at the bathroom door. Gabriel stood behind him.

Hunter pulled away with a growl. Samantha blinked and sucked in air. She looked up at the bathroom doorway. Both men looked as uncomfortable as Samantha felt.

"I figured as much," Hunter said tightly.

"You all right?" Gabriel asked Samantha. He had a hard face and sad eyes. He watched her closely, his brow lifted as he waited for her answer.

"Yes, I'm fine," she muttered. Hunter was shaken. She could plainly see that, felt it in his kiss.

"Gonna need stitches," Gabriel said succinctly.

"I'm taking her to the emergency room. I'll meet you guys back at the station," Hunter answered as though she had no say.

Oh, that was it, the last straw. Now, she was embarrassed as well as aroused, frustrated, and angry. She really wanted to punch something. She glanced back at Hunter, her hard gaze matching his. She could almost hear the crackle of tension between them.

"The hell I am going to the ER," she said through her teeth.

"Stubborn woman," he growled at her. "You may need a tetanus shot."

She glared at him. "Had one, two years ago. I'm current. Just give me the fuckin' Band-Aids."

"Doesn't look so bad to me." Logan stepped into the cramped space. He stood over them, his hands on his hips. His bulky frame was clad in a beige uniform, gun at his hip, and damn, if he didn't make that ugly uniform look good. Samantha felt suffocated. Too many big, controlling men in too small a space.

Logan's eyes were hard as he examined her wound, tilting his head. "Bleeding has about stopped. Put some antibiotic ointment on it. She'll be fine."

She liked Logan. At least one of them was making sense.

Give her the fuckin' Band-Aids. Hunter snorted as he handed her the box of Band-Aids and the antibiotic ointment. He wanted to snarl at Gabriel and Logan, but he wasn't afforded that option at the moment.

Both men were too damned close to her to suit him anyway. As if he wasn't aware of them ogling her long, shapely legs.

He glared back at the two men, frowning fiercely. He didn't like the gleam of amusement that came to their eyes.

"We're leaving the ranch," Hunter told her as the other two men finally filed out of the cramped area. "We're in deep shit here, Sam. Get dressed and re-pack that bag while I get things together with Gabriel and Logan."

"What kind of deep shit? Did you find out something about the kid?" Her voice was filled with excitement now.

Hunter wiped his hands over his face. She would be the death of him. She slapped a Band-Aid over the cut on her knee and followed him quickly as he left the room. He glanced back at her, seeing the glitter in her eyes, the flush on her cheeks, and the intent, determined expression on her face. Hell. He wanted to fuck her, not take her out into a damned war.

"We found something, but I don't know where the child involved is yet," he growled as they entered the bedroom.

He slammed the door shut behind him. His cock was raging, but he'd be damned if he'd let Gabriel and Logan hear the helpless little cries of pleasure that came from his Sam's throat as he made love to her.

"What did you find out?" She jerked her bag off the floor and tossed it on the bed. Glancing back at him curiously, she packed her things.

"You got a pair of jeans to wear out of here?" he asked her, crossing his arms over his chest. She was raring to go, dammit. He had hoped to talk her into staying someplace nice and safe while he, Gabriel, and

Logan moved in to find out what the hell the mayor and his henchmen were up to.

She nodded quickly. "Now tell me what's going on."

He sighed wearily. "We're not completely certain, Sam. But it looks like someone is using Deerhaven's old mines, cave system, and backwoods for human trafficking. We think the network is far-reaching and includes a lot of local and state officials."

Sam stopped packing. He watched her face.

"What?" He narrowed his eyes, seeing a sudden dawning realization in her eyes.

"When I was on the force in Detroit, there was an investigation. I suspected someone on the force of aiding in the transportation of illegals, possibly with terrorist ties and connections to the sex trade, slipping them across the border into Canada. Nothing came of it, but . . ."

"Tom's here, causing trouble." Hunter clenched his fists as he tucked them into his pants pockets. "Was he part of the investigation?"

Sam licked her lips nervously. "It was rumored he was *under* investigation, not part of the investigation," she whispered. "Like I said, nothing came of it." She shook her head desperately. "It was just a rumor."

"In this case, I don't think it's just a rumor, Sam." He sighed. "Gabriel and Logan were investigating on this end. They're part of a national taskforce, and Tom Novak's name pops up in more than one memo concerning problems Detroit is having tracking this situation. When he showed up here, he raised more than a little interest."

Her eyes lit with an angry gleam. "That's treason. Not only treason, it's evil," she said quietly.

Hunter was silent for a moment before he sighed wearily.

"Yes, Sam, which makes Tom incredibly dangerous. We suspect the mayor as well as Rodgers and Decker of conspiring with him. Now get ready, get your stuff together. I have to talk to Gabriel and Logan, and see how we're going to do this."

He walked to her, hating the hurt in her eyes. She looked disillusioned, betrayed.

"I thought he was just an asshole. I had no idea he was capable of . . ." she whispered. "Will they suspect me now? Of helping him?"

They had, Hunter knew. Gabriel had been very blunt in giving that information. Until the incident with the truck. The description Sam had given of the driver matched with a suspected arms dealer involved in kidnapping and the transportation of illegals.

Her injuries, her attempts to stop the truck, and now the attempt on her life pretty much cleared her of suspicion.

"No, Sam," he promised, pulling her into his arms as he kissed her forehead gently. "No one suspects you, baby. But you are in danger now. You can identify the driver, and you know the dangers involved in that. We have to end this."

He pulled back, but he couldn't resist lowering his head to kiss her trembling lips. His hunger for her was unlike anything he had ever known. He craved the taste of her . . . Yeah, that soft trembling moan. His body tightened, his cock raging instantly in demand.

Her mouth opened for him, her tongue tangling with his timidly as her hands gripped his shoulders. She wasn't timid for long, though. Hunter groaned as she moved against him, her hands moving to his hair, her lips opening farther, her mouth becoming hungry now as the kiss intensified. Kissing her was like feeding fire, and it was threatening to rage out of control.

He tightened his grip on his control, easing back shakily as she moaned at the desertion.

"Damn, baby." He sighed, leaning his forehead against hers as he stared down at her. "You burn me alive."

He touched her cheek gently before releasing her. Her skin was soft, though still pale. But the pain was gone from her eyes. They were darkened now, and rich with passion. That look made him want to devour her.

She drew a deep breath, causing her hard-tipped breasts to push against the fabric of his shirt. Damn. He wanted to rip the shirt from her and immerse himself in the heat and fiery passion that belonged to Sam alone.

"Hunter . . ." He saw the emotion in her eyes, the words trembling on her lips, and waited breathlessly. "Nothing."

Disappointment raged through him as she shook her head and moved carefully away from him.

"Sure?" Damn her, she was stubborn. Or was he merely indulging in more wishful thinking than the situation deserved?

He loved her. There was no doubt about that. He had loved her when she was a kid, then at seventeen that love morphed into something completely different. He was so damned crazy about her now he could hardly see straight for it.

"Yeah." She cleared her throat, moving back to her suitcase. "Do whatever you need to do. I'll be ready in less than ten minutes."

Hunter sighed. "I'll finish out things with Gabriel and Logan. We'll be waiting on you in the living room."

He left the room, his cock hard and ready, his heart and mind whirling in confusion. Dammit to hell, she had to love him. Why was she being so hesitant? He shook his head, promising himself he would find out soon. As soon as he had her safe.

God help her, now was not the time. Samantha wanted to tell Hunter she loved him, that she always had and always would. There had been something in those eyes of his. Something mesmerizing, something powerful that pulled at her. For a moment she thought he might actually be in love with her too. This was the worst possible time, and she was too vulnerable. Best she clear her head; she couldn't let herself go there. Not now. She'd made a fool of herself over Hunter Steele too many times. She wouldn't do it again.

Her heart was still pounding, her nipples sensitive, sending pulses of need radiating through her. She closed her eyes and bit her lip. Her pussy throbbed, and every step caused a silken sliding friction that made her want to plead for release. With her love came this all-consuming lust, hunger, desire. Whatever the hell it was, it wasn't like anything she'd ever known, and it wasn't something she could easily ignore.

She pulled off her shorts and with a grimace, her

underwear. She was gonna need panty liners with Hunter around all the time. Quickly she pulled on clean panties, followed by her jeans. She stuffed her toiletries into her overnight bag and folded the clothes she just took off and put them in the outside pocket of her bag.

Tom certainly hadn't made her yearn like this. Tom, what in God's name had she seen in him? She'd thought maybe she loved him once. She had admired his strength, his intelligence, his independence. He had never demanded of her time; he had his thing and she had hers. She sighed and sat on the edge of the bed, just for a moment.

At the time, it seemed the perfect relationship until the abuse started. Samantha shuddered at the memory of his tirades, the threats and accusations, the name-calling, deriding her in front of fellow officers. It had been too much, so she broke it off, or tried to. She swallowed the knot lodged in her throat, clenched her teeth, ran her shaking hands over her hair. Her braid still in place, she took a deep breath. All this time he was a monster.

And now he was trying to use her. Had she been used before? It made her skin crawl to think about it. She wanted the weasel to feel pain. Lots of pain, hideous, gruesome, tremendous pain. And she wanted it to be at her hand. Although she was pretty sure if Hunter got to him first, there would be very little left of him to hurt. Well, she thought, as she stood and slung her bag over her shoulder, ignoring the bite of pain, she'd just have to get to Novak first now, wouldn't she?

chapter nineteen

Hunter stood with his back to her, his hands on his hips, talking to the state cops. The man looked good from every angle, his ass was no exception. Even with all hell breaking loose around her, she thought about how she'd love to bite it. Samantha gave herself a mental head slap. God, she was a mess. It didn't matter what was going on, just the sight of him turned her into a wanton inferno of lust. Her insides melted, her vagina clenched. She nearly moaned out loud. Damn. Gabriel and Logan didn't look bad either. Yep, she was losing it.

"We intercepted a transmission reporting another delivery in a month," Gabriel said. His voice was a commanding deep bass.

"From where was it sent?" Hunter asked.

"Morocco," Gabriel answered.

"Let me guess, the report was meant for Novak," Hunter suggested.

Logan nodded.

Gabriel glanced briefly at Logan then fixed his gaze on Hunter again. "We suspect this isn't something as simple as human trafficking this time. There very well could be a terrorist cell involved with this one. We know there's a small cell in Deerhaven now that will be moving on. We're expecting activity within the next day or two. Just lay low and watch. If you observe anything, report it immediately."

Hunter's back stiffened. Samantha would be willing to bet that his gray eyes were narrowed.

Logan sighed, reading Hunter's body language. "Look, I completely understand how you must feel, but if you go Rambo out there, you'll blow the whole thing."

"I'm not a stand-by-and-watch kind of guy, but I'm not wet behind the ears and I'm not an idiot either. I'll do what needs to be done," Hunter bit out.

"Good." Gabriel's frown deepened. Did the man never smile? "We'll be heading to Los Angeles today to coordinate with the taskforce being prepped there."

Samantha cleared her throat and their gazes shifted past Hunter to focus on her. With their closed expressions, broad chests, and massive biceps, they were an intimidating sight to behold. Even without the wide, shiny, black gun belt hanging low on their narrow hips. She suddenly felt sorry for anyone who tangled with these boys.

Gabriel stood just a little taller than Logan, his black hair was wavy and a bit mussed from the wide brimmed olive hat he held in his hand. Those vivid green eyes of his were revealing. There was a story there. The corner of Logan's mouth lifted a bit and the half smile made his blue eyes sparkle. Did he just wink? She could have been mistaken. Maybe he had a twitch. Hunter turned and frowned at her. What had she done now? Sheesh.

"Ready?" Hunter's tone was a bit strained. He took her bag and pulled her firmly to his side as she walked up and stood beside him.

Samantha lifted her face and narrowed her eyes. "Yes."

"Let's go." He nodded to the officers, who turned and walked out ahead of them.

The back seat of a patrol car was not designed for comfort. Samantha shifted, trying to relieve the cramp in her thigh.

"Will someone fill me in now?" she snapped.

She met Gabriel's gaze in the rearview mirror, and when he didn't say anything, she lifted her brows and he looked back at the road. She turned to Hunter sitting beside her. His long legs made him decidedly more uncomfortable than she was.

"We believe they're using the rest stop off the interstate as a pick-up and drop-off point. There's a network of caves right above it. You and I are going to camp there and stake it out. Gabriel and Logan are taking us to pick up another vehicle, then we'll take an old back road up to the caves," Hunter said, holding her gaze. "Everything we need is there already. Jacob hooked us up."

"We expected they'd try to take you out, Officer Ryder," Gabriel interrupted. He didn't like explaining himself, she could tell by his tone. "So we had things put in place to send you and Sheriff Steele on the stakeout. That way you're safe and you're useful at the same time."

Useful? Ha. He had no idea. She hated being underestimated.

"And we will be in communication with those two?" She nodded toward the front seat without taking her gaze from Hunter's. She couldn't look away from the storm brewing in his eyes.

"Yes, and others working on the case." He lowered his voice a bit. "Are you up for this?"

Samantha snorted. "I am so up for this." She finally turned away. Her tone did nothing to hide her desire for revenge. She could still feel Hunter watching her. Gabriel too. She knew they were concerned. They probably thought she was too emotionally involved. But she didn't care. There was too much at stake here. The fact that she'd been used, was still being used by that little pissant of a man was just one part of a whole shit storm of things that made her livid.

So was the kid part of a family involved in a terrorist cell or was he or she part of the flesh trade? The thought of either scenario had her stomach churning. He'd sounded so young and that cry was definitely one of pain. Was he sick or injured? Was he being abused? She jumped when Hunter enveloped her hand in his, linking his fingers with hers.

The warmth of his hand, the caress of his thumb, soothed her. It was as though he read her mind and knew how to ease her building anxiety. She closed her eyes. When had she let her guard down and fallen all the way? God, she loved him more than she thought she was capable of loving anyone. If he didn't love her back, she was going to break a little. Real damage that would take longer to heal than any bruise Tom had left on her body.

She squeezed his hand, shifted again, and frowned out the window. The road began to narrow and the homes became farther apart. They turned off onto a wooded dirt road. It wasn't long until the woods became denser, the road rougher. Finally they came to a stop. Logan got out and opened the door for them. Gabriel continued to watch in the rearview mirror.

Samantha got out of the car and stretched her arms up over her head to relieve the stiff ache in her shoulders. Out of the corner of her eye she saw Logan's appreciative gaze. Hunter didn't try to hide his scowl as he went to the back of the car and lifted her bag from the trunk. She lowered her arms and quickly pulled her shirt down, clearing her throat.

Logan's eyes were bright with humor. Samantha could tell he enjoyed pressing Hunter's buttons with his subtle flirting.

"Follow this road about five hundred feet then turn right onto an overgrown path. Take that path about three miles and you'll see a stick in the ground with a neon orange tie on it. Pull it up and turn there into the wooded area. Around the corner and almost on the edge of the cliff, you'll find the mouth of the cave," Logan said, as he got back into the patrol car. "Be sure and watch for it or you'll pass it right up." He smiled at Samantha and winked. She was sure of it this time. "Be careful. We'll be in touch."

Hunter nodded. "Thanks," he said blandly and began walking.

Samantha heard them backing up as she jogged to catch up with Hunter. They walked in silence until they came to the Jeep. It was painted camouflage green, black, and gray. It was fully loaded, indeed. They had night goggles, weapons, two-way radios, a sat phone, food, matches, lanterns . . . everything they could possibly need was there.

She climbed in next to Hunter.

"You good?" she asked, laying a hand on his forearm.

He looked at her as he turned the ignition. She felt a shiver slide up her spine. A mixture of heat and anger gathered there, then softened. He leaned over and kissed her lightly on the lips. "I'm good."

She kept quiet for most of the teeth-rattling way. She held on tight to the roll bar to keep from being thrown out.

"Maybe we should have taken this trip on horseback," she said after a particularly hard bump.

"Nah, still would have been a rough ride and slower," Hunter replied, not taking his eyes off the path. "The work it would take to brush down, feed, and water Buck and Shiloh while we're here would be counterproductive."

"Good point." She nodded, scanning the area. Up ahead she saw the marker. Logan was right; it was inconspicuous. Hunter noticed as well and slowed to a stop. Samantha hopped out and pulled it up, threw it in the back, then walked around the rest of the way.

The mouth of the cave was secluded, shielded by bushes and undergrowth. Hunter drove the Jeep as far into the brush as he could and secured it.

Hunter had to duck to enter the cave. Samantha didn't expect it to be as spacious inside as it was. It opened up into a cavern big enough for all their equipment and a fire if they needed one. Someone had already cleared it out and kindling was piled along one wall with a stack of firewood.

"This will be pretty comfortable." Hunter scanned the room then glanced at her. "Let's get the Jeep unloaded."

When they had everything they needed unloaded and set up in the cave, Hunter put the top up on the Jeep, and it seemed to dissolve into the foliage. Deeper inside the cave, lanterns sent shadows and low light dancing over the walls. It was cool, but not cool enough for a fire. The sun was going down, and Samantha was thankful for the bug repellent. She sat cross-legged on her thick bedroll, loading her pistol.

"Come here," Hunter said without turning. She pulled herself up and went to where he stood right outside the cave. He put his arm around her. "Look, down there is the rest stop. You see?"

"Yeah, pretty clear view." Even with the dim light, she could see the block building through the trees and the people walking back and forth from the building to the various cars, trucks, and campers. "Shouldn't be difficult to get what we need," she muttered.

"We have a video camera with infrared." Hunter nodded.

"Cool." Samantha grinned up at him. "A new toy! I get to use it."

Hunter chuckled and kissed her nose. "We'll see."

She scowled at him. "Oh yeah. You'll see." She looked back down at the rest stop. "What about Tom? Will he be showing up here?"

"I doubt it." She felt him watching her now. Her body so easily responded to his slightest touch. Like honey, arousal spread warmth through her as his hand moved down over her hip and up again, but she tried to ignore it. "Sam."

Conflicting emotions swirled in her stomach as she kept her eyes on the rest stop. Hunter turned to stand in front of her, blocking her view. He lifted her chin and waited till she met his gaze. What she thought she saw in his eyes made her breath hitch. Or was she seeing what she wanted to see?

Before she could decide, his mouth closed over hers, his tongue stroking hers, tasting her kiss. Desire erupted inside her like a flash fire as he pulled her close, his hands holding her body tightly against his. Her nipples tightened against his chest, his thigh moved between hers, and she swallowed his groan. His hands moved over her ass, kneading, lifting her against his hard thigh, then his bulging erection.

"Hunter. We need to be watching." Her words were a moan whispered against his mouth as she threaded her fingers through his hair. "On guard."

"It's early yet. Nothing will happen for hours," he murmured as he nibbled along her jawline, her earlobe, her neck. "Baby, I have to taste you, feel you now. I won't get another chance later." Her body was vibrating with need. Liquid heat flooded her sensitive folds; her vagina clenched, aching to be filled with him. Only him.

chapter twenty

Hunter's mouth devoured hers, his head tilted, his tongue licking then delving past her lips, her teeth, to stroke the delicate interior. He sipped at her tongue and nibbled at her lips as he walked her backward, until she found herself wedged between the rough, cool stone and the searing heat of Hunter's solid body. The provocative way he moved against her, causing the lacy cups of her bra to abrade her erect nipples, heightened her arousal.

He leaned away from her body, but only enough to touch her face, to caress the rounded sides of her breasts. They felt as though they were swelling, filling his big hands with her heated flesh. His thumbs teased her nipples, and she squirmed as his hand moved lower, slowly, as though he loved the feel of her stomach, her navel, flooding her senses with every erotic touch. With a flick of his wrist, he unbuttoned her jeans, his fingers slipped in and trailed lower, just above the elastic band of her panties. Gently, lightly, he stroked her there, she felt like she was going up in flames.

His hand slid inside her panties to the curls covering her mound, and over the pouting lips of her sex. Slowly he traced the crevice between. She tilted her hips and spread her legs wantonly, allowing him better access as he drew her juices over her swelling flesh. His mouth muted her cries as his fingers eased between her slick folds. She ground her hips against his hand as his tongue moved inside her mouth, mimicking the way his fingers stroked her saturated pussy.

Her breath was coming in pants as she clutched at his shoulders. She wrapped a leg around his hip and pulled him closer as she rode his hand. A sound that was greedy and raw escaped his throat, and his hand became rough and hungry.

With his free hand, he shoved her shirt and bra up together, freeing her breasts. He growled, taking one taut peak inside his hot mouth. His tongue flicked over it, and she grit her teeth and swallowed her scream. His finger plunged inside her, stroking her as the arousal flowing from her gripping flesh flooded his hand. Her mind was fuzzy, her whole focus on the building tension growing, throbbing within her. She cried out, unable to stop herself. He was taking her to the edge and she was helpless.

"Shhh, baby," he whispered hoarsely against her throbbing lips.

"I can't," she whimpered, licking her swollen lips as she tore at his shirt. She wasn't sure how she got his shirt off and she didn't care. She loved this man; she wanted this man like she'd never wanted anyone. She was voracious. Her need, her desire was like a wild, hot current running along every nerve.

He jerked her against him, his mouth covering hers as he took her over the edge. Samantha bucked in his arms, her breath caught as pleasure consumed her. He swallowed her moans with his hungry kisses.

It took a moment for the pulses of her orgasm to soften enough to free her mind. Her nails bit into the warm, smooth skin of his bicep. It bulged under her palm as he continued to stroke her gently, not letting her pleasure completely fade. She licked and bit and sucked his neck. Her blood was raging through her veins, demanding more of him. She needed to feel him inside her.

Her hands slid down his chest, unfastened his jeans and freed him. His hot, rock-hard cock filled her hand. God, she loved how his throbbing cock felt in her hand, in her mouth, in her pussy. She kissed him, sucked his bottom lip as her thumb smoothed over his velvety tip. She spread the drop of pre-cum as she explored. She stroked his ridged shaft, feeling the blood pulse through the prominent veins. "Fuck me, Hunter," she whimpered breathlessly in his ear.

He yanked the shirt and bra over her head and threw it aside. She opened her eyes and met his dark gaze. "God, you're making me crazy," he snarled low before possessing her mouth again. She cried into his mouth as he shoved her pants down.

Her world tilted, and she found herself lying on the bedroll. He held her effortlessly, as though she were weightless. He pulled her jeans off with a single tug. She lay there, overheated, naked, watching him as he stepped out of his own jeans and knelt between her legs. His strength and the power of his lust for her had her trembling in anticipation.

He grasped her hips and pulled her forward, and she rose up, straddling him as she wrapped her arms around his neck. His cock nestled between the sopping, engorged lips of her pussy and she gasped. His hands caressed her ass, slowly moving her back and forth. He let the round, swollen head glide against her throbbing clit.

Samantha kissed him frantically, moaning into his mouth. He groaned and cupped her breast, weighing and kneading it as his mouth moved down, nibbling her collarbone, his tongue firmly stroking her other breast. She arched her back as his teeth grazed her nipple, sending her spiraling out of control. She clutched at him, panting as her head fell back.

His hand fisted in her hair and he pulled her to him. She clung to him as the waves of sensation swelled, pushing her toward climax again. He lifted her then, impaling her onto his thick shaft. His mouth covered hers, swallowing her screams as a second orgasm seized her. Helplessly captive to the pounding surge of pleasure, her body trembled from the force of it. Her rippling flesh clutched at his invading cock.

"You feel so good, Sam," Hunter groaned, moving inside her. "So hot and wet."

She pressed against him and rode. Her body, coated with sweat, slid against him. Every brush of her erect nipples against his chest sent new spirals of pleasure surging through her, coiling tighter and tighter, building again. "Harder, Hunter," she croaked.

"Yeah, baby. Wrap your legs around me." He held her

hips still while she leaned back, bracing her body on her arms, her hands fisted in the padded bedroll. "Tighter, hold on tighter." She tried to catch her breath as she did as he instructed, locking her ankles behind his back.

Hunter supported her shoulders, neck, and head with one arm. The other supported her back as he slammed into her. Hard. Every thrust sent mind-numbing pleasure thundering through her. The sound of their labored breathing, the slapping of wet flesh against wet flesh, intensified her need.

She clenched her thighs around him, arching, thrusting upward, taking all of him. She heard the small cries that came from her; they sounded far away. She bit her lip in an effort to keep quiet as she tightened the walls of her sheath around him, intensifying the friction as he withdrew and drove into her again. She was focused only on Hunter, the pleasure that engulfed her, the pleasure that she was giving him.

Another climax shattered, like a million tiny shards of intense sensation. She rose up, clutching at his arms. Her breath caught in her throat and she struggled not to cry out. Hunter plunged deeper and deeper, touching her womb. Samantha couldn't distinguish between the pain and the pleasure. It was all so good.

Her vagina contracted again and again, her slick cream flowing from her with every climax, coating her thighs, his thrusting shaft, his balls as they slapped against her. The ripples of ecstasy she thought were fading swelled and grew and washed over her again. She thought she might die, and she didn't give a damn. Her heart pounded, her body flooded with pulses of pleasure.

Hunter bared his teeth as he surged inside her again, then once more. His gaze locked with hers. He groaned, his hot cum filling her. Her gripping vagina captured him, milking him.

He lifted her body and held her close. "My Sam," he murmured as he changed positions and laid back, her body draping over him, his semi-rigid cock still inside her. She closed her eyes, nuzzling his chest. She felt sated, limp, and so in love, shuddering as aftershocks vibrated through her. If he only knew how much hope she put in those two words.

For a moment she lay still, giving her body time to cool, her breathing to even out. Hunter ran a hand over her hair and kissed her forehead. It was such a tender thing to do, so intimate. She knew he cared, and for now that was enough. She kissed his chest; her tongue caressed his flat, brown nipple. She smiled at his sharp intake of breath, felt the pulses of blood pumping into his shaft, making him swell and lengthen inside her again.

He closed his eyes on a groan and lifted his hips, pushing himself deeper. She rose over him, her hands splayed on his chest, bracing herself above him. He opened his eyes and met her gaze. She moved slowly, pulling away and taking him in again. She flexed the muscled walls of her vagina as she sheathed him, and his lids lowered over stormy gray eyes.

His hands gripped her hips. Hard, rigid muscle rippled under her fingers as they circled his nipples and skimmed over his sweat-dampened body. "You feel so good." She moaned, riding him with achingly slow strokes, his cock like steel, stretching and filling her. His hands cupped her heaving breasts, his thumbs grazing her stiff aching nipples. She groaned as she picked up the pace.

His hand moved down her stomach and glided through the wet thatch of curls to the top of her pussy. He found her clit and rubbed, circled it, as she rotated her hips, grinding against him. She whimpered as his cock pressed against her G-spot. Her head fell forward, letting her long hair trail over his chest.

"Oh yeah, that's good." He grasped her hips again, his fingers biting into her flesh as he arched his hips to meet her circling thrusts.

She spread her legs wider and arched her back, bouncing harder and faster. She fought to contain the small, breathy cries that came from deep inside her as long, violent waves of sensation crashed over her. Her body trembled, bathed in a gripping euphoria. The expression on Hunter's face mesmerized her. She watched the passion darken his eyes. His hooded gaze held hers as he bared his teeth and took control, changing positions with her, carefully turning her onto her stomach without leaving her body.

His knees were between hers, pressing her thighs farther apart. His arm banded around her stomach as he surged into her with deep soul-shaking thrusts that had her gripping the bedroll in her fists. She didn't think she could come anymore; she wasn't sure she could stand the intensity but she didn't want it to end. Her pussy was tender, her clit ached with sharp pleasure every time his balls struck her swollen flesh. A low, needy whimper left her throat as the overwhelming and incredible sensation tore through her. Her name was a groan as Hunter climaxed, filling her with hot cream.

Exhausted, they collapsed together; he lay on his side, pulling her against him, sweeping the damp curls away from her face and neck. He kissed her cheek, her neck. "You're so soft, baby, so sweet." He nibbled and licked at the tender skin behind her ear. "I'll never get enough of you. The way you feel, the way you taste." Her stomach quivered as his hand splayed over her soft skin. "But, I'll let you have a few minutes to recuperate."

Samantha breathed deeply and turned in his arms. She smiled and touched his face. "That's good. I'm afraid I'll need more than a few minutes."

She felt his lips curve against hers. "Yeah, I'm not gonna lie. Me too." He chuckled softly.

chapter twenty-one

It was like she stepped into a fantasy world. Fireflies twinkled everywhere like fairy lights. The soft, sultry breeze carried the scent of honeysuckle and pine. The melodic sound of the gentle mountain stream as it flowed down over the slick rocks was soothing.

Hunter stood waist-deep in the deeper part of the water, watching her from under lowered lids, a roguish grin curving those wonderfully firm lips. Shadows made him look mysterious, dangerous, exotic, like a mystic king enticing an innocent virgin to sacrifice her purity to please him.

Standing naked on the bank of the creek, her arms wrapped around her stomach, Samantha shuddered at the thought, and then smirked. She was the furthest thing from virginal, but she wasn't immune to his seduction. He was too damn enticing to resist. He quickly sank into the swirling water and emerged again with a splash, smoothing his hair back, the water sluicing off the hard planes of his body.

He caught her gaze again.

"You look incredible standing there like that." His voice lowered to a growl. "An incredibly sexy little pixie."

Samantha grinned. "Pest, Pixie *Pest*. Remember?"

"Nah, pest isn't the right word anymore. You're trouble, no doubt about that. There's a whole lot of fire and spark in that tight little body." He sucked in air through his teeth. "C'mere. I need to touch you."

"Again?" Jesus, the man was a sex machine.

Not that she was complaining.

"Hell yes, again." His grin broadened as he walked toward her. "And again, and again . . ."

Samantha watched Hunter's muscles bunch and ripple as he moved toward her. He made her mouth water. Indeed, his cock was heavy and erect, glistening in the waning light. She should back up, she told herself. But her gaze was locked with his, and something held her in place. Her body swayed with the impact of his desire for her. Even in the dusky light she could see it there, plain in his eyes.

He took her hand and helped her step down into the stream. He led her to several large smooth stones. The brisk, clear water rushed over them faster there and didn't rise much over her ankle.

He lowered himself onto a wide, flat stone, careful not to slip.

"Here, sit here," he said, spreading his legs, his shaft bobbing against the current.

"Sit?" she asked wide-eyed with a crooked smile.

"Yes, Sam, turn around and sit. The cool water will feel good," he suggested.

Samantha lifted her brows and shrugged. She really was tender, but she was still aroused, her flesh still slick and tingling, her nipples tight and aching. She turned and his hands circled her waist, holding her, as she eased herself between his legs. He pulled her back against his chest and pushed her knees apart. The water was just cool enough, flowing gently over her swollen flesh, her throbbing clit, washing away her soreness, but it did nothing to alleviate the heat of her arousal.

"Oh, yeah. This does feel nice." She moaned, spreading her knees farther apart.

Hunter cupped the cool water into his hands and let it spill over her chest, over her breasts. Her nipples contracted into hard tips. His hands covered them, warming them as he massaged her. His substantial arousal pulsed against the small of her back. She leaned her head back on his shoulder, inviting him to kiss her. She licked his full lower lip and his tongue darted out to meet hers. She sighed as she sucked it gently, her lips pressing against his. His hands plucked at her nipples, electrifying her senses. Her blood pounded in her ears.

"We've got to get back, Hunter," she whispered hoarsely.

He sighed deeply and kissed her neck. "I hate it that you're right." He arched his hips against her. "I want to fuck you all night." His voice was raw with mounting hunger.

Samantha stood and looked down at him. He'd make a great *Playgirl* centerfold, she thought. She felt his eyes on her as she carefully stepped over the rocks to where the water was a bit deeper to rinse away the dry, salty sweat from her skin. When she turned to walk back, she saw Hunter standing on the bank, leaning against a wide oak with his legs crossed, still watching her. The way he looked at her took her breath away. He made her feel incredibly desirable and wanted.

Samantha's lips curved into a smile as she stepped onto the bank and walked toward him. Naked and unashamed, he stood unmoving, his cock fully erect, his eyes filled with erotic promise.

"You ready to go back?" he asked as he rubbed her arms, soothing away the goose bumps the cool breeze had caused.

Taking his face in her hands, she touched her lips to his, lingering for a moment. "Not yet," she murmured. She craved his pleasure as much as her own, and she wanted to make him feel that the way he made her feel it. His brow furrowed as he searched her face, and she kissed his lips once more before she began trailing kisses down his body.

He held his breath and uncrossed his legs. "Sam." He groaned as her tongue circled his navel and moved lower. She knelt in front of him and grasped his thick erection with both hands. She gazed up at him as she took the broad tip between her lips and tasted the pearl of pre-cum that had welled up there. Her lips opened, allowing the bulging head to glide into her mouth. She ran her tongue along his frenulum and sucked gently, as her fingers moved lightly over his shaft. He grasped her head, his fingers weaving through her hair. "Oh God." His voice cracked just a little.

Her lips drew him in, sucking him deeper inside her mouth as her tongue stroked the pulsing underside. She loved the heat, the way he throbbed against her tongue, the salty sweet taste of him.

The sound of his labored breathing, his fingers flexing in her hair urged her to suck him harder. Her own body responded, warm and slick, gathering in the sensitive folds of her pussy as she brought him closer to the edge. One hand closed over the base of his cock, the other cupped his balls, and she gently massaged the delicate flesh.

She withdrew and sucked him in again. He groaned, pulling her closer, sinking deeper into her mouth. She felt the hot throbbing head of his cock against the back of her throat and swallowed, taking him as deeply as she could.

"Ah fuck," he growled. "My Sam."

She felt his balls tighten, his body go rigid, as he thrust into her mouth. Her tongue stroked, her mouth pulled on him longer and harder. He threw his head back with a strangled cry as his seed shot into her mouth in long, hot bursts. She swallowed him, taking all he had to give. She watched his cock jerk and licked the last drop from the darkened tip. A satisfied smile curved her lips as looked up at him.

He pulled her off her knees and into his arms. "You're so damn good, Sam," he murmured, his breathing still labored. His mouth covered hers, melting her bones, curling her toes. Sighing, he buried his face in her hair and nuzzled her neck.

She held him tight, never wanting to leave that spot, but they had to. Night had fallen and she needed to focus on the job ahead of them now and not on Hunter's hands, or his mouth or his cock. Dammit. Carefully, they made their way back to the cave in the dark. If she was going to keep her mind on her work, she was going to have to keep him at arm's length.

They decided to watch the rest stop in shifts. Samantha took the first watch while Hunter slept close by. He woke around three and took over while she slept. She slept pretty well, considering. She grinned, thinking it was probably the workout that helped. She woke around eight and yawned.

"Hey, see anything?" she asked, stretching.

Hunter looked over at her and winked. "Mornin', gorgeous. No, not yet. Got a call from Gabriel, though."

"I didn't hear the phone," she said, pulling on a clean pair of socks and hiking boots.

Hunter lifted the binoculars and turned his attention back to the rest stop. "It's on vibrate."

"Ah," she said. "So?"

"So, he said they expected activity today. Possibly this afternoon." His expression turned serious.

"Good. Do you think I have time to walk back down to the creek?" she asked. "Girl stuff," she added when he gave her a questioning glance.

Hunter thought a minute. "Okay, but don't take long, and take your gun."

"All right." She strapped her pistol to her hip and headed out.

The rough path that led around the foot of a mountain to the stream looked a bit different in the light of day, Samantha thought. When the path widened and the cover of trees thinned out, she veered off to the side of the path, careful to stay in the shadows.

She had just reached the clearing when the rumble of a chopper overhead alerted her and had her ducking for cover. She glanced up to see it pass over and hover just as an arm grabbed her around the waist and yanked her farther into the undergrowth, under a thick bush.

"Stay down, Sam." Hunter's voice was a hiss in her ear.

"I'm down," she groused back. "Why did you follow me?"

"I didn't follow you. I heard the chopper."

"How?"

"I was Special Forces, Sam." There was an edge to his voice. "I also did two tours."

No further explanation was necessary.

She recalled the conversation she'd had with Clara Abernathy. She figured that if he wanted to tell her about Kelly and his time in the military, he would. She wouldn't ask him. Now definitely wasn't the time to bring it up anyway.

"Well, I guess you're a man of many talents," she said flatly.

He lifted a brow. "You would know."

She narrowed her eyes and chose to focus on the situation at hand.

"It was heading that way." She stood, pointing toward the mountain peak as she brushed the twigs and pine needles from her knees. "Probably landed somewhere up on the mountain, don't you think?"

He nodded, listening intently and watching her. "Let's go."

chapter twenty-two

There were few things in the world as beautiful to Hunter as the California Mountains, especially those in Butte County, "Land of Natural Wealth and Beauty." Lush valleys, clear rushing creeks, and steep rugged cliffs had always fascinated him. The sense of history and continuity kept him grounded, reminded him daily why he had joined the army, why he had fought in the Middle East, why he had taken the post as sheriff in the small town.

Because some things were just worth fighting for. His uncle's murder had shaken his world, had left him questioning values and beliefs that had sustained him all his life. He questioned them because he knew the killer or killers were close to home. Men he had been raised with, had fished with and socialized with. Not exactly friends or men he would trust in a bind, but people he knew.

Deerhaven was a small, intimate community. He

knew about Miss Eunice, the elderly spinster who ordered her adult toys on a regular basis, and her widower neighbor, Charlie Beckett, who watched through the window on scheduled nights of usage. He knew about Tommy Austin and how he thought it'd be a good idea to whip his wife for sassing him one night on a drinking binge. He'd ended up with a goose egg and a mild concussion before he could follow through. She had been her baseball team's heavy hitter three years in a row. Tommy never drank again.

And there were the parties out by the lake, and the regulars he could count on to keep things calm and safe there. The ones he was confident were likely to cause trouble. He knew everyone in the small town, had grown up with them in some form or another, and realizing that several of them were capable of hurting children, capable of treason, of murdering their neighbors in cold blood, it had hit him hard. He had always had a decided innocence where his little county was concerned.

Realizing that one of them could commit murder and still function normally had been a bitter pill to swallow, but that was just the tip of the iceberg.

Naïve . . . He admitted in some ways he had been. His training should have done away with that naïveté long ago. He knew the things men would do for money, for war, just for the hell of it. But seeing it so close to home had ripped away any sense of innocence he may have held on to.

Realizing how corrupt Henderson was had perhaps been the first step. The man was rabid, like a coyote stalking, slinking around in the dark, just waiting to rip

ut the throat of anyone opposing him. And that in-
luded Hunter and Sam.

"Henderson has an old hunting cabin up here somewhere," Hunter said quietly as they pushed farther up
he mountain. "I gave Gabriel the general location as I
emembered it, but from the sound of the helicopter, I
ould have been a few miles off."

He frowned, trying to place the exact location. It had
een years since he had been through this particular
rea. He had been little more than a teenager, and he and
is friends had been more interested in fishing the re-
note ponds than they were in Old Man Henderson's
ricey little shack.

"You think he's hiding them there then?" Sam asked
s she moved close behind him.

"Seems reasonable, but I'm thinking it's probably
nore like a place to conduct business safely. Kinda like
acob's place, only a lot less secure." He grunted, angry
ith himself for his inability to remember the exact
ocation. "The helicopter landed on the other side of
is hill, which is about five miles from the location I
ave Gabriel."

The sat phone he carried helped keep everyone
breast of their location. It would also be some help if
nings went bad. The problem was that often things went
ad entirely too fast. In this situation, he knew that the
angers they faced could be more than either of them
nticipated. He trusted Sam, though. She was smart and
trong. Staying put wasn't an option, anyway. It was
neir job to check this out.

The terrorist element had him most concerned. It was

a very real threat, one that was more prevalent in the US than people realized. His contacts within the armed forces and friends who had served in the Middle East since September 11 reported the growing danger in America, Mexico, and Canada. The investigation into the possible terrorist cells traveling through Deerhaven and other counties was coming to a head. The situation was volatile.

"Hunter, you didn't answer me," Sam hissed, as they wound their way up the mountain, growing steadily closer to the area he believed the helicopter had landed.

"I know he's got something going on up there." Hunter sighed, bitterly aware of the fact that he had dropped the ball on this one. He should have checked the cabin months ago. "If he's hiding someone, it's members of the terrorist cells." He rubbed a hand over his face. "It's all connected, but the people he's helping move for the flesh peddlers are merchandise. They would be run through the cave system. Henderson wouldn't have any regard for them as human."

"Good point." Rage vibrated in those two words.

Henderson wasn't away from town much; he'd never seemed to be a nature lover, so it had never occurred to Hunter to stake out the cabin, or to have Jacob do it. The location of activity so far had been confined away from the cabin, so he hadn't suspected it. Which wasn't a good enough excuse, as far as he was concerned. He'd missed it. Failing wasn't an option. A sheriff had too many lives in his hands and one slip up could cost dearly. That was exactly what plagued him from the moment he was appointed to the post.

"The cabin is a perfect location," he continued, as

they rounded a stand of shoulder-high boulders that looked like sentinels standing watch over the forested valley below. "There's a rough track that leads right into there about a mile from the rest area. It's secluded and not well known. As far as anyone knows, Henderson sold the damned place years ago. The reason I know different is because I happened on it while doing a search of property taxes on Uncle Zachariah's place after his death."

He stopped on the other side of the boulders, leaning against one as he watched Sam lower herself onto a long, flat boulder nearer the ground. Her breasts were heaving beneath the soft material of her tank top, perspiration glistening on her upper chest and neck.

Tendrils of golden brown had fallen from her ponytail and lay along her graceful neck, tempting him to reach out to smooth them back. He wasn't about to touch her. The woman was more enticing than was reasonably safe in the best of circumstances.

"So what next?" She frowned up at him, watching him cautiously.

Hunter sighed. "We're gonna check it out. If nothing else, we'll have verified proof that someone is there, which will give our federal friends a little more leeway in their investigation."

"What about the kid?" she asked him softly.

Worry darkened her eyes and lent a regretful sadness to her expression.

"Sam, the kid is safer than you at the moment." The child weighed on her mind, he knew. "There's a unit working on that right now."

She lowered her head, nodding in acceptance of the

answer. That kid had worried her since the day of the accident. Hunter understood why, and he prayed they'd find him. If they didn't find that kid, he wasn't sure Sam would get over it.

"Come on, let's get moving. I want to get off this mountain by nightfall and let Gabriel know what the hell is going on."

chapter twenty-three

"We're fucked," Hunter breathed out silently, as they watched the cabin from behind a smaller stand of boulders than what he liked.

Lying flat on their stomachs, he and Sam had crawled as close as they dared to observe the activity going on around the large hunting shack. There had to be a dozen men, armed militants, milling around, unloading the helicopter that had brought in either more inhabitants or more supplies.

There was Henderson, by God, in the thick of it, shouting out orders. Rodgers and Decker were there as well, surveying the activity going on around them. Hunter narrowed his eyes, paying attention to the armed men rather than those he already knew. He felt fear strike his heart as he recognized several of them.

The terrorists' faces were flashed across every police bulletin going through the nation the year before.

Updates were sent through regularly, and he knew priority had been given to capturing several of them.

"Shit." Evidently, Sam had realized the danger involved here as well. He could hear the thread of worry in her voice and cursed the moment he had decided to venture up the mountain.

He had left Gabriel and Logan a message, so they weren't without recourse. But dammit, the other men wouldn't think to check on them until nightfall. Hunter had assured them that he and Sam could handle this scouting mission. Information gathering mostly. They were supposed to be their eyes.

"Time to get the hell out of here," he muttered, motioning her back. "Stay down, Sam. Keep behind the boulders until we get back over the edge, then we'll run for it."

They inched back, heading for the small ledge they had worked their way around earlier to get into position to see the cabin. The area they had come through was heavily sheltered, with numerous stands of boulders and large rocks as well as a thick undergrowth. He prayed it would keep them hidden from the men who were no doubt watching for a nosy hunter, or a dumb sheriff. If they were caught, they would die. It was that simple.

Hunter knew Sam was more than aware of this. The merciless intent of the terrorists had been displayed on many occasions. Many of the men now hiding on this mountain had been linked to the planning and details of recent terrorist attacks.

"Hunter, this is bad," Sam whispered, as they worked their way slowly back along the hard ground. "There's too many there. How the hell do they intend to get them out without being seen?"

"Same way they got them in," he growled. "A few at a time, or in campers or RVs. They're smart and they're dangerous. A deadly combination, baby."

Hunter glanced back, seeing the ledge as it came nearer. They were almost home free. If they could get past that without being sighted, then they had a chance of making it off the small mountain and back to relative safety.

They were inches from success when the first shot was fired. The bullet barely missed Hunter's head, burying in the trunk of the tree beside him instead.

"Fuck! Run!" Hunter screamed out at Sam, terror thudding hard and fast through his bloodstream as a stream of Arabic began to echo through the mountain.

He heard Sam curse, but as he jumped to his feet and cleared the ledge, he saw she was already running. He knew the bastards back at the cabin were running too. Running with semi-automatic weapons that could easily take Sam and him out with a properly placed bullet.

"Stay close to the trees!" he yelled as he came up on her, covering her from behind. "Keep your head low."

Goddam it, he cursed silently as he spared a quick look back to see several of the terrorists top the ledge and come over it flying.

"Run, Sam!" He pushed her harder, knowing their chances of outrunning the bastards were slim to none, and their weapons hopelessly inferior. It was damned hard to battle automatic rifles with the standard issue police pistol.

Gunfire began to fill the silence of the mountains. Hunter jerked his revolver from its holster, firing back wildly, hoping, if nothing else, to force them to lose any proper aim they had on them. Bullets buried in the trees, ricocheted off boulders, and kept them zigzagging, dodging the gunfire as they fought to escape to the relative safety of the vehicle at the bottom of the mountains. God, he had to get Sam out of there.

"Run faster, baby!" he screamed out at her as he glanced back. There had to be half a dozen of those bastards coming down the mountain after them and even more behind them.

The air filled with the sound of gunfire, angry voices, and the thunder of his own heart. He pushed Sam harder, screaming at her, urging her to run harder, faster, to get to the safety the caves would afford them. If nothing else, there was communication there, the vehicle. They would have a fighting chance.

He glanced back again, his heart filling his throat as he saw the two men kneeling, raising their rifles.

"The trees," he screamed, jerking Sam forward then coming to a halt and slamming her to the ground as a crazed figure rose up in front of them.

He covered Sam's body, staring up at Jacob in amazement as he stood over them, the M16 in his hand spewing out cartridges like a summer storm spills its raindrops.

"Get!" Jacob didn't spare them a glance as he screamed the word.

Hunter jerked Sam to her feet and pushed her back to a dead run. They were nearly there. With Jacob's help and the damned canon-sized weapon he was carrying, they at least had a chance now.

"Get to the Jeep!" he screamed at Sam. "If we're not in it with you, then get the fuck out of here."

"Like hell!" she yelled back, breathless with fear and flight as they tore from the mountain.

"Keep her running!" Jacob called out behind them. "We have more coming. Let's get the hell out of here."

"Fuck. Fuck." Hunter pushed harder, hope filling him as they broke the line of trees. "Jeep."

They ran for it as Hunter grabbed the keys from his pocket. It was the last thing he knew. He heard Sam scream, but as he fought the darkness overcoming him, he prayed that if this was his last breath, then Jacob could protect her.

chapter twenty-four

Thank God for Rambo, wherever the hell he came from, Samantha thought as she ran. Almost there, almost there, she looked back and saw Hunter and Rambo go down. "Hunter!" she screamed. For just a moment she thought her heart stopped. She started toward them when a hand seized her arm and spun her around.

"Where you going in such a hurry, Samantha?" Tom said with a sneer.

She had no time to think, running on pure emotion and adrenaline. She struck out with her free hand. He caught her and held her against him in an iron grip. Tom had always been ridiculously strong. She stiffened, twisting against his hold. She distracted him enough to stomp on his instep. He grimaced and cursed but held her firm. His fingers dug into her flesh, and he shook her hard, rattling her teeth.

"You bastard, you fucking bastard," she snarled and kicked out. Her knee missed his groin by an inch.

"Stop," Tom yelled.

"Like hell." She grunted as he jerked her against him again. She looked up, surprised to find he wasn't talking to her. She turned and saw two men standing over Hunter and Rambo, guns aimed at their heads.

Panic rose in her and she fought.

"No." The word screamed in her brain, though it escaped her dry throat as a plea. Tom's grip was unyielding as he squeezed her arms harder; she winced but didn't take her eyes from Hunter.

"Don't worry, love. I want him alive." He lowered his head and ran his tongue over her ear. "For now."

The caress made her blood boil, and her stomach clench. She wanted to recoil in disgust. Instead, she turned her head quick and bit his cheek as hard as she could. She tasted his blood and spat onto the ground. He yelped and pulled away from her. She used the moment to wrench free. She made a mad dash for the gun she knew was in the Jeep, only to be caught by Decker and Rodgers, the two idiots. She twisted futilely against their hold.

Tom stalked toward her. His hand touched his face, and then he looked at the blood on his fingers. She saw the rage in his icy glare.

She knew she was outnumbered, but she'd be damned if she'd give in or make it easy for them. "Go to hell, you son of a bitch."

Fury flashed in his eyes. He stood over her, fisted his hand in her hair and yanked her head back, his nose touching hers.

"You will always belong to me!" he screamed, his body shaking with rage. Suddenly he went still and calm.

"Did you really think I'd stand by and do nothing while you whored yourself out to this redneck trash?"

Samantha glared at him, refusing to look away. "I will never belong to you." She pushed the words through her clenched teeth.

He slapped her hard. Her head snapped back. He waited till she turned back to him. His breath was soughing in and out of his lungs, but his voice stayed eerily calm.

"You do. And now that hillbilly sheep fucker is going to see. He's going to see that you are mine, and then he'll die knowing."

"He knows better." Samantha kept unflinching eye contact.

Her teeth marks were plain to see in the drying blood on his cheek. A sinister smile slowly curved his lips. She wondered why she hadn't see this side of him in the beginning, or at least at some point. He was insane. What had ever made her think she could care for this man? Rodgers and Decker were chuckling, standing too close, their fingers digging into her arms, rubbing against the outside swell of her breasts.

"Those trees over there will be perfect for what I have in mind." Tom gestured with a nod of his head. "Tie them up," he said to the armed men.

They hesitated for a moment. One spoke up, his heavily accented words were terse with irritation. "Why are we wasting our time with this bullshit? Kill them. There's too much to do to prepare . . ."

"Do it!" Tom interrupted. "Make sure the sheriff has a good view."

The armed men grudgingly went about doing as instructed.

Rodgers and Decker dragged Samantha to the place where Tom had directed them. He sauntered up to her with the rope from the Jeep, watching the men tie Hunter and Rambo to a tree not far from them. That same smile was still fixed on his face as Tom stepped closer. With a pocketknife, he cut the long rope into three shorter pieces. Samantha struggled, twisting her body, tugging her arms.

"Damn, bitch. Be still!" Rodgers spat.

Tom rolled his eyes at Rodgers as he knelt down and tied a length of rope to her ankles. He backed up on his haunches, measuring distances by sight then motioned for them to bring her forward.

He stood, pulling the ropes, and her feet came out from under her. Rodgers and Decker dropped her. The breath whooshed from her lugs as her back hit the hard-packed dirt. Decker planted his booted foot on her chest. She fought for breath as Rodgers knelt quickly and grabbed her arms, jerking them over her head. He tied them together while Tom gazed down at her as though he was studying her. He motioned for the armed men to come forward. "Grab a leg."

One of the men unwrapped the rope from her ankles then each man took a leg. Realization struck her like an anvil to the chest. She kicked and bucked, but Tom just laughed as the men spread her legs wide and tied them down.

"What the hell?" Henderson was out of breath and sweating like the pig he was as he came upon the scene, taking in what was happening. "Have you lost your fuckin' mind, Novak? Just kill 'em and be done with it."

Tom scowled at the man. "I'll handle this the way I see fit. If you can't stomach it, then take the men and go back to the cabin."

They glared at each other for a tense moment, until finally Henderson waved a hand. "Fuck it. Do what ya want. The nosy little bitch and her fuck buddy had it comin'." Henderson turned and motioned for the men to follow.

The tiny sliver of hope Samantha had faded away. Tom knelt between her legs and began cutting her clothes from her body. She grit her teeth, pulling against the ropes that dug into her wrists and ankles. Her stressed joints burned as she bucked and jerked. Samantha knew what was going to happen. She refused to think about the fact that Rodgers and Decker stood to the side, their arms crossed, their eyes glassy, waiting for the show.

She shuddered with revulsion as she watched Tom. His hands roamed over her, cutting away her shirt, her bra. She held her breath as the knife lightly circled her nipple. Hating that they involuntarily tightened from the shock of the cold metal, she swallowed the knot of fear and anger that rose inside her, threatening to choke her. He sat back and let his gaze travel over her naked body hungrily, predatorily.

"Wake him up," he said with a grin.

She wanted to cringe but she didn't. She faced him, hated him with everything in her for what he was about to do to her, to Hunter, to their relationship. She'd feed on that hate. Tom's hand replaced the knife, trailing over her breast. He squeezed. Her stomach lurched and she swallowed.

"You disgust me," she snarled.

His gaze locked with hers, his features contorting as his fist plowed into her jaw. Pain flashed through her skull as her head bounced off the ground. Breathing deeply through her nose, she tried to resist the need to puke. Glaring at him, she worked her jaw to assure herself that it was still intact. An ominous growl reached her ears, and she knew it came from Hunter.

"You stupid whore," Tom grunted. He turned, facing Hunter. Samantha clenched her teeth as Tom shoved his fingers inside her, sending sharp pain radiating through her. "This is my cunt. I'm taking it back. You're going to watch," he snarled and began unbuckling his pants.

She turned her head then. Hunter was watching her, his gaze locking with hers. Fury reflected in his hard, cold eyes. He strained against the ropes binding him, his expression murderous. The muscle in his jaw jumped, the muscles and veins in his neck bulged.

If somehow they lived through this, it would never be the same. Once Tom raped her in front of him, Hunter wouldn't be able to get that out of his head. He'd never look at her the way he once had. She would be lost to him. The only man she had ever loved. No matter what Tom did to her, her heart, her mind, her soul would belong to Hunter. Only him. She couldn't help the tears that fell across the bridge of her nose. So many things she never said. "Hunter," she said, whispering his name.

chapter twenty-five

"No! Goddamn you, Novak!" Hunter screamed, every bone and muscle in his body rioting as agony flashed through his soul. Novak was daring to touch her. He would kill the son of the bitch; if he had to do it from the grave, he would kill him.

Sam. His Sam. God, why hadn't he told her he loved her, told her what she meant to him? He saw the tears slide along her bruised face as the bastard touched her. He felt his own tears searing his eyes. Fucking bastard, he was going to kill him. He would kill him with his bare hands. He fought the ropes at his wrists, refusing to watch what Tom was doing to her. He kept his eyes locked with Sam's trying to show her he loved her, to give her the strength he knew she would need to get through this.

God help him, he prayed. *Please God, don't let that bastard rape her.* He felt his skin breaking beneath the ropes, felt the warm sticky moisture of his own blood, but he couldn't stop, wouldn't stop. He had to get free, how could he let his happen? Sam would never survive such brutality.

Jacob had called in the highway patrol. Hunter knew that. How Jacob knew what the hell was going on, Hunter didn't know, but he knew help was coming. He just had to distract Novak, had to delay him.

"Novak, you don't want to do this!" he screamed out again as Sam flinched, her eyes dazed as Tom shoved his hand between her thighs.

Novak pulled his hand away and licked his fingers as he turned his head back to sneer at Hunter.

"She tastes good, doesn't she, Hunter?" he called out. "Our little Samantha gets so hot and wet. Does she beg you like she used to beg me?"

A red haze of rage went over Hunter at those words.

Sam mouthed the word "no," repeated it over and over, as though she needed to deny his claim.

"Only a weak, cowardly piece of shit forces a woman, Tom." He fought to hold the other man's attention. "You know Sam, man. She'll kill you when she gets free. And if she doesn't, then by God, I will."

"Samantha!" Novak screamed as he came to his feet. "Her name is Samantha, you stupid sheep fucker. She's not a pokey hick Sam."

"Then Samantha will kill you," he snarled bitterly. "Your ego is making an ass of you, Novak. She doesn't want you."

Novak glanced down at Sam's bound body, watching her struggle as Hunter fought to get free.

"Doesn't matter," he sneered. "She belongs to me. I'll take her anyway and you'll watch. Watch as I fuck her and as I kill her. And you'll die knowing I was the last man to have her. That I took back what belonged to me."

"No. Stop." Hunter's lips curled back from his teeth as Novak went to his knees again, his mouth latching onto the flesh between Sam's thighs as she screamed out in pain.

The sound tore through him like a thousand blades. Her eyes closed as she strained against the ropes, fighting like a demon, demented, unable to accept what was happening to her.

"I . . ." He started to tell her he loved her but he stopped. He couldn't tell her like this. She couldn't associate those words from his lips with this brutal assault. "Sam."

He kept struggling, fighting the ropes as terror lit a fury inside his soul that threatened to drive him insane. He screamed out Novak's name again, heaving against the ropes that restrained him like an enraged bull.

Then he heard the disgusted hiss behind him. "Shut the fuck up before they see me, you moron."

The unfamiliar female voice was filled with anger, as she tucked a gun into his hand. "Hang on, I'll cut you loose."

Hunter started praying. He watched in horror as Novak's mouth came away from Sam's thighs, a sneer on his lips as he rose to his feet, his hands going to the crotch of his pants to pull his penis free. Then he glanced at Hunter. The knife sliced through the rope as Novak's eyes widened.

Hunter wasted no time. With Sam's screams still echoing in his ears, he brought the gun around as he went to his knee and fired. He took out Novak and

Decker, each with a shot to the forehead, as four CHP vehicles screamed into the clearing. Then Rodgers fell as Jacob, freed by the same mystery woman, came out firing as well. Hunter swung around then for the three terrorists.

He shot low, taking out a knee, an ankle, but Jacob went for the heart. The third was dead before he hit the ground. Before he could think, Hunter was on his feet and running for Sam.

The woman who had cut him loose, obviously known to Jacob, was already cutting Sam loose and kicking Novak's lifeless body to the side.

"Sam." He caught her as she began scrambling hysterically away from Novak's body, her desperate sobs cutting into his heart as he jerked his T-shirt off and forced it over her head.

She fought him as he dressed her, strangled cries pouring from her throat as she begged him to let her wash. To let her clean Novak's touch from her body.

"It's okay, baby." He pulled her into his arms as the hysteria began to slowly ease. His arms tightened around her, rocking her as police officers poured into the area and an official helicopter flew low overhead.

"Hunter." She clutched at him then, burying her face against his chest as she shuddered in reaction. "I didn't. I never belonged to him." Her voice was hoarse, dazed and shocked, as her nails bit into the skin of his shoulders. She fought to get closer to him as his arms tightened around her, his body bending over her, sheltering her, holding her as close as possible.

"It's over, baby." His muscles were still taut as he fought his own reaction. He held her tighter, rocking her, holding her close, his eyes closing as emotion washed over him. Again the words "I love you, Sam" whispered through his brain, but he refused to say them. Not yet. "I've got you. Do you understand me, baby? I won't let you go. I've got you." He rocked her, whispered the strangled words in her ear, as he felt his own tears dampen his cheeks.

So close, he had come so close to losing her, and she hadn't even known that she held his heart and soul. He swore that as soon as he could, he'd tell her and he wouldn't let a day go by without making sure she knew how much he loved her.

Hell had erupted around them. Troopers were yelling orders back and forth, men cursing, screams filled the air as more sirens joined the melee going on around them. Hunter lifted Sam in his arms and carried her down the hill to the stream. There he held her as she washed, as she sobbed and fought to get past the terror she'd felt at a madman's hands.

She had known him, and though she hadn't loved him, hadn't liked him, she knew he was bad news. But she had never believed that such evil existed in him. That innocence had been stripped from her, and though Hunter knew she would survive it intact, she would never forget it.

Back in the cave, he helped her dress after drying her carefully, thankful that she was slowly calming down, the color coming back into her face. He carried her to the farthest corner of the cavern, allowing her the privacy she needed to come to grips with it.

Outside, Gabriel was calling his name, his voice fierce, imperative. There were reports to make and a briefing to get through, but Hunter hadn't observed the rules since taking office, and he figured now wasn't a hell of a good time to start. They would get what they needed when he got around to giving it to them.

"Hunter." Her voice, soft, husky from the tears she had shed earlier drew his attention to her.

He turned around on the crate he had been sitting on, watching as she came from the shadows of the back of the cave. She was dressed in jeans and his shirt. Her wet hair brushed back, her face no longer so pale. She walked into his arms.

Without hesitation, without the fear he had worried would be there, she came to him.

"I want to go home, Hunter," she whispered. "Take me home."

She sounded fierce, angry, his Sam. He listened to the commotion outside, thought again of all that needed to be done.

"We'll have to sneak away," he whispered with a smile of anticipation. "They're looking for us."

"Let 'em look." Her lips caressed his neck as her arms tightened around him.

epilogue

Samantha whimpered as she watched Hunter from lowered lids while he licked and sucked her toes. She never knew the nerves in her toes were directly connected to the nerves in her core. She sighed as his tongue moved to her ankle, her calf, the back of her knee. He paused there nibbling, sucking, driving her crazy.

His silver eyes glittered with naughtiness as his hands caressed her. He looked up at her through dark lashes. "Feel good?"

"Mm-hmm." She closed her eyes and submerged herself in Hunter, his scent, his touch.

He sucked at her inner thigh and she gasped, liquid arousal spreading through the sensitive folds of her pussy. She parted her legs for him, the short stubble on his cheeks rubbing against her swollen lips. Her blood heated as he kissed her there, his tongue delving inside, drawing her juices through the narrow slit. He paused and waited until she opened her eyes and met his gaze. "Tell me if you need me to stop, Sam."

"I don't want you to stop, Hunter. I want you to wash the bad away."

Without a word, he nestled himself between her thighs again and plunged his tongue inside her, drawing it up and over her clit. He stroked her, making her moan and writhe. Gently spreading her apart, his thumbs rubbed over the sensitive folds as he slid a finger inside, then another. She felt him firmly, slowly stroke her G-spot as his tongue circled and rasped over her swelling clit.

"Rub your breasts, baby. Rub those gorgeous nipples for me," Hunter mumbled, his voice vibrating against her cunt. "Damn, I wish I had more hands."

"Me too," she panted as she cupped her own breasts, rolling her nipples between her fingers.

He chuckled against her and added another finger. She groaned and arched her back, crying out at the sharp pleasure that fired through her. His long fingers stroked her more intently, sliding deep insider her then withdrawing slowly as he took her clit between his lips, sucked gently, giving it little flicks of his tongue.

"Oh God, Hunter," she groaned as he sucked harder. She bucked up as the climax slammed through her. He didn't stop until she collapsed in a panting heap.

He kissed his way up her body, pausing at her navel and her breasts. His mouth closed over one pert nipple. His hand molded the other breast, and she moaned as his thumb rasped over it. The ripples cascading over her didn't have a chance to subside before they grew again.

Hunter slid farther up her body, his mouth possessing her, muffling her moans as he entered her in one smooth stroke.

The weight of Hunter covering her body, pressing her into the soft mattress, felt more than wonderful. He kissed her bruised cheek, whispering sweet things in her ear. His hand supported her head as his hard body, slick with sweat, slid over hers, the length of his cock moving inside her with long, slow thrusts. With every stroke, waves of pleasure flowed over her, each one deeper, more powerful, pushing her toward another climax.

Samantha wrapped her legs around his and tilted her hips, taking him deeper, reveling in the power of his desire for her. Feeling his body tremble, the muscles in his back ripple as he struggled to take it slow, intensified her own passion. Her hands traveled downward to grip his tight ass, pulling him in deeper, arching her back more. She whimpered, not sure if she could take this pace much longer. The sensual ache emanating through her body made her yearn for release, but at the same time the friction of Hunter's substantial cock slowly pumping felt so good, she wanted it to last forever.

He withdrew slowly then plunged into her. She arched up her head, fell back on a cry. "My Sam," he moaned against her neck, sucking and licking as he picked up the pace.

"Yes," she cried as he grasped her hips and rose to his knees. She gasped and bucked up, her hips pistoning up to meet his driving thrusts. "Hunter," she pleaded breathlessly. His ravenous mouth moved over her jaw, her neck, her mouth, their tongues tangling, lips nibbling.

She wrapped her legs around his hips and her arms around his neck and hung on as sensations burst along every nerve cell. Hunter stiffened and plunged deep inside her, calling her name, his body trembling. She moaned and cried though her orgasm as it swept over her in long undulating waves. Hunter groaned, filling her with hot jets of his cream.

He rolled over, taking her with him. She lay on his chest, listening to his heart pound.

"Sam," he said hoarsely after his heart rate slowed.

"Yes?" He rolled onto his side but kept his arms around her. He made her feel safe and cherished. She didn't want anything to take away that feeling.

"Look at me." Reluctantly she lifted her face to look into his eyes. "Sam, I love you."

Samantha held her breath and blinked. "You do?"

"I think maybe I always have." He kissed her forehead and then her nose. "I know I always will."

Time stood still and her heart felt like it may expand out of her chest. "I love you, Hunter. I know I always have and I know I always will."

Hunter feigned an exasperated sigh. "Woman, does everything have to be a competition?"

"No, not if you just accept that I know best."

With a growl, he rolled over on top of her and tickled her until she begged for mercy. Soon the tickles became caresses, and kisses and she was begging for anything but mercy.

"Time to get up." Hunter nosed aside Sam's hair from her nape and kissed the sensitive skin gently.

Sleeping on her stomach, her body relaxed and

flushed, she was a temptation he was hard-pressed to ignore. Getting her back to the house after the arrest and general cleanup of the traffickers and terrorist cell had been hell. Unfortunately, Gabriel had caught them trying to sneak away and had delayed them by several hours. In the debriefing, they discovered what Hunter had suspected after looking at the files on the flash drive. Lillian had discovered the unscrupulous activities and shared her information with Uncle Zachariah. When Uncle Zach started nosing around, he ended up having an unfortunate accident. Lillian must have been afraid for her own life after that and passed the flash drive on to Dottie in case anything happened to her. When it did, Dottie started asking questions and met the same fate.

Reports were filed and the cleanup was nearly done, but the investigation was not closed. Henderson's corruption was long-reaching but he was not the main source. He was just one component of a criminal machine. It would take more probing, more reconnaissance to eliminate the entire organization. But they had done all they could on their end and were finally allowed to head home.

Home. It had been a long time since any place had been home.

"Sam," he whispered against her neck again, his hand moving slowly over the curves of her rear as he pressed her to wake up. He had plans, and they had an appointment, one he wasn't about to cancel. He had spent the last hour setting it up and getting everything ready. There was no room for excuses, no way for her to wiggle out of it.

"Wha . . . ?" she mumbled into the pillows, trying to burrow deeper in the mattress to escape.

"Wake up, baby." He chuckled as she scooted away from him.

"Go 'way," she growled, pulling the pillow over her head.

Hunter pulled the pillow away, amazed as he always was, how his heart could just soften, melt with the smallest things she did. She fascinated him, captivated him, made him so damned horny that half the time he was in a haze of lust. And he loved her. Loved her in ways he didn't think was possible.

"Sam, this is important. Wake up." He pulled the blankets from her as she tried to burrow under them once again.

She flopped over on her back. Her firm breasts peaked with those pretty little berry nipples, making his mouth water. Her eyes were narrowed in warning.

"The house on fire?" she asked huskily.

"No." He shook his head, his gaze going to those perfect breasts once again.

She cleared her throat. "You got produce or strange sex toys you're wanting to try out?" Her eyes gleamed in interest.

"Nope." He grinned

"Oh. Well, I'm going back to sleep then." She went to flip back over.

"Oh no, you don't." He laughed, gripping her arms and pulling her up in the bed. "Get showered and dressed. I laid out that pretty, cream-colored dress that was hanging in your closet, and everything else you need. We're in a hurry."

She grumbled under her breath, pushing her hair out of her eyes as she stared up at him. "What's the hurry? A dress? Where the hell are we going that I need a dress?"

"Church." The word hung in the air around them as she shook her head in confusion.

"Today's Sunday? Are you sure?"

"Today's Friday."

"Are you trying to deliberately confuse me?" She frowned then, the sleep slowly clearing from her eyes. "Why are we going to church, Hunter?"

"To get married."

"Oh, that's okay th—" Her eyes widened, then she blinked, as she swallowed tightly. "Married?"

"I won't let you back out of it either, Sam," he warned her fiercely. "We're getting married."

"Married?" she whispered, shaking her head. "When did you propose?"

"Propose? No way." He shook his head, fighting his irrational fear that if he didn't marry her now, then something would happen, some way, somehow, someone would destroy the chance.

Hunter wasn't a fool. Had Novak managed to actually rape her, then Sam would have healed from it. But she would have left Hunter, would have fought any chance they had of surviving it together. If he tied her to him and did it now, then no matter what happened, she was committed. She was his.

"Hunter." She shook her head. "You're supposed to propose," she protested as he pulled her from the bed. "You know? Wine, a ring, all that good stuff?"

"Rings are at the church. We'll celebrate with wine

afterward. Now shower." He pulled back the door and started the water.

"Hunter, I want to marry you. But why now?"

He stilled, his heart lodging in his throat as he sat down slowly on the edge of the tub. He stared up at her, his heart breaking as he remembered her screams. She had screamed out his name, begging him to help her. If Jacob's lady hadn't been there, he wouldn't have Samantha now.

"I can't lose you, Sam," he whispered then, jerking her to him, his face buried at her stomach as he fought the emotion surging inside him. "Do you understand me? No matter what happens, no matter what anyone else does, you're my heart. You're my world."

"What time is the ceremony?" she asked softly, sliding down until she rested on her knees, staring up at him with a wicked glint in her eye.

"Two hours." He touched her face, marveling at how deeply he loved her.

"So when did you intend to make the actual proposal?" She arched a brow curiously.

Hunter grinned. "During the honeymoon."

She shook her head, laughing up at him then. The sheer pleasure and love he saw in her filled his world.

"Marry me, Sam," he whispered, needing to know it was what she needed as well. "Please?"

"Yes, Hunter. I'll marry you."

Hey, y'all! We hope you enjoyed reading *One Tough Cowboy* as much as we enjoyed writing it. We also hope you'll come with us on our next Cowboy adventure in the little town of Deerhaven, California. Find out what happens when Jacob Donovan's well-ordered world is turned upside down! Thank you so much for spending time with us and our characters.

Love!
Roni Chadwick and Lora Leigh